The TWILIGHT ZONE

Book 3:
DEEP IN THE DARK

JOHN HELFERS

ibooks
new york
www.ibooks.net

DISTRIBUTED BY SIMON & SCHUSTER, INC.

For Karen, who made this book possible.

An Original Publication of ibooks, inc.

The Twilight Zone
TM and © 2003 CBS Broadcasting, Inc.
ALL RIGHTS RESERVED.

An ibooks, inc. Book

Distributed by Simon & Schuster, Inc.
1230 Avenue of the Americas, New York, NY 10020

ibooks, inc.
24 West 25th Street
New York, NY 10010

The ibooks World Wide Web Site Address is:
http://www.ibooks.net

ISBN 0-7434-7978-5
First ibooks, inc. printing January 2004
10 9 8 7 6 5 4 3 2 1

Edited by Karen Haber

Special thanks to John Van Citters

Printed in the U.S.A.

PROLOGUE

For hundreds of years the town of Geiststadt had slumbered, buried beneath the churning, drowning, overheated world. Everything had changed around it—the ice caps melted, the oceans rose, and every continent was reshaped by relentless rising waters. Change engulfed the strained planet as millions swelled into billions, the 21st century begat the 22nd, and the small village once known as Geiststadt became Geistad, just another borough of the city of Greater Metropolitan New York.

But not even the floods could stop the city's growth. Its builders had simply moved upwards rather than outward, bending science and engineering to their will and piling level upon level, building upon building, creating stratoscrapers of previously unimaginable height.

Much like the unstoppable city, the Noir family had similarly endured and advanced. NoirCorp, the family business, had become a vast empire of wealth and power that reached into every nook, every cranny of every citizen's life. At its helm were its relentless masters, Mason and Antonia Noir. They, too had endured, but not without paying a price...

The Derlicht family had not fared so well during the last century and a half. Their family had suffered a reversal of fortune, their influence and power dissipated under the mighty Noir juggernaut. The kinder rumors whispered that the Derlichts simply couldn't embrace the future, that they were stuck in the past and had been left behind. Now the clan were scattered across the area, and the once proud bloodline was but a shadow of its former self.

And as the modern world and its engines of technology and commerce beat steadily onward, Geistad continued as well. To all outward appearances it was a harmless little neighborhood with a proud history that could be traced back before the founding of New York City proper. But underneath, the dark heart of the community, born in fire and blood, continued beating, its legend and original name remembered by only a few elders of the area, and never spoke about.

Despite its charming appearance, travelers coming through Geistad never stayed any longer than they had to. They couldn't explain their strange uneasiness, the general feeling of foreboding coming from the buildings and even the people of the area.

The residents of Geistad dismissed these notions as ridiculous, but some of the older men and women would get a strange look in their eyes, as if recalling some of the stories their parents had told them, stories that had passed from truth to tall tale to legend, as if the passage of time could make them any less true. Stories that

Geistad itself was somehow...different, a locus point for the strange, the unexplained, the mysterious.

That was one thing that hadn't changed, not in more than four hundred years. Geistad had been founded in blood and fire...but the events of the next forty-eight hours would make those violent, haunted days pale in comparison.

For its slumbering soul was about to awaken....

CHAPTER ONE

Peeking around the edge of the doorway, Shizume Mader spotted the body immediately. The still form of a Greater New York Metropolitan Police Officer lay in the center of the abandoned room.

Her optics adjusted to the dim light in the burned out level of the derelict stratoscraper, revealing crumbling, scarred walls composed of barricaded floor-to-ceiling windows, any failed electroglass in them stolen or broken long ago. Litter covered the floor, most of it detritus from floorsquats, roving families or gangs that moved from floor to floor in the downlevels. Something sparked in a corner, and she saw a malfunctioning condom wrapper attempting to execute its virtad, the celbatts expending their power in a vain effort to entice a previous user one last time.

"Where's his partner?" she asked. Although her lips barely moved, her partner heard every subvocalized word.

A calm voice replied in her head. *"I have opened a channel to him now, Officer. He is on DL 26. He was pursuing other suspects and the pair got separated."*

"I thought partners were supposed to stay with their assigned officer at all times."

"He claims his officer gave him specific orders to move ahead. Apparently the officer was caught by surprise while alone. When the partner could not raise him, he radioed for us."

"Note that for the file," Shizume replied. "Patch into his vitals, then give me a floor plan and hotsight for the entire floor on screen one with overlay from my location."

"Working, Officer Mader."

An instant later, the schematic she had requested popped up in the lower left quadrant of her vision. A heads-up display, it would stay with Shizume wherever she looked, with a small red dot marking her location in relation to her surroundings. Next to that was a small readout indicating the physical condition of the prone officer in front of her. His heart rate and pulse were steady, and there was a flesh wound on the scalp above the parietal bone, indicating a possible concussion. The readout suggested summoning a skymed unit for him.

Yeah, yeah, I was just going to, she thought. "Metro 5-1, Metro 5-1, this is Officer Mader requesting assistance at downlevel 24 in grid—grid—"

"G-7."

"Shang, I knew that," she said. "Officer Mader requesting assistance at downlevel 24 in grid G-7, officer down, repeat officer down. Requesting backup for three by three floor sweep and a Skymed unit for evac. Hotsight shows that suspects may still be in the area. Request permission to charge my weapon."

"Permission granted, Officer Mader," a different, female voice said inside her head. *"Proceed inside and secure the area. Apprehend any suspects encountered."*

"Copy that, I am proceeding inside," she replied, feeling the comforting tingle of her stunfinger going online. The power meter on the left side of her sight rose from red to yellow to green, indicating full capacity. Shizume held her hand out, palm down, index finger leading the way in approved GNYMPD fashion. Her hotsight had located two human-shaped perps, each one hiding behind ragged terrocene walls at the far end of the room. Shizume felt her heartbeat accelerate, every sense on overwatch. *This is what it's all about,* she thought.

"I res two targets behind far wall."

"Stunfinger has acquired two target bios."

"Set for twenty minute incapacitation, and get his partner up here to help secure the area." Never taking her eyes off that doorway, she crept to the form on the floor and verified that he was still alive. *Where's his helmet?* she wondered, scanning around for the standard issue plasticine-Kevlar riot helmet all downlevel cops were issued.

"Officer Mader, please take another look at the human on the left."

Glancing at the hotsight again, she saw that one suspect's head was slightly misshapen, bulging at the top, and his face was flattened. *He's wearing the damn thing,* she thought.

"Fliv, lights."

Halogen spotbeams flooded the room and the far doorway. "This is the Greater New York City Metro Police requesting that the two people on the other side of that wall drop any held or concealed weapons and step into this room one at a time. Failure to comply with my orders—"

Both suspects broke and ran, boots slapping the bare floor as they headed for a bald iron door on the far wall.

"Stop or I will shoot!" Shizume said. When neither complied with her command, she pointed her finger, aimed, and fired.

There was no explosion, no flash of flame or bullet expelled, but one suspect suddenly lost all control of his movements and dropped to the floor, skidding into the wall as he did so. Unfortunately, his body had shielded the other suspect from her shot, and he burst through the door and pounded up the stairs.

"Shangit! Fliv, on me, let's go!" she said, shooting across the room into the next one and pulling the door open.

"Suspect is heading uplevel, two stories ahead of you."

Shizume didn't hesitate but took the stairs two at a time. "Metro, one suspect is incap. I am now in foot pursuit of the other suspect leaving DL 24 and heading UL."

Above her, a door slammed, and Shizume stopped for a second. "Give me a readout."

"Sonic rangefinder indicates he took the next exit door. Approach with caution."

"You got that right." Shizume kept her finger ready and, staying close to the wall, walked up the stairs. "Fliv, ready the floor plan and open the door when I say."

"Affirmative."

Shizume crouched down so that most of her body was

7

hidden by the grimy stairs and wall. Holding herself so that only her head and finger would be exposed, she gave the signal. The door swung open with a loud squeal, but Shizume ignored it as she swept the corridor, searching for the slightest movement.

"Hot sight on," she said. Moments later the familiar red and orange dot popped on the floor plan, pulsing in the middle of what used to be a small nest of offices, torn apart long ago and rebuilt into a rat's warren of tunnels and hallways, depending on who lived there and for how long. Shizume exhaled, finding her center and rebalancing after the short chase, then began creeping down the hallway.

The red dot stayed put as she approached. There was something strange about it, but she couldn't put her finger on it. Maybe Fliv could. "Fliv, give me ultraural."

Seconds later a cacophony of sounds burst in her ears as her partner adjusted the volume. Shizume now heard the wind whistling outside the stratoscraper, and far-off creaks and groans as the constantly moving building expanded and contracted. Underneath it all, she noted the distant, continuous lap-slap of the ocean against the submerged lower levels.

"Filter environment," she said. Seconds later, all of the background noise faded away, and a rapid *lub-dub, lub-dub* could be heard. *Got him,* she thought, taking a few more cautious steps forward. She readied her helmet light to activate as soon as she saw him. Her HUD indicated he was just on the other side of the wall—

"Metro Police, don't move!" Shizume cried as she came around the barrier. The man froze in front of her, his eyes squinting under the glare of her spotbeam, crinkling his face into a crow's nest of dirt-seamed wrinkles. Half-raising his hands, he rocked back on his haunches. His stench, a combination of crashsweat, mold, grease, and another unidentifiable odor, filled the small area. Catching a whiff, Shizume tried to take small, shallow breaths to avoid inhaling any more of him than she had to.

"Stand up, slowly, and keep those hands where I can see them. When I tell you, turn and walk to the wall, placing your hands on it. Do you understand?"

The man trembled once, his fingers curling into claws, then relaxing with an effort. He nodded, a single jerk of his head.

"Erratic pulse, pinpoint pupils, traces of blood on his breath. I'm reading evidence of a crashburn. You have a dustjunkie on your hands."

"Thanks for the update. Where's my damn backup?"

"Channel says all units have been diverted to a three level fire in G-4."

"Great," she said. "All right, you—"

A flicker of movement caught her eye, and she pivoted, looking for a possible threat. "Who's there?"

In the corner of the room stood another man, dressed unlike anything she had seen before. Unlike the addict in front of her, this man was clean and handsome, with clear blue eyes, all his teeth, and tousled blond hair framed by a smooth-skinned, almost feminine face. He was dressed in *muy* retro clothes, like he had stepped out of a history triholo; a loose-fitting, puffy-sleeved white shirt, some kind of pants that looked more like leggings, and square-toed, tanned hide boots. He reached out with one hand, his mouth moving with no sound coming out, looking as if he was trying to say something, to make contact with her. What was even more incredible was Shizume's distinct feeling that she had seen him somewhere before.

"Who are—" was all Shizume got out before the duster leaped at her, ramming his shoulder into her chest and sending her sprawling against the back wall. Her helmeted head thumped hard against the floor, and even with the protection, her vision blurred for a second. The footsteps of the escaping junkie echoed in her ears as she got to her feet.

When she was standing again, she wagged a finger at the other guy. "Stay here!" she said, then took off after the runner.

Shizume caught up with him just as he was trying to wriggle into a heating duct that disappeared into the wall. Spotting his legs slithering into the tunnel, she dove for them, managing to grab an ankle before it disappeared.

A howl echoed through the ductwork as the addict jerked to a halt. Sitting up, Shizume braced her feet on either side of the duct and pulled with all her strength. Squealing and struggling, the man fought his capture every centimeter of the way. The moment she got him out of the duct, he lashed out with his other foot, driving her backwards and tearing his leg from her grasp. Instead of trying to flee again, he snarled and came at her, a grimy fist cocked and ready.

Shizume didn't wait for him to try anything else. When he closed to within a meter, she lashed out with a booted foot, hitting him square on the kneecap. With her hearing amplified, the crack of his patella popping loose was like a board snapping in personal defense practice. The man buckled, clutching his injured leg and trying to limp away. Before he could, she kicked out again, sweeping his feet out and sending him crashing to the floor. She was on him in an instant, twisting one arm up behind his back as she read him his rights. After Shizume had secured her prisoner, she marched him back to the other room, looking for the third man.

He was gone. In his place stood a potted, seven-foot tall ambulatory Venus flytrap, its gaping pink-mouthed leaves gnashing back and forth, chewing the air for something to eat.

"All right, Fliv, I know this isn't part of the training. What happened to that other g—?"

"Sensors have detected an unknown energy surge outside the program. I'm stopping the scenario—now."

With a sideways wrench, the dirty levels of the building shimmered into nothingness, replaced by the walls of Shizume's studio apartment. A soft chime rang in the living room, and a voice announced, "water ration available on this floor for the next thirty minutes."

Shizume rolled her head around on her shoulders, adjusting to the sudden shift from virtraining to real time. Her head ached and her arms and legs felt leaden and stiff from the aftereffects of the simulation. Even though what she had been doing was all in her mind, it still exacted a physical toll on her body.

"You should get a shower while you can." The voice came from a one meter in diameter doughnut-shaped machine hovering in midair next to Shizume. "Fliv," as she referred to it, was the standard GNYCMPD Patrol Assistant. Each officer was assigned one in training, and

11

it accompanied them throughout their careers, or until one or the other was damaged or killed. Hovering on a small anti-gravity field and powered by a tiny self-renewing hydrogen fuel cell, the devices served as a combination of forward scout and mobile sensor platform. They also recorded each officer's activities to corroborate their own internal recorders in case of internal review or when needed to testify in court. The partners contained, among other useful data, the entire fifty-three-volume GNYCM justice code, and could act as an impartial mediator when circumstances warranted. Partner, teacher, and mentor, the PAs were programmed with a level 4 near artificial intelligence, allowing them to adapt to most situations on their own. During an officer's training, the PAs ran virtual simulations and response tests when the cadets weren't at academy, reviewing and strengthening the core curriculum.

Shizume was an advanced student, so she only reported back to the academy about once a month and had even mobilized twice with the regular officers during times of civil unrest in the downlevels. But right now training was the furthest thing from her mind.

"Fliv, you're my partner, not my mother. Besides, I've got to check something out first," Shizume said as she toweled sweat off the back of her neck.

"Yes, but we also have to review the training module."

"Oh, right."

"Exactly. Your mistakes were not what I had expected from a third-year trainee."

"What, so I forgot which grid I was in, it could happen. Review scenario from three minutes in to end, double speed."

The wall flickered, and Shizume watched herself running across the large room, through the door and up the stairs from the perspective of her partner floating over her shoulder. She cleared the door, then crouch-walked to the wall and took the guy by surprise.

"That is not the only error you made today."

"Yeah, yeah. Okay, wait for it—freeze there. Camera angle on southwest corner, illuminate."

The view changed to reveal a filthy corner identical to every other one on that level, empty except for scraps of paper, discarded chugpaks, and assorted human waste dried in piles on the floor.

"What the—all right, Fliv, where'd he go?"

"To whom are you referring?"

"You know who, the third man, the guy who was standing in the corner. The guy who turned into the six-foot tall carnivorous plant."

"This sim had only two suspects in it, and you encountered both of them. And about that second encounter—"

Shizume listened with only one ear, the rest of her attention focused on that frozen corner of simulated room. *I know what I saw,* she thought. *But if that's true, where did he go?*

HAPTER TWO

Mason Noir stood at the window of his penthouse office, watching nature rage all around him. A wind that could only properly be described as eldritch screamed around the stratoscraper's 550 floors, attempting to batter its way inside the room. Sheets of gray rain battered against the electroglass, drumming against the impenetrable barrier like hails of watery bullets. Occasionally jagged silver lightning split the heavens, and moments later the world reverberated with the sound of the very sky cracking as thunder fragmented the atmosphere.

There'll be flood warnings in the city downlevels tonight, he mused. Mason was unconcerned with anything happening more than four kilometers below him as he had not bothered to set foot on solid ground in more than fifty years. There was no need. Everything he needed was up here, among the clouds. *Well, almost everything,* he thought, raising a highball glass of century-old single-malt scotch and draining the last swallow. He savored the taste, knowing full well that the alcohol would be eliminated from his body without causing a bit of inebriation or damage. He could have drained the entire bottle in one long swallow, and it would do him as much harm as mother's milk.

Just one more advantage of living in this brave new world, he thought, running a hand absently through the thick black hair that was part of his family's heritage. His original body had contained a tendency for a receding hairline, as well as several other less-than-desirable genetic traits, but he had eliminated all those flaws in this third edition. He had also made several improvements, including eidetic memory, keen eyesight, and superb physical reflexes.

His body also contained the latest versions of all the vaccines against the rare but very deadly 23rd century diseases that still troubled mankind. Biotech had finally succeeded in finishing off the thousands of varieties of common colds and flus, but generations-removed mutations of viruses such as ASARS and 3bola still thrived in the last of the Third World nations, although they were gradually being brought up to speed with the rest of the planet.

New technology had brought with it new dangers as well, including GHUS, or Genetic Helix Unraveling Syndrome, which his DNA was also protected against. The treatment guarded against the rapid and irreversible degenerative disease that had terrorized the small human clone population for almost thirty years in the mid 22nd century. When cloning was in its infancy, GHUS had almost wiped out the field's research and technology. Mason's own contribution to reproducing human beings, the MIND-NET, a way to literally download a person's entire memory into a computer, was heavily dependent on cloning moving forward. When GHUS broke out in mass, he threw every bit of resources his fledgling company had toward finding a cure. Only an inspired effort on the part of NoirCorp's research labs had brought about a preventative vaccine and saved decades of study.

When the MIND-NET procedure had been perfected, Mason had been the first volunteer. When the time was right, the first cloned Mason had informed the world of his success in an Ultranet press conference, and he had reaped uncounted benefits, including being awarded the Nobel Prize in medicine. His company thrived as well, with NoirCorp's success with the GHUS vaccine and MIND-NET ensuring its absolute domination in the fields of cloning and mind transferal technology.

Mason also found other advantages to his new fame and fortune. He had lobbied for years to allow the cloning of human organs, and once it was approved, he wiped out the organ transplant waiting list in less than a decade.

Cutting edge regenerative and medical processes weren't the only fields NoirCorp worked in either. In the past half-century his company had branched out into almost every aspect of worldwide business, from importing to telecommunications to agriculture. Advancements made by the multi-national corporation's branches and subsidiaries had raised the standard of living for billions, terraforming arid deserts, bringing technology and communication to remote areas, and truly doing its part to join the world together.

A world created, more or less, by my family, Mason thought. *Building it up to reach to the skies, these towers that leave the earth behind. Creating living space, breathing room for billions of people, each one's life shaped every day, in some minute way, by a NoirCorp product.*

He reached out with one hand, placing his fingertips on the humming glass, feeling the impact of the thousands of raindrops on the other side of the thin sheet of glasteel, their velocity reduced to impotence by the sheath of electric energy protecting the building. He imagined each one spiraling down, landing on the hair or head or shoulder or back of a man or woman far beneath him, trying to get to shelter before the waves whipped up and crashed over what remained of the streets of Old New York City.

Not much time now, he thought, aware of the time ticking down to the second. His task tonight, like many of the things he had done over the past century, was guided by a document written more than two hundred and fifty years ago. Mason hadn't gotten to where he was by deviating from its directives, and he wasn't about to begin now. In fact, he had one minor matter to take care of before beginning the project that would mark the next step in his family's legacy...

The massive double doors at the other end of his plush office swung open without a sound. Turning, Mason set his glass down and walked around his black horseshoe-shaped desktop that floated in mid-air, suspended by a silent anti-gravity field underneath it.

"I trust you have it, Adam?" he asked.

The man silhouetted in the hallway light walked into the office, a sealed plasticine envelope under one arm.

As he approached, Mason marveled at the grace and fluidity in the man's stride, his apparent single-minded determination as he approached. His face was calm, smooth, and androgynous with a closely cropped buzz cut and two narrow, trimmed lines for eyebrows. The man's cool grey eyes evaluated everything they saw in a millisecond for the potential of possible harm to Mason, for that was what he had been programmed to do.

Adam came to a stop in front of Mason and extended the file to him. "As you requested, sir."

Adam was the only one of his kind, a brilliant fusion of man and machine. Since the landmark *Carpenter vs. Clonetics* genetic identity case in 2046, clone creation had been divided into two rigorously sanctioned classes. Infertile parents wanting a cloned child could have one safely and legally without difficulty. The other class was clones without brains, created for those fantastically wealthy who could afford to "body-hop," as the term was known, living for century after century, downloading their memory and personality engrams into a new body at the appropriate time.

Wanting a completely subservient bodyguard that was more powerful than a human but wouldn't attract attention like a common robot, Mason had alpha-tasked his midnight R&D team to fuse human and machine together into an indistinguishable facsimile of a man with ten times the strength, speed, and reflexes. Adam was answerable only to Mason and was the only protection he needed. Maybe in another twenty years, he would reveal Adam's existence to the world, but not just now.

"Any trouble?" he asked as he took the envelope.

"No sir, the drop went as scheduled. Will there be anything else tonight?" his bodyguard asked.

"No, Adam, thank you. Take the rest of the night off," Mason said.

"I will await your command in the antechamber, sir."

The corner of Mason's mouth quirked upward in what passed for a smile as the cyborg turned on its heel and walked out of the room. *Absolutely no sense of humor,* he thought. Mason sobered as he tapped the envelope against his fingers. He tossed the packet on his desk and walked back around it, sitting down in his high-backed antique leather chair that had once belonged to the long dead real estate mogul Donald Trump.

"Wedding day, go."

The empty floor in front of him lit up in a profusion of light, color, and sound, showing a three-dimensional hologram of the afternoon of Mason's wedding. A few meters away stood a simulation of his wife, Antonia. Resplendent in a cream-colored Chinese silk gown, she walked down the aisle, straight towards him. Like him, she looked no different today than she had on that spring day more than 150 years ago.

"Freeze holo," he commanded, and Antonia's three-dimensional image glided to a halt in front of him, her lace-sheathed hand reaching out to him, the invisible groom. Mason had edited the ancient digital film of their wedding—the events after their handclasp were ones he still didn't want to revisit, although he had had the footage analyzed for years by everyone from scientists to paranormal experts to purported mediums. The "supernatural disturbance" captured by the cameras that had survived the event had shown a maelstrom of spirits, with Antonia and Mason at the very center. Caused by the wraiths of his own ancestors, Thomas and Jon Noir, the psychic storm had been stopped by the lovers working together. *That grasping bastard making his final play to stop me,* he thought. They had almost succeeded, for the effort had very nearly cost Antonia her life. She had been weakened for years afterward, and their original union had never borne that which he had most wanted—an heir.

Since then they had both been reborn, although Mason's ultimate goal—a child—still eluded him. Artificial insemination, in vitro fertilization, bodyform DNA reweaving, genetic fetal cloning—none of the standard or new methods had worked. Mason had grown increasingly frustrated at the lack of progress and had never stopped trying. With every new advance in cloning and reproduction, he had insisted Antonia try every one first. All had failed, despite his skill and vast resources.

"We have all the time in the world," Antonia would tell him after each new failure. Mason had always been willing to believe her, at first simply because he loved her. After all, she was right in one respect: thanks to the cloning, they did have all the time in the world. But as the decades had passed, he began to suspect that she was holding something back from him. With 99.9 percent of infertile couples being assisted by technology, it seemed inconceivable that Antonia was beyond help.

Finally, Mason had gone to get a second opinion of his own. Obtaining a body scan of his wife before their family physician had seen it, Mason had sent it to the best ob-gyn hospital in the nation, on what remained of the reshaped West Coast. Adam had just delivered the results of that evaluation to him.

Mason spun the envelope on the marble desk, his eyes never leaving the face of his wife, lover, and companion of more than 150 years. The expression on her face radiated pure adoration, at least, that's what he saw when he looked at her. Reaching for the envelope flap he undid it with trembling fingers, both drawn to and unwilling to read the findings. Removing the thin sheaf of real paper—which he had requested to prevent electronic interception, as no one used hardcopy anymore—he quickly scanned it, his eyes locking on the one phrase he had been searching for:

"It is my opinion that, based on the data and bodyscan image supplied, Mrs. Noir is perfectly capable of conceiving and carrying a normal, healthy fetus to term and is an excellent candidate for impregnation at any time."

Mason stared at the sentence, the words burning into his mind...

...perfectly capable...

...carrying a normal, healthy child to term...

...excellent candidate for impregnation...

The papers slipped through his numb fingers, and Mason raised his head to stare at Antonia's frozen image, forever looking off to the left. He felt strangely disassociated from what he had just read, as if he was examining someone else's life and had just read something that didn't impact him at all. The woman who had married him, who had supported him in his endeavors for more than a century, who had helped build and make his company what it was today, the woman whom he had thought was in love with him had been deceiving him from the very first day of their union. Part of Mason's mind wanted to scream his incoherent rage at being tricked for so long, but his resolve asserted itself just as quickly, and he tamped down his anger. His perfect memory cursed him now, as every conversation they had had regarding children replayed in his mind.

"Just a few more months..."

"...still too weak from the wedding..."

"...the latest treatment didn't work...don't worry, my darling, we have all the time in the world..."

And finally every doctor's damning words:

"Frankly, Mr. Noir, even with today's best technology, for some—inexplicable—reason, your wife cannot conceive, and I don't know if she ever will."

Even as his anger at the deception slowly burned away to ironhearted resolve, part of him marveled at the incredible intricacy of the web of deceit she had spun around him over the long years, involving the doctors, medical experts, everyone. *I knew she was good,* Mason thought with an ironic chuckle, *but I had no idea she was* that *good.*

The overwhelming question now was why? *Why would she prevent me from having an heir?* He thought back to the research his wife had been doing when they had first met in the early 21st century. It was one of the reasons they had gotten together, something he had casually dismissed at the time, caught up in the potential of his MIND-NET prototype. Antonia had been examining the records of her family and had uncovered the uneasy peace between the Noirs and the Derlichts.

It all clicked together for him in an instant. *She found something else as well. Something to do with our families, something Antonia discovered is why she has been keeping a child from me all this time.* His pragmatic side did not waste any more time berating himself over being deceived, it would have been a waste of time. *I was in love, and, for all intents and purposes, she is still the ideal wife for me.*

A soft chime from his desk indicated an incoming message.

"Cancel wedding day," Mason said. "Receive incoming message."

The likeness of his wife flickered and vanished, to be replaced by a man with his hair shaved in multi-colored horizontal bands around his head. Despite his appearance, which Mason understood was one of the popular styles of the day, he was calm and completely professional.

"Mr. Noir, we have completed the primary impression and are ready for the genetic sample."

"Thank you, Kar. I'll meet you in the imprint chamber in five minutes."

"Yes, sir, we'll be ready."

Mason rose from his chair and headed for the wall. A panel opened as he approached, and he stepped into the empty small round chamber, floating in midair. Mason looked down at the black void beneath him and said two words.

"The vault."

The gravator, or anti-gravity elevator, dropped him four hundred floors in just under thirty seconds, decelerating him to a gentle stop at his chosen destination, a room he had not visited for several decades.

The wall in front of him was indistinguishable from any other wall in the building, but when Mason placed his hand against the polished glasteel, a two-meter section recessed inward and swung away, creating a dark portal.

"Light." The word brought up a gentle indirect glow, illuminating the space and the single item it contained. Mason entered and walked to the center of the room, feeling a long-gone hand of history settle on his shoulder. He breathed in the still air and for a moment felt himself transported back more than three centuries to when Geistad, the modern borough, was Geiststadt, a small, isolated farming community on the distant outskirts of New York City.

The room was small, almost claustrophobic, barely five by six meters. Hewn from a single massive block of New England granite, it was the chamber where his great-great grandfather, Benjamin, had conducted his research and experiments so long ago. Dark experiments, all with the sole purpose of unlocking the secrets of the universe, among them things that mankind was meant to forget or perhaps should have never known in the first place.

Benjamin Noir's true will and addendums had specified that the 13th Noir male in each generation would be responsible for the room, and funds were always set aside for its upkeep. If a generation didn't have a 13th son, the responsibility fell to the next sibling.

In the mid-22nd century, the greenhouse effect had risen to alarming levels, taking the worldwide levels of the oceans with it. Mason had spent millions of dollars to wrest the room from the ground beneath his family's mansion before it had been claimed by the Atlantic, placing it securely in the bowels of his corporation's headquarters. The bribes to the contractors and building inspectors alone had been astronomical, but it had all been worth it. He was the only person who knew of its existence, and even if someone else did find it, Mason was the only one who could enter it unscathed.

He had last visited the vault when it had been laid to rest, making sure its contents weren't disturbed. He had continued the research as dictated by his relative, but his own experiments, while carried out in this same room long ago, had taken a much different turn. While his forefather had delved into the spiritual and metaphysical worlds, Mason had embraced technology with an unyielding passion, bending the modern gods of electricity, physics, and biotechnology to his will and reaping benefits even Benjamin Noir couldn't have imagined.

Mason breathed in the musty, centuries-laden air, remembering his early tests performed in this very room, the thrill of advancing past what had then seemed to be insurmountable barriers. *Today I know how Alexander felt when he thought there were no new worlds to conquer,* he thought. *If only he had even attempted to look beyond his borders, he would have found challenges beyond his wildest dreams.*

But after his long, successful quest to unlock the potential of the human body and conquer death itself, Mason found himself growing restless as well. His past achievements no longer satisfied him, but it also seemed that he had run out of new avenues to explore. Even with his immeasurable advantage of potential cloned immortality, Mason was beginning to think he had reached the limits of what could be accomplished. Until he had turned the page of the codicil to his great-great-grandfather's will that morning, and a smile had spread across his face for the first time in a long while.

He walked to the antique ironbound seaman's chest in the middle of the room. The container should have been falling apart, but, while worn from years of use, it was still as solid as when it had been placed here. It sat patiently, as if waiting for its owner to hoist it over a shoulder and carry it to his ship's berth, bound for a shore somewhere over the distant horizon.

Not today, not ever again, Mason thought. From around his neck he removed a brass key, worn smooth from years of rubbing against his skin, and inserted it into the keyhole. The key turned with no resistance at all, and the trunk *clunk*ed open, the sound swallowed by the thick walls. Pushing open the lid, he removed the single object inside.

A creamy white alabaster jar about fifteen centimeters tall rested in his hands. It was sealed with a cover that fit flush with the opening, and atop that rested the sculpture of a woman's face with a basket balanced on her head. It was Nephthys, the Egyptian goddess of rebirth, who was also responsible for protecting the dead. Around the seam where the lid met the jar was a line of black wax etched with demotic hieroglyphs, a written language dating back to the Ptolemaic period. Mason read the symbols as easily as that morning's holopapers:

Protect this mortal's ka, O Nephthys, Mistress of Reincarnation.
Keep his soul safe from Ammon the Devourer.
Under your watchful eyes will he rise again.
And walk in life everlasting.

Canopic jars had been designed to hold a mummified person's vital internal organs; the heart, believed by the Egyptians to be the center of all thought, liver, lungs, stomach, and intestines. Mason smiled as he remembered reading how ancient embalmers had discarded the brains of the deceased, believing them to be useless. He picked up the jar, feeling its weight, heavier than anyone might have believed. *Wrong, they were all wrong,* he thought. *The brain is the center of thought, but it is the* blood *that contains the ability to live again, nothing else.* He tipped the jar, ever so slightly, feeling the sluggish shift of the precious liquid inside, full to the very top.

During his own research into his family's lineage, Mason had learned that Callie, Benjamin Noir's Caribbean housekeeper and *mambo*, or voodoo priestess, had collected enough blood from her master to fill this very canopic jar. She had then warded and sealed it, protecting the contents for as long as necessary. Until today.

Mason's long-lost ancestor had quested to live forever. Benjamin's long-ago research had told him that, even if he had not been able to find life eternal in the 1800s, there would be a chance to be resurrected in the future. To this end, Benjamin had ensured that a sizeable part of his fortune, the part that had been withheld from his betraying child, Thomas, would be kept in trust and looked after by his other offspring, Daniel, Seth, and James, until the right child came along. Mason had been that child, a true 13th son, and had been directed to marry into the family of the Noirs' old enemy, the Derlichts, to gain access to the fortune, sire an heir, and continue his forefather's research. Now, more than three centuries after his death, it was time for Benjamin to live again.

But it will be the wonder of science that will make my ancestor live again, not magic, Mason thought as he stepped back into the gravator. And, even though he never would have admitted it, even to himself, deep down inside, a small part of him hoped that this experiment would renew the spark of life that had been dampened in him as well.

"450th floor," he said. "And summon my wife."

Mason stepped out of the tube into an airlock, the canopic jar secure in the crook of his arm. After a thorough body scan, he exited into a gleaming white room surrounded by an electroglass dome that offered a view into yet another large chamber surrounding it. Mason walked to the center control room, ready to oversee what was about to happen. The area bustled with glowing energy-shielded lab technicians and engineers, all making last minute tests and adjustments. Snatches of conversation swirled past him as he entered:

"—primary bodyform is at stable optimum transfer temperature of 94.5 degrees—"

"—Mind-net transfer protocols are all functioning within optimum parameters—"

"—we are ready to begin DNA print as soon as we have received the sample—"

Kar, the department's chief cloning technician, walked over to him, his colorful hair and youthful face blurred and indistinct behind a protective energy field.

"Sir, we're ready when you are."

"Excellent. Where's Antonia?" Mason asked as he walked over to a small airlock and placed the jar inside.

"She's on her way. For protocol's sake, I have to ask if you are aware that that is not a sterile container?"

Mason's mouth creased again into his peculiar quarter-smile. "Duly noted, Mr. Da'hasian." He hit the button to cycle the jar into a separate, sterile room, then nodded to the lead technician. "Energy sheath on."

His surroundings blurred for a moment, then refocused into crystal-clear sharpness. Mason was now literally a part of the room, the energy current that provided his environmental protection also bringing him the data needed to bring about this vital transference. Readouts on the bodyform they would be using as well as information on the jar itself scrolled in front of him, revealing that the body was ready, and more importantly, that the container and its contents were intact.

"Arms," he commanded, holding his own out, fingers ready. Inside the small room, two shapeable anti-gravity fields shimmered into existence, virtual reality image projectors making them resemble a pair of hands hovering over a long row of instruments.

"Remove seal," he said, pointing at the wax with his finger. Inside, one of the floating hands fitted an industrial crystal to the tip of its finger and a thin blue beam of light shot out, melting the ancient wax and obliterating the demotic hieroglyphs that had bound the jar for centuries. The black wax bubbled and flowed down the side of the jar, dripping down over the pearly-white alabaster. Mason made sure no trace remained on either the lip of the jar or its cover. He was just about to open it when the airlock door cycled behind him again.

"Mason? Please don't tell me you've started already?" The dulcet tones of Antonia Noir rang through the room. Turning, Mason saw his wife. Even after what he had discovered earlier, she still took his breath away.

Unlike Mason, not a thing had needed to be changed from one incarnation of Antonia to the next. Immaculately dressed in a Ceyline Marie sheathsuit, her long, glossy hair was bound up in a businesslike bun at the back of her head. Despite her Palatine Germanic ancestry, his wife's skin was dusky, forming a perfect canvas for the rest of her face. Dark eyes glowed underneath gracefully arched brows that never seemed to frown or furrow, no matter how hectic business got. Her nose was pert and perfect, leading to rich, full lips that Mason remembered kissing with pleasure over the decades, always with the same intoxicating blend of spirit, intelligence, and desire.

Behind those beautiful features was a mind that was as sharp as a medical laser and quick as NoirCorp's fleet of sub-orbital spacecraft. Sometimes Mason thought she knew more about cloning and the human body than he did. She stayed on top of aspects of international law, national government as it pertained to business, and the ever-shifting world of global finance with an ease that intimidated both partners and rivals alike. Until several minutes ago, every time Mason had thought of her he'd known he was the luckiest man on the planet. Looking at her now, noticing the way everyone in the room, even Kar, paused in what they were doing to steal a glance at her, almost kept those feelings alive. Almost.

"Antonia, darling, you knew when this was going to happen." Mason marveled at how calm he sounded. He would have liked to think it was his decades of running a multi-national organization, but dealing with balking lunar manufacturers threatening to strike was one thing, talking with one's own wife after discovering her century-old deception was another matter entirely. Still, his voice didn't quiver or break, but stayed in the same calm, measured tones he had spoken in for decades.

"Dear, I couldn't just rush out of the Pan Singapore-Australian Combine board meeting at a moment's notice, could I? You do remember the supply shortages we're having down there?"

"Of course, that's why I rely on you," he replied. "To handle all those details that might escape me." She moved to embrace him, but he shook his head, "I'm already suited."

"Yes, how silly of me. Suit on, please." The energy field enveloped her as well. "Where do you want me?"

"I'm just about to open the seal, so please monitor the bodyform's core readings. Once I have the sample in storage, we can begin the transfer process."

"Gladly." She moved over to the bank of floating holographic tri-dee monitors that provided constant readout on the blank-faced form contained in its own "amniotic" fluid, actually a closely-guarded cocktail of oxygenated vitamin and nutrient-rich liquid that protected the clone body and encouraged rapid cell growth.

This form had been especially prepared for this moment, grown from the top tissue samples NoirCorp possessed. They had spliced together DNA from cross-sections of the healthiest male subjects they could find to create the finest body ever grown. All it needed now was the mind that had been trapped in the individual cells contained in the blood that had rested in that white jar for centuries, awaiting its time of rebirth.

Mason returned his attention to the jar, wielding the anti-gravity fields with deft skill. He lifted the lid off to reveal the ancient but still-vital dark crimson liquid inside.

"Suction." One of the hands brought out a small nozzle and sucked the blood away, cleaning the inside of the canopic jar back to pristine whiteness.

"The hemoglobin, corpuscles—all are still viable," Antonia reported, surprise evident in her tone. Mason waited for her to ask the next logical question, but another voice beat her to it.

"Are you virting me?" Kar said, heedless of whom he was questioning. "You're telling me that blood is still—alive?"

"Yours not to reason why, Mr. Da'hasian," Mason replied. "Voodoo or whatever we might call it today, it seems that Callie certainly knew her abilities. Begin DNA extraction and replication. Prepare bodyform for helix overlay and memory transferal."

In the early 21st, a popular theory had been advanced that the body itself was a living recorder, that every cell contained the ability to recreate the person it had come from, including memories and personality. In 2028, an ultranet virtual behaviorist named Martin LeConnell proved that each cell not only contained the blueprint for a person but they also contained the genetic blueprints for every ancestor that had come before them. He then topped himself by discovering how to access those stored memories and create a perfect pattern of human cell division, defeating the problem of irregularly dividing cloned cells that had stymied genetic laboratories around the world. A week after accepting the Nobel Prize in medicine, he was visited by Mason Noir himself, who wrote Dr. LeConnell a blank check to continue his research.

The advances in cell research were fused with Mason's MIND-NET technology to unlock the capabilities of every human being's DNA and perfect the cloning process by the late 2030s. Now it was going to be put to the ultimate test—successfully bringing back a man who had died more than three hundred years ago. Much-publicized experiments had been tried using DNA samples from Napoleon Bonaparte, and rumors had swirled around for a while that a group of hard-line Marxists in Russia had attempted to clone Lenin, but the attempts had all ended in failure. *Or*, Mason thought, *if they had resurrected the Communist leader, he was keeping his mouth shut and doing something much more lucrative than reviving his long-dead social experiment.*

The womb containing the bodyform slid over to the main view port so everyone could watch the procedure's progress.

"All bodyform readings are at optimum levels," a female tech said.

"Sample scan will be complete in just under 30

seconds," Kar reported from his console. We will begin transferal on your mark, sir."

Mason regarded the smooth blank face of the body-form as the seconds ticked down. *This is certainly not the world you left, Benjamin. How will you adapt to such things that even you could not foresee while alive? Stratocraft that can cross the globe in an hour, a permanent base not only in space but on the moon and Mars as well. And a Geistad and New York City the likes of which you have never imagined. You will be a child in the world's largest candy store and know that this has happened in no small part because of what you began those many years ago.*

"Sir, we're ready," Kar told Mason.

"Initiate helix overlay on my mark. Three... two...one...mark."

The walls of L-cell supracomputers hummed quietly, running through their programs and doing exactly what they had been made to do—reweave the genetic double helix in the body into the one that had been extracted from the serum sample. The first time Mason had reworked the DNA in a subject—a clone of himself—it had taken a month to finish. Now it would be done in just a few minutes, each of the billions of connections recoded to match his ancestor's blood.

Once that was complete, the computers, now containing the memories scanned from Benjamin's blood sample, would download the data into the hippocampus of the clone body, which was alive but dormant, a blank slate waiting to be filled. Mason knew he was taking an incredible risk by using Benjamin's blood. Usually the personality and memories of a transferee were taken directly from their brain's hippocampus, the center of long-term memory, and loaded directly into the new one, often via a direct computer link that monitored the transfer and kept the data flowing steadily so as not to overwhelm the bodyform. The same process would then be followed with the cerebellum, which processed skill memories, and the basal ganglia, which housed the memory of coordination and body movement.

But with no brain to sample, Mason and his team had been forced to experiment using the blood itself. Kar and his team had performed tests using the blood of trained lab animals to transfer skills and memories into cloned animalforms and had succeeded about 75 percent of the time. This was the first time they had tried to load a human from a blood sample, however. It was the ultimate gamble, and Mason's pulse quickened as he thought about what a successful transfer would mean.

"Helix overlay 80 percent complete...85...91...96...100 percent. The bodyform is ready for hippocampus download."

Mason looked back at Antonia, who was engrossed in the displays in front of her. Even though all of his attention should have been on the process, he still couldn't help wondering, *Why? Why, if you professed to love me as you claimed, did you do this—*

"Sir?" Kar asked.

"Yes, begin hippocampus transfer immediately," Mason replied.

"Mason, you should take a look at this," Antonia said at the same time.

"Put it on v-screen for me," he said. A small holoscreen

pinholed open in the bottom left quadrant of his vision. He saw thousands of cells bursting and dying in massive waves.

"Antonia, what am I looking at?"

"It's the sample we took from the jar—it's dying," she replied.

"Even in the plasmagen unit, it's still decomposing?"

"Yes, we're down to 43 percent, and more is going every second."

"But the memory scan was completed, correct?"

"That's affirmative," Kar piped in.

"Kelvin the rest of the blood before it deteriorates further," Mason said. "How is the transfer coming?"

"There was a strange bit of resistance at first, as if the bodyform's hippo didn't want to take the download, but the transfer is proceeding as scheduled," Kar replied.

Playback the initial implant, upper right," Mason ordered, still keeping an eye on his ancestor's dying blood cells. By now there were only scattered survivors, and they were rapidly succumbing to whatever was killing the rest. *You've served your purpose*, he thought. *It will be interesting to find out what killed you, however. Perhaps that will be Kar's next project.*

Another monitoring window opened in his vision, and Mason saw spikes of bioelectrical activity in the hippocampus and the ambient area surrounding it. As he watched, the waves ceased and the information flow progressed unimpeded. *That is strange,* he thought, checking the monitoring levels all around him. Everything was in the green, no abnormal waves showing.

"Sir, hippocampus transfer is complete."

"Drain him," Mason said.

The container with what he hoped was his great-great-grandfather—now implanted in a body younger than Mason's own—was raised upright so he, Antonia, and the rest of the team could watch. Valves opened, and the nutrient liquid the clone had spent all of its short life in drained away, streaming from the man's mouth and nose, then sucked away as a mask dropped down and cleared the remaining liquid, replacing it with fresh pure oxygen. The clone's hairless chest rose and fell in a rhythmic pulse.

"Blood pressure 107 over 65...pulse 65 beats a minute," Kar called out. "He's slowing a bit...now 58...now 54...stabilizing at 54 beats per minute. All other vital signs look good."

"Mason, when will he awaken?" Antonia asked.

"Any second now, I'd imagine." Mason shut down the room with the jar inside and walked over to the window separating him from his new creation. "Open the tank."

He heard the hiss of the seal being broken, and the transparent cover cycled up and away. The body inside began to flex and shift. The eyelids, still sticky with fluid, fluttered open. His dripping hands twitched then rose to clear the dripping fluid from his face.

"Shouldn't I get him to the cleansing room?" Kar asked.

"No, I want him to see us first." Mason activated a communication channel into the room. "Can you hear me? Are you all right? What is your name?"

At the sound of the first words emanating from nowhere the clone started, looking around for the source of the noise. His mouth opened and closed, but nothing came out.

Mason tried again. "What is your name?"

The naked, glistening man grasped the edges of the tank and made to pull himself out.

"Shall I contain him?" Kar asked on a private channel.

"No—no, let's see what he's going to do," Mason replied, his eyes never leaving the clone. He activated the comm channel again. "Welcome home, Benjamin."

At the mention of the name the man looked up again, apparently seeing the windows around him for the first time. His hands clenched the sides of the tank as if holding on for dear life. Suddenly he jackknifed over, bent double in what looked to be total agony. He reared back, then forward again, his entire body taut, every muscle bulging, every vein throbbing.

"Kar, what's going on?" Mason asked.

"I've got spikes across the board—brain waves, heart rate, blood pressure—he's seizing!"

"Get him back in the tank, now!" Mason commanded.

But it was already too late. The clone's head lifted, its bright blue eyes pinning Mason under their unfocused stare. As he watched, the man's face aged in front of him, becoming lined with wrinkles, its skin sagging into octogenarian pouches and folds up and down its body. The once-taut muscles withered and drooping into infirm uselessness, his firm legs contracting and shriveling into two sticks. Mason's ancestor was dying before his eyes.

"Move, goddammit!" When the tech at the window didn't comply fast enough, Mason lunged at her, shoving her out of the way, their energy shields flaring as they impacted each other. "Transfer all control to me now!"

He activated the anti-gravity fields in the other room and scooped the disintegrating body that had fleetingly been Benjamin Noir back into the tank. The cover swung down with agonizing slowness. "Kar, you'd better be ready with that mix, or I swear—"

"Nutrient flowing now," Kar said. Mason watched the fluid climb up the glass, covering the quivering, seizing body until the entire form was enveloped. Only then did he turn away.

"What the hell happened?" he asked everyone in the room.

"Hypothetically speaking, the same thing that happened to the sample," Antonia, calm Antonia, was the only one to reply. "Incredibly fast cellular decomposition, quicker than anything I've ever seen, only without the normal accompanying cell renewal. He literally aged a century right before our eyes."

"What is his condition now?" Mason asked, dreading the answer. *Please, don't let her say what I think—*

"I'm sorry, Mason, but we were too late," his wife replied. "The clone is little more than a vegetable now. Minimal brain function, I'm afraid."

Mason's exhilaration fled as quickly as it had come. "Everyone out," he said. "Now!"

The technicians all looked at each other, then at Antonia, who nodded. They filed out one by one, their personal energy fields deactivating as they left the laboratory.

Mason did the same, then buried his face in his hands. On top of what he had read in his office earlier, his failure to resurrect his ancestor cut even more deeply into his soul. Antonia took a step toward him, then just as suddenly turned away.

"Mason, what is that noise?"

He lifted his head and listened. For a moment, he heard nothing, then, in the silence, a clicking, as if an old analog speaker was being powered on and off in a succession of dots and dashes:

".- -- .. -. -. --- .. .-. .-.-.-.- .. .- -- "

Antonia was looking at him with a puzzled expression on her face. "No doubt just residual data from the failed transfer. Shall I have the room swept?"

"No—no." Mason sprang to the nearest station, activating his energy shield as he did so. "Track source of frequency disturbance. Enable audio translation link." When the computer indicated this had happened, Mason spoke again, "Who's there?"

As if from a thousand miles away, an unmodulated voice replied, faint at first, then gathering strength with each word. Antonia and Mason stared at each other in utter astonishment.

"I...am...Benjamin...Noir."

CHAPTER THREE

After suffering Fliv's painstaking evaluation of her training for what seemed like hours, Shizume couldn't stand it any longer.

"Look, I know what I saw. There was a third guy there, and whatever bug was in the program turned him into a 1.5-meter tall Venus Flytrap. Just let me bring it up on my optics, and I'll show you."

During the second year of training, after the wannabes had washed out, all New York police officers underwent transplant operations, replacing organic body parts with cybernetic ones. The degree a person was altered depended on their assignment. Since Shizume wasn't going into any ultra high risk assignments like Narcotix, Vice, or Special Purpose Assault Teams, she just had the basic package. Her cybernetic eyes used a technology developed more than a century ago to replace the natural rods and cones in her retinas with hundreds of thousands of nanoscopic electrodes. Because they were configurable for different situations, she could record to Fliv or just about any wireless data storage device within her range. She also had the ability to see across a variety of spectrums, including limited telescopic vision equal to an eagle's—enabling her to spot a pigeon from a mile away—low light, and thermal. Her hearing was also improved, able to hear a human heartbeat like she had in the simulation. As she was still a trainee, her partner controlled the implants until she became completely acclimated to using them by mental commands.

Her standard police weapon, the stunfinger, was a cybernetic device connected to a small implant battery that was recharged by kinetic motion and worked by amplifying her body's own electrical field into a focused bioweapon. The replacement cyber-finger, designed and manufactured by NoirCorp, emitted a beam of energy calibrated to scramble a target's central nervous system, rendering them unable to move. It worked through all clothing and some physical barriers, although most metal hybrids used in building construction during the past thirty years stopped it. Even a top-flaming firedust junkie could be brought down without a problem, although the beam was completely absorbed by a human body, which is why the second perp in the scenario had managed to escape. The weapon could be set for one person or widened to a sixty-degree cone that could incapacitate up to a dozen people at full power. The partners were also equipped with a more powerful version of the stunfinger for crowd control. The weapon system had made riots almost a thing of the past, as half-a-dozen equipped officers and their partners could face down ten times their number and pacify a crowd with little difficulty.

The mods also included a tightly guarded spinal implant that rendered every officer immune to the stunfinger's effects. Officers were constantly monitored by their partners and central command, so in the unlikely event of an officer going rogue, the implant could be deactivated, ensuring that they could be pacified with relative ease. Every few years the black market claimed to have invented a way around the stunfinger, but nothing the chopdocs came up with ever worked even half as well as they claimed.

Shizume's eyelids flickered, and the wallscreen split in half. She and Fliv observed the training run again, this time from her perspective, all the way up to the takedown of the second suspect.

"Okay, stop—here. He should be..."

"Who should be where?"

"No, shang it, he was right there. I looked right at him," she said. "Good-looking guy, maybe 20 years old, blond and blue, dressed like someone in one of those Renaissance Age hover-cruises, puffy shirt, tight pants, leather—where could he afford leather in this city?—boots."

"Having reviewed both recordings of your scenario—yours and mine—and other than your flagrant disregard for following orders—I found nothing else out of the ordinary."

"What! I followed the orders I was given—" Shizume said.

The voice of the command computer rebuked her as its words echoed inside her mind. *"Proceed inside and secure the area. Apprehend any suspects encountered."*

"That does not include leaving a wounded officer to pursue a fleeing suspect."

"His partner was nearby—"

"Nearby and on scene are two different things," her partner replied. *"The fact remains that you left a downed officer alone without assistance and left the area you had been told to secure. Your back up would have helped you clear the area and track the suspect."*

"But—" Shizume stopped in mid-protest, aware it wouldn't get her anywhere. "All right, I screwed up. But I know what I saw in that corner."

"And apparently you're the only one who saw it. I think we've done enough training for today. You'd better take that shower while you still can."

"Yeah, yeah. Say, Fliv," Shizume began while shucking her skinsuit, "I know the procedural error is going to be sent in, but do you have to report the mystery man as well?"

"You wouldn't be asking me to withhold information, would you?" The voice in her head sounded insulted.

"No, no, I was just wondering—what are you going to say?"

"As I did not see this—person—that you claim you did, I am going to report that your attention was distracted by an unknown stimulus."

"Won't that look funny to the board?"

"If it does, you'd better hope that you can explain it better than you did to me."

Ouch. "Good point," Shizume tossed back over her shoulder at Fliv as she headed for the shower stall, which had unfolded from the wall. "Four minute steam cycle, one minute rainfall, three-minute air dry," she commanded. Even though a recently completed project to convert submerged levels of many sky- and stratoscrapers into water purification and hydroelectric plants was up and running, with 60 million people spread up and around the traditional seven boroughs of Greater New York City, not to mention the tens of millions in the surrounding area, water was still at a premium, and recent shortages had forced the city to introduce rationing measures.

The more things change, the more they stay the same, she thought as she scrubbed herself clean in the billowing clouds. The shower cycle finished and the same jets that had released the water now blew warm air over her, drying her and the shower stall as well. Shizume stepped out of the unit, which quietly melted back into the wall it had sprung from. She took a look at herself in the mirror, seeing the ever-popular blend of Mexican and Asian-American blended with the polygenesis of various American ancestors who had settled the county centuries ago, resulting in a face with brown, slightly upturned eyes, a skin tone somewhere between cream and mocha latte, silky black hair, and a round face accentuated by high, small, gracefully-curving cheekbones. All in all, certainly not bad-looking, judging from some of the admiring glances she had received at the academy. Shizume had been too focused on her training to explore the men behind those stares any further, and besides, a lot of them probably would have been scared off when they learned where she wanted to be stationed.

Brushing her shoulder-length hair back, Shizume activated a snake clip that wound itself into her locks, binding them in one of a dozen pre-programmed styles. Wrapping herself in a truesilk red short robe her mother had given her, she walked to the formchair near the window, sitting down and tucking her legs underneath her, feeling it gently wrap around her and automatically begin massaging and heat therapy.

Leaning back in the chair, she stared out the 224th floor window of her studio apartment, looking at the endless vertical rows of hoload-covered windows surrounding her, the stratoscrapers that encompassed several city blocks, each built on the backs of the ones before it. Along their sides ran vehicles belonging to the round-the-clock transport system that raced up and down the sides of these huge buildings like technological cockroaches. At the bottom, now covered by several dozen meters of water, were the streets and buildings of an older New York she had never seen.

Shizume, however, was comfortable where she was, living in a middle-class three-by-three block apartment complex in the middle of Geistad, which had been deeded to her by her surprisingly rich grandfather ten years ago, to be held in trust until she came of age. When her parents had moved to the New West Coast four years ago, she had elected to stay and never regretted the decision.

There were, however, sacrifices made for her current lifestyle. She had rarely seen real ground. The last time had been on a university trip to one of the last pockets of wilderness in the reforested area that used to be the Gobi desert. *More of NoirCorp's environmental terraforming at work,* she thought. With the world's population ballooning to more than 30 billion, living space was at a premium, and new, inhabitable land was worth its weight in platinum an acre. Inhospitable steppe, taiga,

and tundra had been altered with nanotech and biologic-
ally engineered plants and animals to create new, sustain-
able temperate biospheres. Even now she remembered
being among those spruces and pines in that far-off
forest and shivered, above all remembering how dark it
was out there, away from all the lights.

For if there was one thing Greater New York had an
overabundance of besides ocean water, it was light.
Apartment buildings and businesses sold space on their
sides to advertisers, who could never get enough room
for their "advirtisments," as the slang went. Despite all
their advances and increases in culture and technology,
America had never been able to shake its consumerist
tendencies, and how could it with Madison borough and
the companies always finding new ways to sell, sell, sell.
Still, for all its faults and foibles, Greater New York was
her hometown, and Shizume wouldn't have traded it for
anything.

"News on," Shizume ordered as she walked back to
her closet and slipped into a one-piece temperature reg-
ulating bodysheath. Over that went a standard holo-
jumpsuit, a plain piece of shapeless gray fabric. When
she zipped it up, the logo of the company she worked
for, Trioptics, Inc., appeared on her shoulder and chest.
A matching holo-hat completed the uniform. Even
though she was working in private security for a maxi-
mall downtown, she wasn't allowed to use her stunfinger
until she was a graduated police officer, so she made do
with an ordinary shock glove and battery, which still put
a 100,000-volt taser in the palm of her hand.

On the screenwall behind her, a blandly pleasant
newscaster face droned out news items tailored to Shi-

zume's interests. Like every home in the city, one wall of the main living room was a theater-sized screen that could project life-size 2-D, or 3-D in more advanced models, programming on every conceivable subject. It was also connected to the Ultraweb, a limited level AI that served as a computerized library, communication port, entertainment center, and VR simulator. Voice-controlled like everything else, it could execute complex commands and simulations, anything from a visit to the base on Mars that a watcher could participate in to teaching someone how to make a soufflé, not that they would ever need to.

Going to the wall that served as her kitchen, Shizume ordered a protein shake from the building's basic food-stuff dispenser, what all tenants called the "foodtap," another ubiquitous product of NoirCorp. The microwave-sized device could assemble thousands of meals out of basic synthetic amino acids, proteins, and carbohydrate building blocks stored in vast vaults in the building's protected lower levels. Each meal was prepared to order, and the machine could also plan menus by the day, week, or month based on an individual or family's variant tastes. Whether it was boiled oatmeal, devilled eggs, or prime rib marinated in port wine sauce with shitake mushrooms, everything was calibrated to provide the maximum amount of vitamins and nutrients. Between gulps of her breakfast, Shizume continued dressing, letting most of the news snippets bounce off her mind until she heard one that caught her attention.

"The boroughs of Greater New York were rocked yesterday evening by what city officials are still calling a 'regionalized atmospheric disturbance,'" he said. "The violent storm that swept in caused localized power outages that were quickly handled by NoirCon Electric, which assured the city that there were no problems with the power systems and that electricity had been restored by 0600 hours this morning. Turning to the weather forecast for the tri-borough area—"

Shizume told the wall screen to mute itself during the weather report and bring up the ultranet, one site in particular.

"Eyes Wide Open," she said.

Instead of the flashy graphics and 3-D bells and whistles other sites used to lure readers, Eyes Wide Open was a no-frills site that existed, like millions of others, on the fringes of society. Dismissed by the mainstream as yet another conspiracy platform that listed and investigated unusual occurrences around the world, Shizume would have been inclined to agree, until she actually began reading some of the material posted on it. This morning's column was no different:

<u>Geistad Continues Its Usual Mysterious Ways</u>
by J. H. Payne

It is the morning of June 22nd, 2157, and already events are off to their abnormally strange beginnings in and around the neighborhood of Geistad in Lower Greater New York City. No doubt many of you have heard or maybe even witnessed the strange power disruptions that began last night all over the city. At exactly midnight, multiple energy spikes were recorded all over the seven-borough area, not just in Geistad, but also from White Plains and Yonkers all the way down to Kings County and Staten Island.

Oddly, surrounding areas were unaffected, but that doesn't mean it couldn't happen again. For regular readers of my column, you all know that Greater NYC, and Geistad in particular, is an epicenter for the bizarre, the unusual, the unexplained. And if the signs are correct, it's all going to get a whole lot weirder. Already the following events have been reported occurring yesterday night or early this morning:

—Police reports confirmed that a man and woman were found embedded in the floor of their apartment just after midnight on the 305th floor of a luxury apartment in Northern Manhattan. Even more disturbing, they were apparently both *still alive*. Police removed the entire section of floor and transported it to NoirCorp North General Hospital, where the doctors on staff were perplexed as to how it could have happened. "The victims had somehow become fused with the material they were standing on, as if they had dematerialized for a half-second and resolidified in the flooring itself," an anonymous source said this morning. "The even more puzzling thing is why they are still alive and in, from what we can determine so far, relatively stable condition."

—A natural-born cat with two heads, one next to the other, is alive and healthy today at an undisclosed location in Geistad. While the current fad for genengineered, multi-headed pets shows no sign of stopping, among normal animals such a mutation is extremely rare and usually is born dead or dying. This one (see linked bi- and trideo below) is in what appears to be the best of health and is eating and responding to stimulus on both sides. Long thought to be a harbinger of evil by the superstitious, this freak of nature's appearance may be much more ominous than people realize.

–The Greater New York City Urban Planning Department has called an emergency meeting to discuss the apparent disappearance of the 79th floor of the cube apartment building at Roosevelt Avenue and Junction Boulevard in Queens today. Visitors to the floor have reported the elevator doors opening to reveal nothing but solid metal. It is unknown at this time the fates of the more than 350 families that had previously occupied the level. Several dozen residents who were away from the floor at the time of the transformation returned to find their families and lives apparently gone. The Council has yet to release a statement about this amazing phenomenon, but EWO will keep you updated as soon as we have any more information.

So what does this mean for you, my discerning readers? Well, if you're reading this from anywhere outside the tri-state area, probably nothing. It's just idle amusement to pass the time as you shake your head and cluck at those 'crazy Greater New Yorkers.'

However, those who follow my columns and have been keeping up with my game of playing historical connect-the-dots, you know what's coming next. All the way back to the Dunkelstad massacre circa 1668, the Founder's Day deaths of 1710, the infamous Summer Storm of 1822, the Hessian Murders and the Derlicht House Fire in 1842, the Great Kills Harbor incident of 1906, the disappearances around The Raunt during the summers of 1946-47, the society wedding to end all weddings (and perhaps society as they had known it), the merging of Geistad's two most prominent families, the Derlichts and the Noirs, and the events of that fateful day in 2003, the Pet Plague of 2034, and, last but not least, the Great Whiteout of 2087 (see previous columns on each of these), you know that this long-ago trail, the beginnings of which began almost five centuries ago, is building to something. What I'm not sure of, but something, and something big.

The next few months, weeks, or maybe even days will be ones to watch as the strangeness intensifies, culminating in something big that none of us will have ever seen before, and if we're lucky, something that we just might be able to live through. If you've come to EWO looking for answers, sorry friend, right now your guess is as good as mine. But one thing you can be sure of is that I'll keep looking for the answers, wherever and whatever they may be. Of course, how soon I find them may all depend on how many more two headed cats are born tomorrow.

Underneath it was a blinking message to Shizume: *Hey, Shi, what do you think of the new column?*

"Reply to Mr. Payne: A bit dark for light summer reading, don't you think, Grandfather? Although there's a lot to say for the oddities that happened last night and may be still happening today."

As soon as her words were transcribed onto the wall, a screen opened up and the face of a twenty-something man with receding blond hair and three lines of braided beard, one in the middle of his chin and two diagonal trailing back from the corners of his mouth, appeared. He seemed to be floating in mid-air, surrounded by a simple, empty black background.

"Grandfather, it's me. You can drop the public persona," Shizume said, shaking her head.

"All right, all right, just a second," he said. A second later the hip face disappeared, replaced by a man sitting in a simple wooden chair in front of a log cabin wall. His hair was white and full, his face lined by the passing decades, but his eyes still sparkled when he looked at her, and his voice was as jovial and loud as she had always remembered him being, even when he was still in his own body.

Shizume's grandfather had chosen another option for people coming to the end of their natural lives: he had downloaded himself into the web and now existed as a virtual person. Nothing had changed for him. He still ran his site, investigating unusual phenomena in Greater New York City and around the world; only now a portion of his income went to the company that maintained the computer keeping his memory engrams functioning.

J. H. Payne, as he insisted on being known, had been

investigating the events in Geistad for the past forty years. He had also gotten his niece interested in the region and its checkered past. During her first collegiate years, she had worked with him on attempting to untangle the coiled, knotted history of Geistad, all the way back to its Germanic and Dutch roots in the middle 17th century, figuring it might make an interesting sociological study. When Shizume had decided to go into law enforcement, her research had taken a back burner.

Payne had continued his investigations, focusing on the two primary families of the area, the Noirs, currently running their multi-trillion dollar corporation, and, some claimed, the city itself, and the Derlichts, an even older, proud family that had waned as the Noirs had grown stronger. In the early 21st century, the aforementioned marriage between the two families had taken place, and the incredible disturbance that was rumored to have happened on that day was still referred to under people's breath in Geistad as "Noir's Folly." Her grandfather had made it his life's work to write the definitive history of Geistad in all its incarnations throughout history and uncover as much about the strange events that had happened there over the centuries as possible. Much of the past two decades had been spent tracing the various families that married into the Noir family, including a long lost ancestor of Shizume's, a gentleman who appeared then faded from notice within a generation. Usually the project and his site took most of Payne's time, but right now all of his attention was focused on his granddaughter.

"So, do you have something you wanted to add?" he asked.

"Well, I don't know if it counts–" Shizume began.

"First rule of living in GNYC today, and especially where you live: never discount anything," her grandfather interrupted. "Go on."

"All right." She sketched out her training module encounter, including seeing the young man standing in the corner. "Fliv has scanned both my recording of the scenario and his, and he claims that the suspect and I were the only ones in the room. But I know I saw someone there." When she described the young man, Payne's eyes lit up.

"Hold on a nano, did he look something like–" A blank white screen appeared beside Payne's head with a familiar-looking picture on it. "–this?"

"Yeah–yeah, that's him," Shizume said. "He had longer hair, though, mod-pirate style, drawn back into a small ponytail. Where'd you get that?"

"You should know; it was part of our research into the Noir family. I recreated this picture based on a diary of a young woman, Trudi Derlicht, nee Schmidt. She had married Roderick Derlicht in 1843 and wrote about meeting Jon Noir and his brother Thomas during the spate of killings and that Hessian business that the author Washington Irving investigated the previous year. She wrote about him a lot, but by then Jon was already gone, killed in a fire that had started under mysterious circumstances."

"What happened to her?"

"From what I can gather, she died of consumption, tuberculosis, you know, about twenty years later. Her husband apparently lived a relatively unspectacular life in Geiststadt, as it was known back then, and died in 1907 at the ripe old age, back then at least, of 85.

"Meanwhile, with Benjamin dead, supposedly killed by the Hessian, the house went to Thomas, who did nothing with it. After his death in 1912, the rest of the Noir clan picked up where he had failed and built Noir-Corp into the entity it is today," Payne said. The current owner/operator, Mason Noir, has been in control for the past century and shows no signs of stopping anytime soon. He's the one who got the corporation exempted from being classified as a monopoly, although how he did it only God knows, and the Almighty ain't telling. That man's got pockets so deep you need a gravator to reach the bottom."

"Jon Noir, eh?" Shizume had her wallscreen save the picture of the long dead young man for her. "So, what do you think?"

"Hmm, actual contact from beyond the grave?" Payne asked. "Well, you've read the column; stranger things are certainly happening."

"It also could have been a glitch in Fliv's programming."

"Excuse me?"

"Hey, it's not a complete impossibility, you know."

"It most certainly is," Fliv replied. *"I ran a complete phase seven diagnostic. There is nothing wrong with my programming or my internal matrix."*

"What time did your spectral encounter happen?" Payne asked.

"About 1410 hours, give or take a couple minutes. Why?"

"Of course, you were invirted. That's why you didn't notice anything," Payne replied. "At precisely 1409 another "disturbance," as the city is calling it, swept through, and more strange stuff happened, not only here, but in other areas up and down the coast. I'm getting scattered reports in, but whatever is happening is disrupting communications systems as well. I'm surprised our conversation has lasted this long."

"It's affecting communications...that might explain what happened just before the scenario cut out," Shizume mused.

"What do you mean?"

"Well—this is going to sound mindfried, but—Jon Noir, if that was Jon Noir, turned into a man-sized Venus Flytrap. A very hungry Venus Flytrap."

"If it was a malfunctioning VR program, that's not outside the realm of the possible. If it's something else, however, I have absolutely no idea what it might mean," Payne said. "I suppose Fliv didn't see that either."

"Of course not."

"No, although what I am seeing right now is that Trainee Mader is going to be late for work if she doesn't leave immediately."

"What? Oh, damn it, I've got to go. Stay rezzing on this, and we'll talk later, okay?"

"Hey, no problem, I live to serve," he answered, then winked out.

Shizume stepped into her boots, snugged the shock glove on her hand, and ran out the door.

Behind her, Fliv anti-graved the robe from the back of her chair into the closet that sprang out to meet him then settled down in a corner to wait for her return.

CHAPTER FOUR

W hat the hell is happening?" Mason asked, pacing across the length of the room only to whirl at the end and retrace his steps. "There's been no change? Not one word, not one damned sound?" He hated being out of control like this, and ever since the first fragmented bit of speech they had heard, there hadn't been a sound from the computers. But something was happening inside...

"Not for the past, oh, eight hours and seventeen minutes," Antonia said, sitting in a formchair as she watched the streams of data flow by a wallscreen. "Whatever is in the system is accessing—well, the entire knowledge of humanity.

"What I don't understand is why you're letting this happen, why you didn't you let me purge the system like I wanted to at the beginning?" she continued, regarding Mason with a frown. "This anomaly could have corrupted valuable data, perhaps even fragged other stored engrams."

"Because one of the things I've learned during the past century is to never jump to conclusions," Mason replied, looking over her shoulder. "Besides, the transfer program in completely enclosed. There's no way a virus or any anomaly could escape to the mainframe or net. So once we had determined that it was something more, I thought we'd see what it wanted to do.

"Here's a bigger question: if the botched transfer did save a memory engram, whole or fragmented, into the mainframe, how can a consciousness more than three centuries old understand the complexities of this system, our data, our files?"

"As much as both you and I both hate this answer, I don't know," Antonia replied. "I'm only going by logic here. The last transfer we were doing was of Benjamin—which I was unaware that we were even attempting today," a chill had crept into her voice, and she altered her tone with an effort. "But as that was the last transfer, and a scan of the system shows no others active, then I must assume that the one we did was partially successful, at any rate.

"Here's what I can tell you: it hasn't accessed any of our encrypted data, but it did try to pierce the icewall, which went up immediately when the system detected the foreign consciousness. When it was rejected, it didn't bother trying again. My guess is that the sentience, again assuming that it is Benjamin, is trying to catch up on the last three centuries it missed while it was comatose in that jar. As to how it's doing it, I don't know—yet."

"Sentience? Are you saying that we can—speak to him?" Mason asked.

"Not yet, although we know he's there, and I'm fairly certain it knows we're out here as well," Antonia said. "The internal program safeguards have shunted it into a closed node, and I've given it a read-only link to the ultranet, which is all it's been accessing since. My suggestion, which hasn't changed from when I mentioned it several hours ago, is that we just wait for it to contact us again. Eventually he—it will to run out of things to learn, and, if intelligent, will look outward, make an attempt to communicate."

Mason looked at his wife for a second, remembering all those countless times where her direct speech and problem-solving acumen had served him so well. Though he had been awake for more than thirty hours, he wasn't fatigued at all, although he did wipe at his eyes, finding wetness on his palms when he took them away.

"Mason, have you heard a word I've said?" Antonia asked. "Are you all right?"

"Fine—I'm fine," he said. "Very well, we'll wait."

"Would you care to sit down?" she asked. "I've got room for two."

Just a few hours ago that offer would have brought a smile to his lips, but now Mason's mouth hardened into a thin line. "Sorry, I'm just too wound up over this. I need to know what we saved, and what condition it, or he, or whatever we've got in there is in. You know I've always hated waiting—"

"A not unadmirable trait, Mason," a voice said from the walls around them. The accent they had heard before was now subdued, gentler, but there still lurked a trace of hard Germanic consonants in its tone. *"It means that you are always looking ahead to what is going to happen."*

Mason and Antonia exchanged glances. "Benjamin?" Mason asked.

"Yes, I am Benjamin Noir, or I was a very long time ago. Now it appears I am something—else."

Both of the Noirs swallowed hard before replying. "You are correct, Benjamin, you have been transferred from—whatever state you existed in before now, into a—machine called a computer," Antonia said. "This machine—"

"Young lady, I am not an idiot," the voice replied. *"Why do you think I was studying your data? Once I mastered the skill of using these streams of electrons to move from one area or another, or to manipulate data for my viewing, then it was a simple matter of 'catching up,' I believe the phrase is, or was, at any rate, on the advances that have happened in the last three hundred years."*

"But—how are you able to comprehend what we have achieved in the last three centuries?" Mason asked. "In your time there were horse-drawn carriages and homes were heated by open fire. You had not split the atom, or harnessed hydrogen, or anti-gravity, or sent a man into space, to the moon, to Mars—"

"Hmm, I had hoped that my offspring would be a little less verbose, however, it seems that is something I shall grow used to."

"Excuse me?" Mason tried not to gape in astonishment, ignoring Antonia's attempts to silently calm him. "That's certainly an interesting perspective, considering without me, you wouldn't even be here—"

"Ah, there you are mistaken," the voice continued. *"For without me, you would not be here. And without my fortune, none of* this *would be here."*

Mason began to retort, then decided silence was the better part of valor, shutting his mouth with a snap.

"That's better, now—is there some way I can appear in front of both of you?" Benjamin asked. *"Surely technology has advanced that far. Just the illusion of being outside this contraption for now would be a relief."*

Mason and Antonia exchanged smiles, and he nodded. "Of course, Benjamin. Activate holoform template, human, standard Caucasian male, forty-five years old—"

"Make that fifty-five, if you please," Benjamin said.

"—Right. Fifty-five years old," Mason said.

There was a flash of light, and the body of a human man stood before them, dressed in a simple one piece bodysuit, his eyes closed, as if he was sleeping on his feet. His hair was black, cut short, and topped an average face on an average body.

"Benjamin," Mason said, glancing around at the walls. "Where you are, there should be a flashing doorway—"

"I am already here, Mason," the hologram said. "Although my appearance leaves something to be desired."

"Of course. Holoform, edit mode," Mason said. "Just picture yourself in your mind, and the hologram will adjust itself to match."

Benjamin closed his eyes, and the image began to flow and reshape itself. The top half of the bodysuit transformed itself into a rough-woven linen shirt with loose, billowy sleeves rolled up to expose tanned forearms, its collar secured with a leather thong threaded through three eyelets on either side. Dark brown trousers flowed down to tuck into high black boots, the toes of which were scuffed from long hard use.

The shape of the body was altering itself as well. Along with the more defined muscles came height, a full ten centimeters past the standard 170 that was the norm for an average male. Although the holo was designed to stand with perfect posture, somehow its spine stiffened just a bit more, not in a haughty or overbearing way, but imperious, as if the inhabitant was the lord of all he surveyed. The shoulders drew back, and his booted feet came together with a click.

The head and face changed to match. The short black hair sprouted out into wavy locks that cascaded down to the shoulders, which were then were gathered together and secured with a length of silk ribbon. His eyes shifted from a neutral brown to a dark black, giving his hooded gaze a piercing directness. His nose elongated, becoming more pronounced and aquiline. On anyone else it would have been overpowering, but Benjamin's jaw was firming and reshaping itself as well, becoming a sharp-edged line that blended into his angular Roman chin. Over that sprouted a large iron-gray beard held in check with rows of small gray-blue stones entwined in it that rustled and clicked when he moved. All in all, he was a very handsome, if imposing, hologram.

Mason noted a subvocal channel message opening via his energy sheath. He activated it to hear Antonia's whisper. "Well, he does resemble a middle-aged Benjamin, at least from how the family histories described him."

Mason brought up a holoscreen. "According to the data we have on this, the 'sentience' is emanating from the banks that had previously stored the scanned memories from Benjamin's DNA sample, although they've—changed somehow—become—alive, for lack of a better word. May we can ask him in a bit—"

"I can see you both now, and I—feel the room—the very air—around me. How is this possible?" Benjamin asked, staring down at his new self with an amazed look on his face. He raised an arm, moved his hand, looked around the room, all with the joyous expression of a child who has just learned to walk.

"The 'sensations' you are feeling are actually constantly updated data being fed to you by the room itself, " Mason said as he walked across the room, Benjamin following his every move. "As something happens in real-time, the data is updated, so you have the option of following me or continuing to watch whatever you were previously looking at."

Benjamin's attention returned to Antonia as she picked up Mason's explanation. "This is the really incredible thing about it." She tossed a test tube at Benjamin's head, smiling as his hand shot up and grabbed it. "Not bad for three-hundred-year old reflexes. The hologram projector uses anti-gravity fields to hold and move objects. You can carry something, or," she motioned for him to throw the tube back, which he did after examining it for several seconds, "give something to someone."

"Amazing," Benjamin murmured. "I had foreseen many incredible things in the future, but nothing like this." He walked over to Mason and extended his hand. "You have done well."

There was a crackling flare of light around Mason's hand and arm, and Benjamin's image wavered and fragmented before reshaping itself. "I didn't get a chance to tell you," Mason said, "both my wife and I are encased in a standard issue protective energy field that prevents any potentially harmful contaminants from contacting us," Mason said.

The holographic Benjamin shook his hand in absent reflex. "Effective."

"The protective program autosets itself depending on the threat level," Antonia said. "No doubt it sensed your approaching anti-gravity field and moved to block it. However, I don't think we're in any danger, do you, Mason?"

"No—no, of course not."

With another brief flare of light, Antonia deactivated her sheath. "Ah, much better."

"Well, in that case, it is my pleasure to greet you first," Benjamin said with a smile.

About to interject, Mason was forestalled by his ancestor turning on his heel and striding over to Antonia. With a courtly flourish, he took her hand and kissed it. Antonia appeared nonplussed, but Mason could tell that the move had impressed her.

"At least I haven't forgotten everything while being away," Benjamin said with a smile. "This is a great improvement over the past few centuries. But, to continue our earlier conversation, in a sense I have always been here."

"In spirit, you mean?" Antonia asked.

"You have wit to match your loveliness, despite your parentage, no offense intended, my dear," Benjamin said.

"None taken," she murmured, frowning at Mason.

"Yes, here in spirit alone, unknown, unseen, forgotten,"

Benjamin said. "Only after my unfortunate demise did I realize just what 'ghosts,' as the ignorant, superstitious peasants called them, really were.

"Now that I had become one, I had all the time in the world to study where I was, and more importantly, *why* I still lingered in this world. Along the way, I saw the advances that changed the world, even in pitiful, backwards Geiststadt.

"But perhaps we should start at the beginning. Popular theory, which, I see, hasn't advanced very much in the last century-and-a-half, still claims that ghosts or spirits, or whatever you want to call them, are the leftover spiritual impressions of people killed by violent death."

"Yes," Antonia said. "There was a small movement in the early 22nd century that based their studies on the theory that ghost sightings were a limited form of time travel, a kind of 'spirit echo' that appeared in the present day. A man named Archel, Carter Archel, was the progenitor of this idea."

"And what did you think of his hypothesis?"

"I—I didn't give his theories much credence," she replied.

"Mason, you *did* choose well."

"Yes, Benjamin, I thought so as well," Mason replied, noticing his wife's darkening countenance. STEADY, DEAR, LET'S HEAR HIM OUT. He wrote to her.

GOOD TO KNOW THAT CHAUVINISM WAS STILL ALIVE AND WELL IN THE 18TH CENTURY. She replied on his screen.

Mason shook his head and returned his attention to Benjamin. "Please, continue."

"Archel was an idiot who had no idea what he was

talking about," Benjamin said. "The old theories are much closer to the truth.

"Ghosts are impressions of people, but they are not tied to emotion, or violence, or even a particular place. What you call spirits are nothing more than thought engrams—engrams that are powerful enough to exist on their own, without a corporeal body to house them. Free-form psychic activity, one might call it. When paranormal investigators find 'evidence' of spirits in certain houses, they are sensing the thoughts of people, thoughts strong enough to survive decades, even centuries later. That is why many people feel chills in the air in haunted houses or castles. In those homes, it was always cold and drafty, so of course the latent psychic impressions are going to concern heat and cold."

"What about the theory that spirits are trapped in one place, tied to it, kind of like how you were connected to the blood I used?" Mason asked.

"That part also contains an element of truth to it," Benjamin continued. "The entities called ghosts 'exist' only because of the intensity of certain thoughts and psychic impressions, ones so strong that they can exist independently on this plane. Only the most focused engrams survive, which is why so many are tied to acts of violence, hate, destruction, et cetera. Consequently, these engrams are repeated, sometimes strong enough to actually cause the person they came from to appear. Other times it is just a destructive physical force, the *poltergeist*, they named it, noises, cold spots, or the like. As there is no guiding force to continue the thought, it is trapped in an endlessly repeating cycle. Only a very few, such as myself and other members of my family, retained the consciousness to break free and roam, although what we are able to do on this plane is vastly overrated."

"So the entire theory of ghost and spirits is nothing more than leftover psychic activity in the material world," Antonia said.

"I would hardly call myself leftover, but yes, you certainly have the basic premise. I would have thought that when you figured out how to capture and download, as you call it, the engrams and memories of a person, that someone would have come up with the idea of trying to scan a place where a spirit has been reported to see if they could get a reading," Benjamin said.

"Uh—proprietary technology patents make that impossible for anyone else, I'm afraid, but that is an interesting idea." Mason said, mentally kicking himself for not thinking of it seventy-five years ago. "But that doesn't explain how your—free-roaming thoughts—for lack of a better word, mystically found their way back here. All of my research had shown that memory and thought patterns are encapsulated in every cell of the body, blood, bone, hair, whatever. Now we resurrect you and you're telling us your psychic self has been flitting around New York City for the past three centuries?"

"I do not expect you to believe it, indeed, it is a tale I would scarcely give any credence to myself," Benjamin replied. "I can only tell you what I experienced.

"Although I had researched the concept of life after death for decades, trying to unlock that ultimate mystery, immortality, it was only after my death at the hands of my cowardly son, Thomas, that I finally understood.

"In a sense, every human being is immortal, if only

by the fact that the dead themselves can still survive and be conscious of their existence, depending on the strength of their psyche at the time of passing over.

"Once I realized this, I began to explore this new world and found myself severely limited in both power and ability. My world had shrunk to Geiststadt, my existence bounded by the demarcation lines of the village itself. Imagine my shock to discover that I was just as trapped as those poor souls who lived here, including my betraying son, Thomas, who stole what he thought was rightfully his. But I had the satisfaction of seeing him receive his just reward.

"I have watched Geiststadt survive, change, and grow for hundreds of years. I have observed endless generation after generation scratch out their meager living from this damned dirt, only to return to the dust from whence they came. If fortunate, they left a pitiful legacy of children doomed to the same fate, if not, their lineage vanished out of this world as if they had never existed on any plane.

"I have seen the land altered, raised, lowered, built on and destroyed, all the while unable to interact with a single person, unable to influence even the smallest event, forced to spend my days sitting idle, watching the pitiful world I was trapped in go by, day after endless day." Benjamin paced the length of the room as he spoke, as if measuring the walls with his eyes. He looked at Mason. "Could I leave this building if I wanted to?"

"Our projectors only work in here," the younger man replied. "If you were completely on the web, you could create any place you wanted, but it would all be an illusion, albeit real to you."

"So instead of the world being real and myself being intangible, now I am as real as possible and can have the world be an illusion around me," Benjamin said.

"Something like that, " Antonia said. "So, you were saying, you were stuck in Geiststadt, like any other psyche?"

"True," Benjamin replied. "In that respect, I was not like those fragments, forever repeating their strongest memories. But three centuries of imprisonment have been long enough, and when I felt the pull of my consciousness being regenerated, I simply followed it here. Now, one of the things I cannot explain is how my psyche existed outside my body and was able to meld with the materials you extracted from the blood I left behind. Perhaps it was a synergy of some kind, the recreation of the body and mind drawing me back to a more stable environment. But if that is true—"

Benjamin was interrupted by a distant dull rumbling that reverberated through the room. It was followed by a small but distinct tremor that rattled the building to its core, including the laboratory.

"Was that what I think it was?" Mason asked, opening a monitor to look outside. "There haven't been any earthquakes here since the Shock of 2113. Afterward we developed the NoirCorp Seismic Neutralizer, which has kept this area stable for more than forty years. Antonia, please see if this was a local occurrence or if it was throughout the region."

"I was afraid of this," Benjamin said, causing both Mason and Antonia to look at him. "That was a shock-wave, but not the kind either of you are thinking of,"

Benjamin said. "You are familiar with chaos theory, I assume?"

"Naturally," Mason replied, trying to keep the smile off his face as he spoke. "The theory that, given a defined set of parameters, an object or event will continue to exist or occur in a proscribed order until a stressor is introduced. The ordered system will not achieve total randomness immediately but instead react to the chaos being introduced and create subsystems that still attempt to maintain order. As more chaos is introduced, the subsystems continued to take on that chaos and break down themselves until the whole system is in complete turbulence. A good example is a pot of boiling water on a stove. At first the heat energy excites columns of water, and they bubble upward to the surface in controlled chaos. But as more heat energy is added, the system breaks down until the entire mass of water is boiling furiously, having achieved total chaos as a function of its basic systems. However, you can boil a million pots of water, and no two of them will ever boil in exactly the same way, even though the conditions under which the stress, or heat, was introduced are exactly the same for the first as they are for the last."

"Excellent," Benjamin said. "Of course, we had no idea that chaos theory existed in my day, but it fits what is happening perfectly."

"And that is?" Antonia asked, her attention divided between the ongoing conversation and the holoscreens in front of her.

"Picture your existence—the two of you, New York, the world—as that pot of water, if you will," Benjamin said. As he spoke, a hologram of the earth appeared in front of them, city lights of major population centers twinkling as the globe rotated in mid-air. "My, this technology is amazing. Anyway, my existence here is the stressor, which is having an effect on the entire space-time continuum. Its reaction is to try to bring natural order back to the universe by causing my dissolution as a man existing out of time—in other words, out of the psychic level—and restoring the order of things as they are meant to be."

As he spoke, a small pulsing dot appeared over New York, followed by other areas in the world, cities, oceans, everywhere, rippling outward until they covered the entire planet in expanding waves of red light. Wherever they appeared, the city lights vanished, leaving an empty, dark void in their wakes.

"In the course of this, the waves that your city, and eventually the world, will experience will cause an awful lot of physical turbulence until the anomaly is corrected."

"So, just because you're not in a physical body, the universe itself is trying to destroy you?" Antonia asked. She turned towards a bank of holoscreens, where several flashing dots had appeared over the last few minutes. "Although we are now getting reports in from several of our subsidiaries around the world regarding similar tremors, I find it hard to believe that you're the cause of it all."

"I certainly can't fault your reaction," Benjamin replied. "The universe exists in a relatively ordered state, expansion and contraction and all that, but within it are layer upon infinite layer of chaos to its very core, contained in billions of interlocking subsystems. Given the right change-inducing stressor, the ripple effect of that chaos spilling across space and time will be very destructive in both the short and long term. But as you said earlier, Mason, there hasn't been any seismic activity for decades, and now..."

"You're standing here in front of us telling us oh so calmly that, as far as you know, reality itself is going to just unravel, until we, everything, is gone?" Mason asked. "And to fix everything, all we've got to do is place you back into a human body? Why didn't you tell us this right away?"

Benjamin looked at him for a moment. "Just because there was the chance of it happening did not mean it was automatically going to," he replied. "I had hoped that the transferal would have gone off without any problems. But it hasn't, so now we all have to deal with it, and the sooner we get started, the better."

Mason's lips pursed as he strode to the wallscreen and began bringing up files. "I just hope your little education hasn't caused the destruction of the entire world. Can you at least give me an estimate of just how long we've got?"

"Given that I've never tried to calculate the destruction of the space-time continuum before, and going only by the interval between the two waves and their relative intensity, my rough guess is about eleven hours, maximum," the simulacrum replied. But all this is going to be for naught if we cannot figure out why the first try wasn't successful."

"I think I may have the answer to that," Antonia said, her every movement calm, crisp efficiency. "Look here."

She set up a holoscreen to replay the transfer from the point Benjamin was supposed to have awakened.

Watching it as well as the other two, Mason saw Benjamin wince as his body decayed before his eyes. He also saw Antonia watching the hologram's reaction, and he noticed a small, satisfied smile flit across her face. *Vindictive little minx*, he thought. *Of course, I should know—now.*

"I hope your little display is meant to reveal something pertinent," Benjamin grumbled.

"Of course, Benjamin," Antonia said, her voice honey-sweet. "Although we were able to extract your primary memory engrams from that live blood sample, it appears that your psyche is not strong enough to awaken a cloned body—without help."

"Interesting, but that doesn't explain the onset of rapid aging that occurred as soon as the bodyform awoke," Mason said.

"Yes," Benjamin said, staring at his immersed vegetative self. "How do you account for that?"

Mason heard the hint of pride in Antonia's voice as she answered. "Even though we overlaid Benjamin's scanned and constructed DNA helix over the bodyform, the instability caused by the sample's exposure to air began immediately. It just wasn't picked up right away. As a result, the scan was flawed from the beginning. Although the helix overlay seemed to take, the moment the body came out of the nutrient cocoon, cellular breakdown was inevitable."

"So a standard clone form isn't sufficient," Mason said. "To put you into a compatible body, we have to go to the source," Mason said, pacing the floor again.

"But all the samples were lost," Antonia said. "Kar's been trying to salvage what he can, but his latest report says he's only recovered nine percent of the helix, and he doubts there will be much more living DNA to assemble."

"What are you talking about," Mason asked, his face darkening. "How can genetic material be destroyed simply because the blood cells have died?"

"First, it's not me, its Kar saying this," Antonia replied. "Second he's at just as much of a loss as well, but he says the double helix of the sample has unraveled as they died, and then each chain fragmented into individual nucleic acids. He's tried to reassemble them, but it's going to take time—time we don't have."

"True, very true, but you're forgetting one thing," Mason said as he pointed to himself. "I'm a Noir too. In my blood flows the history of the Noirs, including—"

"—my genetic contribution," Benjamin finished.

"Exactly," Mason said. "The real problem is that I don't have a bodyform made up, as we usually don't worry about replacement before age ninety. We've found that if you store a cryogenically-frozen body form for longer than a decade after you've grown it, it basically does the same thing your blood did—begins to break down at the cellular level."

"But to grow a form for Benjamin based off your DNA will take years," Antonia said. "If what he said is correct, we're already doomed."

"Not necessarily," Mason replied. "There's that project Kar and I have been dabbling with off and on for the past decade or so. We had first conceived it as an emergency overlay system, for that occasional case that was already too old to survive until their replacement body could be grown, or someone who was involved in a severe enough accident to require immediate transferal.

"The subject is placed into suspended animation, and the helix scan is done and overlaid directly to a new body, which is given certain illegal growth hormones to advance its development to the young adult stage. Because of the inherent risks in the entire process, there is a higher chance of body abnormality, quickened aging, gigantism, that sort of thing. However, it is usually stable for several years, which means that another, normal body can be grown during this time. However, it wasn't deemed cost effective when compared to the frequency of use versus maintaining a unit."

"Despite the risks, it sounds like that is our only option to provide me with a body before the entire universe comes crashing down around us," Benjamin said.

"Mason, I don't like this," Antonia said. "There's no proof that anything is happening because of what we've done here. Even though there are other tremors, even with the coincidence of them occurring at the same time, I think we need more data before drawing any kind of conclusion."

"I'm afraid I must disagree; time is of the essence," Benjamin said. "The longer we wait—"

"According to you, and you haven't given me anything I'm willing to risk my husband over," Antonia said. "The more I think about it, your entire theory sounds more and more preposterous—"

"That's enough, Antonia." Mason's head snapped up, and the determined look on his face was laser-like in its focus. "Regardless of who is right and who isn't, if there's even a chance of what Benjamin has told us coming to pass, we must take whatever steps we can to try and prevent it.

"So, we'd better get started, because the shortest scan time we got was a bit over ten," he continued. "This overlay has to be the newest possible, which is why it takes so damn long. Even our parity DNA computers take a bit of time, and we want to make sure this is done right. I'll prep for stasis immersion immediately."

"Is there any way I might be of assistance?" Benjamin asked.

"Yes, you'll be my link to Antonia while I'm under," Mason said. "Let's get moving, people."

He headed for the door, with Antonia just ahead of him, her lips set in a tight line of disapproval. As they walked Mason saw Benjamin's face reflected in the smooth glasteel of the computer banks. For a moment he thought he saw a satisfied, covetous smirk on Benjamin's face, but the hologram passed the bank so quickly that he couldn't be sure. *And who wouldn't be satisfied regaining even a semblance of life after so long?* he thought as he headed out the door, his mind already moving on to the complexities of what they were about to try.

CHAPTER FIVE

Shizume ran down the hallway again, stunfinger at the ready. Rounding the corner, she ordered the dustjunkie to freeze, but he didn't. He just stood up and turned towards her, and then he wasn't the addict anymore, his features morphing into those of the man in the corner, and he was standing right in front of her, and his mouth opened. He tried to say something, but she couldn't hear anything but a dull roar, like the ocean whipped up against the bottom floors of New York, and the roar was getting louder and louder—

With no warning at all, the floor dropped away, sending her spiraling down, down into an endless tube of blackness. Shizume screamed, her mouth locked open in terror, but any sound she made was absorbed into the darkness around her. Just when she thought it would never end, she found herself in a room unlike anything she had ever seen before. It was a room made of wood with rough beams framing a pitched roof and plaster walls that could only be made of that antique material. One end of the room was burned, blackened, the walls and floor charred and sooty. Ancient wooden boxes and *chests were scattered around the area with no rhyme or reason to their arrangement.*

And in the middle of it stood that man again, Jonathan Noir, if her grandfather was right. He was dressed exactly as he had been in her sim and reached out to her, beckoning her forward. Unable to stop herself, she took a step, then another, almost to within reach of his hand. It was close enough to touch, and she reached out for it—

—only to see a burned, blackened body attached to the other end, pale white teeth grinning from a charred, lipless mouth under gaping eye sockets. Shizume tried to pull away, but his hand had now curled around her own and held her in its unbreakable grip, crisped fingers digging into her skin—

Shizume jolted awake, trying to recall the simple command to banish the darkness that kept eluding her memory. *Wait a minute—*"Lights."

A soft glow emanated from the walls revealing her sparse bedroom with only a shelf nightstand next to her low anti-grav mattress sleeping field. Shizume took a deep breath and rolled out of bed, simultaneously coming awake and trying to hold on to the already elusive elements of the dream that had awakened her.

Or was it just that? she thought as she padded to the bathroom. After finishing there, she trotted out to the kitchen and got a chugpak of water from the cabinet. Activating it, she watched the frost creep up the sides as the chemical reaction in the plasticine container cooled its contents. After a few seconds, she popped the tab and took several long gulps.

"Is anything wrong, Trainee Mader?" Fliv asked from the corner.

"No—yes—I'm not sure," she said, moving to the bar that formed part of the kitchen and slowly sitting down. As soon as she began, a single-stemmed stool grew from the floor to support her. "I dreamed about him."

"About who?"

"The mystery man in the trainer sim today, who else?" Shizume said.

"The mystery man who does not exist."

"Funny, very funny."

"And the techs say I have no sense of humor," Fliv replied, still deadpan. *"It's not uncommon for the subconscious to utilize elements of events and people encountered during the day as part of your REM-sleep dreamtime."*

"Huh, that's funny, I thought you just said he didn't exist," Shizume said.

"I do have a theory about the whole incident, but I don't think you'll want to hear it."

"Oh?"

"Given your penchant for what I can only describe as apparent hallucinations, I'm afraid my diagnosis would suggest a psychotic break, indicating perhaps that you are on the verge of a fugue state of some kind during which you see things that aren't there," Fliv replied.

"You're right, I didn't want to hear it," Shizume said, tossing back the rest of her water.

"Do you wish to make an appointment with the mental health department?"

"No, thank you." Shizume paced between the kitchen

and her window. After a few laps, she turned to the wallscreen. "Screen on, J. H. Payne, Eyes Wide Open."

The screen winked on, and seconds later, Payne was blinking at her, his own wallscreen on behind him.

"Don't you ever sleep?" she asked.

"As my own great-grandfather said, that's for when I'm dead," he said, the grin on his face fading as he caught her expression in response to his humor. "Hey, what's going there, Shi?"

"What happened to Jon Noir?" she asked.

"I told you, killed in the Derlicht House Fire."

"Tell me everything you know about it," Shizume said.

"Whoa, why the interrogation, officer?"

"I dreamed about him, just now," Shizume replied. "He was standing in an old, old room, framed in what had to be wooden beams, with part of it burned away. It was so real, I thought I smelled smoke. So, please, if you would."

"Sure, no problem." Payne opened up a screen to reveal a picture of an ancient oil painting, cracked and darkened with age, depicting a large square three-story mansion going up in flames. Despite its obvious status as an aristocrat's house, the surrounding grounds were deserted, with no bucket brigade or any attempt to combat the blaze to be seen. The only sign of hope was the paradoxical storm cloud filled sky overhead, seemingly about to deluge the conflagration.

"This is Thomas Cole's legendary lost painting, *The Burning of Derlicht Haus*, which he completed in 1847, just two years before he died. More famous for his masterful landscapes, this was found more than a century later and was thought to have been his statement against

man's claiming more and more forest territory for urban-
ization."

"Great, it's a nice painting, I guess, but what does that
have to do with anything?" Shizume asked.

"Because this was the fire that Jonathan Noir lost his
life in, sort of," Payne replied.

"How so?"

"The only witness at the house was a butler named
Pompey, who said that Jon had come to visit Agatha
Derlicht, the head of the family, who was in ill health at
the time," Payne began. "The fire began soon after, supposedly started by an Irish thug in Thomas Noir's employ,
and the building went up in flames. But, according to
Pompey, a sudden squall appeared out of nowhere, right
over the manor house, and doused the flames before they
could spread to the attic. Witnesses later claimed they
found fish and plants from the nearby river there, as if
the water had been sucked up and flown over the burning
house, but Cole wisely decided not to illustrate that part.

"Anyway, Agatha Derlicht was found in the attic, alive,
mind you, with Jon's body around her, dead not from
the flames or smoke but from a stab wound to the chest.
Rumors rezzed that someone else's bones had been found
in the debris as they were clearing the site away for
rebuilding, but by the time a formal investigation was
made, any evidence of an unknown assailant was gone.
Agatha recovered from the ordeal and lived in the rebuilt
house, complete with the surviving attic, for several more
years."

"Hmm. Can you give me an approximate location of
where the Derlicht House was located in relationship to
modern-day Geistad?" Shizume asked.

"Sure, why don't I just whip up Jon Noir himself to answer your questions while I'm at it?" Payne asked. "Keep in mind that with the flooding of oh, the last seventy-five years, what used to be Geiststadt, or even Geistad proper, is now completely underwater and has been built on so many times that who knows where the original location might be."

"Nevertheless, I'm sure someone with your resources can find it, right?"

"Flattery will get you everywhere," her grandfather replied. "All right, let's see what I can do here. Pull up map for Kings County, New York, years 1840-1845."

The painting disappeared and a black-and-white map with hundreds of notations in spidery calligraphy appeared. Shizume recognized the outline of Long Island and half of Staten Island.

"Overlay with a topographical map and zoom in on Geiststadt."

Altitude lines crossed the map, and a portion magnified itself to enlarge a dot that read "Geiststadt."

"Cross reference with the most accurate census map of the town from 1830-1870," Payne said. The dot expanded even further, and a census map of the town appeared with a date of 1850 in the corner.

"That makes sense. The 1850 census would have been a major accounting throughout the nation, and by that time Derlicht Haus would be rebuilt," Shizume said.

"You know my methods," Payne said. "Even then, the Noirs and the Derlichts were still the most prominent families in the area. Therefore they will have the largest houses. Now Benjamin Noir, the patriarch of the family, was either a visionary or a complete mindfry, take your pick, and built a glass greenhouse at no small expense, it was whispered. So, if that building is contained on this estate here—" yet another portion of the map magnified to reveal a large house with a rectangular building off to one side, both of them surrounded by several smaller outbuildings, "—then the other main house should be Derlicht Haus."

The overhead view panned to a square, three-story home on a barren plot of ground with almost nothing surrounding it. Just seeing the square gave Shizume a momentary chill. "Is that it?" she asked.

"Apparently so," Payne said. "Now comes the really fun part, trying to figure out what happened to the site during the last tri-centuries or so. So, let's see, the Dutch came here in the middle 1640s, and Kings County was created as one of the twelve original counties in New York in 1683. The first town was the village of Breuckelen, the oldest township in NYC, founded in 1646. Eventually it became Brooklyn, and the rest is history."

"Yeah, speaking of history, could we skip a few centuries and get to somewhere closer to the here and now?" Shizume asked as she ordered a bowl of hot Toflex cereal from the foodtap and began eating while she watched.

Payne's face took on a faintly injured look. "Kids these days, no sense of the years gone by. All right, we'll quicken our pace a bit, little miss speed-D. Geiststadt existed on a kind of bubble between Queens and Brooklyn, near what later became Bushwick and Glendale, several miles north of East New York. After the Dutch left the area or died out—and I've never been able to uncover what happened to them, and not for lack of trying, either—they were replaced by Palatine Germans in the early 1800s. The Palatines were just as stubborn as their predecessors and didn't join the city of New York until 1898, right about the time the locals 'modernized' the name to Geistad. That leaves about two and a half centuries to cover. Let's move faster, shall we?

"Extrapolate population and building patterns on three-dimensional map of Geiststadt, no, let's see Kings County in general, 1900 to present. Go."

The wall screen showed two views, one of the population density of Geistad and surrounding Brooklyn, already at more than one million people by 1900. The other showed the landscape and how it had changed since the beginning of the 20th century. Shizume and Payne watched as houses and buildings rose and fell in waves, saw the expansion and growth of the now legendary Coney Island amusement park. A large stadium appeared almost instantly at the corner of Sullivan Place & McKeever Place.

"What's that?" Shizume asked.

"That...was...Ebbets Field Stadium, where an old baseball team named the Dodgers played," Payne replied.

"What, on the ground?" she asked.

"Hey, I've never claimed to understand all this stuff. Just watch," Payne said, as enraptured as she was.

The years marched inexorably forward, and construction continued in the area, with ever-larger buildings appearing. The population ballooned, growing to 2.5 million people by 1930 and remaining relatively stable for the next six decades. The baseball stadium disappeared a little more than halfway through the 20th century, but the amusement park survived. The Verrazano

Narrows Bridge sprang up to connect Staten Island and Brooklyn. And still the town of Geistad kept going, surrounded but never absorbed by the borough around it. Buildings sprang up, aged, and were demolished like a time-lapsed city of sand, rising and falling with the tides of time and fortune. Throughout it all the two colonial homes remained, Noir Manor and Derlicht Haus, two old warriors that refused to bow to the other but stayed eternally vigilant, each guarding their part of the township.

New York City continued to thrive and grow, devouring more of the surrounding land, its appetite insatiable. In 2001 the World Trade Center disaster happened in a blink and two of the largest buildings on the skyline vanished, leaving a crater that was slowly filled in during the next several seconds. Still Shizume's eyes stayed glued to the spot where the Derlicht house stood.

Both houses remained into the next century, when the global warming trend submerged the entire area from 2061-2070, destroying the old neighborhoods and causing the waters of the Atlantic to lap at the feet of the Statue of Liberty, completely submerging Staten Island, Coney Island, and almost washing over Long Island itself.

But the people of New York City fought back, reclaiming the lost land by raising the entire island in a three-decade-long terraforming project that must have cost tens of trillions of dollars. Dykes and dams wound their way around the coastline, protecting the fragile earth. Coney Island had been deemed lost to the hungry waters and was broken off from the main island, a curiosity only sought out by powerfin divers looking for submerged New York nostalgia.

"Wait, stop it right there," Shizume said, leaning forward to examine the map more closely.

"What, what did you see?" Payne asked.

"This—what happened in—2072?" Shizume asked.

As soon as the island was stable, there was a brief period when everything in Geiststadt, now renamed Geistad, and the surrounding environs had been leveled and removed. The area was a barren wasteland with not even a scrap of foliage to be seen.

"Cross-reference development of Geistad from 2069-2073, go," Payne said. Newspaper articles and columns scrolled up, too many of them to read quickly. "Outline and highlight...ah, after the flood they dumped about two trillion tons of earth infused with nanoanchors to seal it to the underwater remains of Long Island and create a base for further development. The essence of it is that in the late 60's, Mason Noir bought all of the land that had been flooded and destroyed and made an offer for anyone who could prove they were descended from a Geiststadt resident to return to the area, selling land parcels at very reasonable prices, even for New York. They had even voted on whether to rename things or keep them the same, and the citizens kept the old names, modernized somewhat for the times. Let's continue forward."

They kept watching the tri- and quad-hundred level apartment buildings climb into the sky, bringing with them the attendant businesses, virt- and maxi-malls, and everything else the residents of an overcrowded city thought they needed. "When the second Global Tide hit, during the Euro-Asian Depression of 2094-99, Mason paid for the construction to raise the town above the water, building the first of the blockpartments. Noir's architectural and engineering innovations set the stage for the next fifty years of development in Greater New York City, and soon it was like 'vertical living' had always been here."

"Shang, my head's spinning," Shizume said. "Okay, so, in between all of this, have we been able to keep track of the Derlicht house?"

"Sure, haven't you been paying attention?" Payne asked with a smile. "Right now what's left of the Derlicht house has been knocked down, paved over, buried under a few million tons of earth, then built on for the past century. I'd say it's right about here."

A glowing red dot blinked deep underneath modern day Geistad with a small readout saying that this particular point was 53.8 meters below sea level. Shizume shook her head.

"Where's the nearest modern building to that point, preferably directly above it?"

"Uh—that would be Grid C-8, block 41A, built in 2092, 12,000 family units," Payne said, a frown crossing his face. "Oh, wait a flash, you're not planning to—"

"Shang right I am."

"Whoa, whoa, hold on a nano. What possible reason do you have for going there, a couple of bad dreams?" Payne asked. "And you can see the view here, there's nothing there but dirt. Hey kid, I love you, but I'm also starting to think you've been reading too many of my columns."

Shizume shook her head. "Something is going on, Payne. I rez that tri-centuries-old dead guy this afternoon, then dream about him again, and it all corresponds too perfectly to what you've just told me," Shizume replied. "My mother's always said there was no such thing as coincidence, and while I didn't always believe her, I'm sure listening now."

"Yeah, but your mother also told you when you were five that the Ursa Major would come down from the sky and eat you if you weren't good, remember?" Payne asked. "And besides, maybe you haven't been keeping up on current events, but from what I've heard, that area of town isn't the best anymore. Since the GNYC Authority collapse out there, some less than hospitable elements hang around, especially in the downlevels," Payne said.

"Relax, I'm almost a cop, remember?" Shizume replied. "I'll zipper over, hit the lowest floor, and be in and out before anyone rezzes me. You wanna come?"

"You mean as a patch, right?" Payne said.

"Of course. You can watch my back, so to speak," Shizume said.

"Yeah, and call for help if you get in a jam," he replied. "You taking Fliv too?"

"I was rather curious about that myself."

"I'd be going as a civilian, not as a officer trainee, Fliv, so how does that stack up in your logic?" Shizume asked.

"A trainee or officer is the patrol assistant's responsibility at all times, except when they are specifically designated by the Department to be working in another capacity not related to the Department," Fliv said.

"Yeah, I sure wish I could take you with me to work at that shanged virtmall," Shizume said. "Well, as your 'responsibility,' let's go," she said, grabbing her shock glove and strapping it on. "Fliv, please patch Mr. Payne into my optics."

"I don't recall that being part of the deal," the hovering unit said.

"Oh, just call it off-the-job training," she replied. "Besides, it'll be good for me getting used to witness and officer walk-alongs."

With the advent of nanotech and cybered officers, police and forensic units could "accompany" street officers on crime scenes, patched into their optic systems. They would see everything the other person saw and could point out suspects and/or evidence, review crime scenes, and assist in the investigation while still in-lab. While it was rare for civilians to accompany the police, occasionally court cases assigned officers to crime scenes while the jury patched in to review evidence at the scene.

"So noted." A flicker later, Payne's face appeared in the lower left quadrant of her vision.

"Hey there," Payne said. "Fliv, I don't suppose you could talk her out of this crazy idea?"

"Trainee Mader's decisions on where she wishes to go are her own business," her partner replied.

"How did I know you were going to say that?" the old man said with a grimace. "So this is what the rest of your apartment looks like."

"You should know," Shizume said. "Shall we?"

With Fliv leading the way, she left the apartment, stepping onto the automated slider that took her past the several dozen other apartments on her level to the Zipper port at the end of the hallway.

"I've already called for one, so it should waiting for us," Fliv informed her.

"I knew there was a reason I brought you along," she said.

"Several reasons, if I know you," the flitter replied.

A revolving plexsteel chamber waited to transfer her to the zipper. Shizume stepped in and the cubicle rotated 180 degrees, opening to the transportation that would take her wherever she wished.

Faced with an ever-growing urban population that still wanted at least the illusion of personal transport craft, the city government knew only endless gridlock would result if people continued to drive themselves around. Add to that the total ban on fossil-fuel vehicles, and something new had come along. As a compromise, the public transportation system known as Zippers, small craft that rode the electrical field generated by the stratoscrapers, went online in 2055 and was an instant success. Hovering a few inches away from the building, they also utilized anti-gravity technology, much as Fliv did. Larger models served as cheap public transportation, while people who were better off could rent smaller ones to take them wherever they wished to go. Automated, non-polluting, and efficient, they were the perfect solution to the mass transit problem in the 22nd century.

Shizume settled into the padded seat with Fliv locked into a socket designed for him.

"Destination, please, Shizume Mader," the Zipper's program requested.

"Grid C-8, block 41A," she answered.

"Travel distance is 9.72 kilometers, and the fee will be 26 credits with your student discount."

"Acceptable," Shizume said.

With an imperceptible whir, the craft began moving down the side of the building, looking exactly like the device that had given it its name. Around her were dozens of other Zippers, from the multi-unit public city transports to luxury Zippers capable of hosting a private party for a select group of citizens with too much cash to spend. Shizume's was somewhere in the middle, private, basic, affordable transportation. She leaned back and looked out the glasteel window, her pulse quickening at the thought of her destination and what she might find there.

CHAPTER SIX

Antonia Noir paced the length of Mason's office over and over, her designer shoes leaving rows of dots in the priceless hand-woven antique carpet.

"If you keep this up, my dear, you're going to wear a hole in the floor," Benjamin said, observing her repetitive travel across the room from where he was leaning against Mason's desk. He was also moving, but in an abstract way, seemingly more to glory in the range of motion, however illusionary, that his electronic body afforded him. He was especially fascinated, Antonia noted, with picking things up, holding each object and looking at it from every angle, then putting it down slowly, as if hesitant to part with it. *I suppose I'd feel the same way if I had been trapped outside the physical world for the past 300 years,* she thought. *But for all his wide-eyed wonder, he's still entirely too much at ease here.*

"Penny for your thoughts?" he asked, as if aware of just what she was thinking. "I suppose you don't even have those anymore. Well, whatever the current mode of currency is."

"I don't think this is a good idea," she replied, meeting

94

his hooded eyes with her own cool gaze. "This technology Mason mentioned is not perfected, it could have serious side effects, it is a risk taken without full knowledge of the consequences."

"But you already know what the consequences will be if this is not done. You've felt them yourself, that tremor—"

"Does not necessarily mean anything," Antonia said, cutting him off. "They could just be normal seismic activity for this area. Perhaps Mason's dampeners are malfunctioning, I don't know, although our teams are checking them right now. What I do know, and, as you heard, don't exactly agree with, is that he's doing this all on your say so because he believes you are his long-gone ancestor."

"And like me, Mason will not hesitate to do what he thinks is best. But what do you think?" Benjamin asked, his eyes dancing with either anger or amusement, Antonia couldn't quite tell.

"The empirical evidence, such as we have, says that you are who you say you are, which I take at face value," she said, whirling around to pace the office once again. "But your story is just what Mason wanted to hear and confirms that he had done what he set out to do, which is fine. But why you are doing this, I am beginning to wonder."

Benjamin straightened up, regarding Antonia with a sober stare, and bowed his head. "Perhaps if you had been around 300 years ago, the Derlicht family could have prevented some of the tragedies that had befallen them. During my time I dismissed your stock as ineffective, but apparently your line simply hadn't—flowered yet. Ah, if you had been alive then, how different things might have been—" he shook himself out of his reverie. "It is good that you are skeptical, Antonia, from what I've seen, it is a trait that is lacking in this world. Too many people are all too willing to accept what is put in front of them, take it at face value, as you put it yourself."

Antonia kept watching him, trying not to let her puzzlement show. *It's almost like he's trying to win me over to his side,* she thought. *Well, Mason may have been swayed, but I won't be.*

"Whatever you may think of me, know this: my bloodline and my descendents are the most important thing in this world or any other to me. They are what I spent my lifetime providing for, and their continued success is all I care about," Benjamin said. "All of this—" he waved his electronic and anti-gravity arms around at the lush office and its surrounding building, "—is just the means to an end. It has taken three centuries of waiting to get this far, and my plans could not have been completed without my progeny. If Mason hadn't harnessed all of his ability—and from what I've seen, you had to be behind some of it—towards this goal, I wouldn't even be this close."

His expression grew thoughtful. "Speaking of progeny, one thing I am curious about is why you and he never had any children of your own."

Antonia turned on him, her face twisted. "You may be Mason's relative, but some matters are still none of your business." She schooled her features to stillness, but nothing could disguise the anger flashing in her eyes. The opulent room, with its vaulted ceilings and priceless paintings and sculptures, suddenly seemed to close in on her. "If you'll excuse me, I have business to attend to."

Benjamin's face was calm, but it was all too apparent that he knew he had scored a direct hit with his question. But instead of reveling in his discovery, he looked truly saddened by the knowledge. "I am sorry to hear of your—inability."

Antonia opened her mouth to protest, but was stilled by his upraised hand. "I meant no offense. Given my family's interest in siring successive generations, it is only logical, I'm afraid, that the difficulty is on your side of the family. There is nothing like seeing the fruit of your loins grow and mature under your guidance and tutelage." His own handsome features darkened with remembered pain. "What I told you earlier is true, but it took me a long time to realize it. I was not a good man during my life, grasping, selfish, always pursuing more power at any cost. I sacrificed much chasing after what I thought was more important, and in the process I lost my sons, all of them, and by the time I realized it, it was too late to regain them—for by the time I realized it, I was already in the spirit realm."

"Why are you telling me all this?" Antonia asked, caught off-guard by his sudden change in demeanor.

"What I'm saying is that while I understand the pain of losing children, I cannot imagine what your grief must be never to have had any in the first place," Benjamin said.

Antonia continued to stare at him in silence, trying to fathom exactly what he meant. *What game is he playing, arrogant one moment, sympathetic the next? It's like he's adopting personalities to see which one suits him best.*

Across the room, the wallscreen flickered on and Mason's face appeared, his head shaved and pale in the harsh lights of the lab. "Have I interrupted anything?"

"No, my dear, Benjamin and I were just talking," Antonia replied. "Are you almost ready?"

"Kar and I are running one last diagnostic on the program. He's made a few upgrades which has added another 5.65 percent to our chances of success," Mason replied.

"And just what do you two put the chances of success at right now?" Benjamin asked the question that was foremost in Antonia's mind.

"Our most informed guess puts it at seventy-two percent," Mason answered. "The scan itself rates at eighty-nine percent, but for some reason the computer estimates that encoding your engrams and memory only has a sixty-four percent chance of success. Keeping in mind the results the first time we tried this, I'd say that's a much better chance of pulling it off."

"I need to talk to you before you go under, it should only take a minute," Antonia said.

"We're about ready to enter the preliminary scanning now, and there's not a lot of time," Mason replied. "I would appreciate it if you would monitor the process once it's started."

"Please, Mason—you know I wouldn't insist if it wasn't important," Antonia replied, suddenly feeling a desperate urge to see him, touch him one last time.

"Very well, if this cannot wait, I'll be down in a moment," Mason said. "Benjamin, why don't you come up to the lab? I'll have Kar give you a basic tour of what's going to happen."

Nodding at Antonia, Benjamin said, "I'm on my way. I have to say, the one thing I could really get used to is this pseudo-teleportation, disappearing in one room—" he winked out of the office in a shimmer of light, "—and appearing in another room in an instant. Now *that's* progress," he finished from the laboratory, looking over a tech's shoulder. "You there—Kar, is it?—what's this readout tell me?"

Before Antonia could begin to frame her thoughts, Mason walked out of the gravator, clad in a skin-tight bodysheath. "Now, what is so important that you feel the need to interrupt us at this *particular* moment?"

His frozen tone took Antonia aback. Mason was pronouncing every word distinctly, a sure sign that he was very upset. *Tread lightly here,* she cautioned herself, then began. "Mason, are you sure this is the right course of action? I cannot see why—"

"No, I suppose you cannot see why I am doing this, can you?" Mason said, his handsome features schooled to preternatural calm. "Nor, might I add, is it necessary for you to see, comprehend, or understand it, either. Even when Benjamin has provided the proof about these tremors, about what could happen to the entire city, even the world, you are still the skeptic."

He took a deep breath. "Normally, that is a good thing. It is something I have come to rely on over the years. But I am telling you now to believe in what Benjamin is saying. A man does not float in nothingness for three centuries only to come back to a semblance of life just to destroy the world. He wants to live as badly as I want him to—"

"Which is fine, Mason," Antonia said, crossing to him and draping her arms around his neck. "Bringing Benjamin back successfully opens up a whole new vista for cloning; I just don't want you risking your own life to do it. After all, Benjamin is the only truly dead person we've brought back, and look where he is. Are you sure he doesn't have an ulterior motive in mind with all of this?"

Shaking his head, Mason reached up behind himself and removed Antonia's arms from him. "You still don't understand, do you? This is not about the company or breaking new boundaries. It's about family and doing what's right. Even if Benjamin did have a trick up his sleeve, I would do this anyway. And I haven't even addressed the tremors either, which is more than reason enough to do this, even if there is only a slight chance of success."

"All I need from you," he said, is to oversee the process, not to agree with me. You just need to help me survive the whole thing, that is the only reason why you'll be up there." His voice took on a familiar tone of finality. "I'm bringing my ancestor back, and I don't care what the costs might be. Do you understand?"

Antonia knew that there was no way she could change his mind now. Her one chance to sway his stance on this entire operation had slipped away. "Of course, there isn't anywhere I'd rather be," she replied, assuming a game smile. "I'll meet you in the lab right away—there's an urgent matter I simply must take care of."

Mason was already entering the gravator. "Don't be

late," were his parting words to her—no kiss, no endearment, not even a good-bye. The door closed and he vanished, leaving Antonia confused and fearful in his wake.

Has Benjamin gotten to him this deeply already? she wondered as she headed for the anti-grav transport herself. *I have to be there for the whole operation, but I must get some information first...* Shaking her head, Antonia slipped into the gravator and headed down to her office.

Mason tried to relax as Kar ran through the final set of diagnostics for the program, making sure it was calibrated and that the scan of Mason's body was as recent as possible before running the program. Benjamin stood by, absorbing every facet of the operation, asking the occasional question, but mostly observing.

"I find your resolve admirable, Mason," Benjamin said. "After all, there was no reason you had to go through with this whole business in the first place."

Mason frowned at Benjamin. "Why would you say that? Of course I would want you to share in our success, to know that everything you began hundreds of years ago has come to fruition. Your dream was to live forever, and now that is exactly the opportunity I'm giving you."

"And I appreciate that," Benjamin said. "But by trying to revive me, you may be destroying everything you hold dear."

"It's a risk I'm willing to take," Mason replied.

"In more ways than you may think," Benjamin said. "Antonia is not fond of me, I believe."

Kar cut in. "Sir, I'm injecting the DNA markers now."

He pressed a hypo into Mason's arm with a faint hiss. "You'll need to take your place in the chamber in sixty seconds."

"Is there something on your mind, Benjamin?" Mason asked. "After all, it's not like certain elements of my family were for this marriage; quite the opposite, in fact."

"Ah, yes, my wayward sons," Benjamin replied shaking his head. "Strange how each successive generation believes it knows best, yet long experience has told me that is not often the case. However, your union with her was strong from the outset, strong enough to fend off both Thomas and Jon together, although it did cost you, I believe."

"What are you saying?"

"Merely that when I was talking with Antonia, she grew quite—upset when I mentioned children. Why do you think that was?"

Mason remained calm with a visible effort as he replied. "It's true. Despite the medical advances over the past decades, for some reason Antonia is unable to have children by any means. We've worked on this problem for a long time, but to no avail. However, I still have some hope that the matter will resolve itself happily in the end."

"Thirty seconds, gentlemen," Kar announced, his fingers flying over clustered holoscreens.

"Of course, as do I," Benjamin said. "I never had the chance to enjoy grandchildren, so I wish you all the best of luck. I should stop prattling on and let you get on with it. I just want to say one more thing," Benjamin said, smiling with genuine pleasure. "Thank you."

Mason puzzled over his relative's expression for a

moment, then nodded. "I look forward to seeing you in a true body once this is over."

"As do I," Benjamin said. "As do I."

As soon as Antonia stepped into her office, she subvocalized a quick command:

"Office mask on."

Nothing around her changed, but Antonia strode into the suite secure in the knowledge that any electronic surveillance equipment was now recording a harried meeting with one of NoirCorp's European branches. She doubted that Mason would ever check, but she had also learned a long time ago to never take any chances where the Noirs were concerned, even her own husband.

Or my own family, for that matter, she thought, slipping out of her shoes and going to the 20th century antique Art Deco chaise lounge in a corner of the office. Antonia's shoulders straightened and she breathed a sigh of relief. Her office was smaller than Mason's but no less sumptuously furnished. Instead of feeling confined, however, it was her sanctuary, where she forbid anyone else, even Mason, to enter.

"Show the children," she said.

The burnished walls of the office slipped away, replaced by the green fields and joyful sounds of a long lost city park. Children laughed and shouted in delight as they played on various pieces of playground equipment, slides, swings, a whirling foot-powered merry-go-round.

In the middle of it all were two children with dark hair, one a girl with curly locks, the other a boy with straight hair combed back from his forehead, both about seven years old. They played with the other children, unmindful of the woman that watched them from the other side of the playground, their happy voices joining the cacophony of noise and movement that surrounded them.

"Leah! Allen! Come on, it's time to go!" A familiar voice sounded behind Antonia, and she looked behind her to see another version of herself and Mason walking across the lawn. They approached the park and strolled past, arm in arm, oblivious to her presence. Mason looked more relaxed than Antonia had ever seen him, and while she had apparently kept a bit of the weight gain from her pregnancy, the blissful look on her doppelganger's face made it clear that she didn't care.

"Mom, just a few more minutes, please?" the boy—Allen—bargained while the girl took the more expedient tack of trying to hide in a covered play platform, apparently reasoning that possible punishment was worth staying a few minutes longer, and if her parents couldn't find her, then they couldn't leave. Antonia smiled at the ruse. *Good girl,* she thought. *Hang on to this as long as you can.*

"All right, both of you, dinner's waiting, but it won't wait for long," the other Mason said. "You must be hungry by now. You've been here for two hours."

The kids' faces reflected their struggle between food and freedom. Allen was the first to break, edging towards his parents, ignoring the plaintive whispers of his sister.

"Miss Leah, there's Chinese waiting for you if you come with me right now," the other Antonia said with a sly smile.

"Yayy!" Any pretense at concealment was abandoned

as the girl burst from her hiding place and ran towards the rest of her family. As soon as she was close enough, she was snatched off the ground and swung into the air by her father, squealing all the while. Laughing and talking, the family left the park, walking past Antonia again, who watched them leave, blinking back sudden tears.

Of everything I have given up, that is what hurts the most, she thought. *But I did it all for Mason, for us.* The park and the children, the alternate Antonia and Mason, all of it was just a programmed illusion, a trip down a different path, an alternate fantasy that could have been reality if things had turned out differently on that wedding day so long ago. *And to have what I thought I wanted, I had to make the ultimate sacrifice...*

"End scenario," she said. The park and its inhabitants dissolved into nothingness, and Antonia was back in her familiar office. Even though the sight of the children she might have once have had always tore at her soul, Antonia had painstakingly programmed the scenario to watch them grow up, figuring that at least she could see what might have been. *Anything is better than no children at all.*

Adoption had never been an option for her either. With what she had done to herself to ensure Mason's and her happiness, Antonia didn't think she could look at a child that was not her own and feel any kind of tenderness for it. Plus, she didn't know if adoption would activate the curse either. *Oh, Agatha, you vicious bitch...*

Banishing her negative thoughts, she lay back on the velvet cushion, closed her eyes and slipped into a meditative trace with the ease of decades of practice, her hand unconsciously dropping to rub her stomach as she did so. The room around her fell away into a long tunnel of pleasant, soothing darkness, and Antonia soon felt as if she was floating in a warm, comfortable, womb-like environment. Luxuriating in the relaxed feeling for a moment, she began constructing the mental landscape for her upcoming conversation.

When she felt prepared, she sent out a mental summons.

Agatha, where are you? I know you're nearby. I've sensed your presence growing steadily stronger in the past twenty-four hours. Come to me now.

Antonia's psychic abilities had been fully opened long ago during the spiritual battle at the church on the day of her wedding to Mason. She had not been prepared for the powers that had emerged during the fight with the spirits of Jon and Thomas Noir. Three downloads and more than a century later, she still had occasional nightmares about that day—the spirits swirling angrily around her, the strange sense of time slowing down as Mason rushed to her side—the indescribable feeling of power she felt as she grasped his hand—the silent scream of despair from the specters flitting around them as they realized that the union had been completed—

Antonia, my dear, it has been so long since we've talked. I've missed our chats.

With an effort Antonia wrenched herself back to the present. In her mind's eye, she was standing on an endless, featureless gray plain with the calm sky blending into a horizon that stretched off into eternity. Antonia had found this the easiest way to maintain her concentration while in the meditative state. Decorations or furniture just distracted both of them, and Antonia had found it best to have all her wits about her whenever she engaged the long-dead matriarch of her family in conversation.

Agatha Derlicht had been the matriarch and leader of Antonia's family during the 19th century, when it had been a force to be reckoned with during America's early years. In this netherworld she was reduced to nothing more than a floating globe of light that shifted color with her mood. When she spoke, the light pulsed in time with her words. Agatha's consciousness flitted back and forth, causing Antonia to remember Benjamin's theories about psyches remaining trapped between worlds.

Well, she used me, so I'm just returning the favor, she rationalized. In their seminal conversation more than 150 years ago, after the conflict in the church, Agatha had revealed the hex that had been laid on the Noir family. A prophesy had been foretold that said if a Noir ever married a Derlicht and the union bore children, the Noir family would be destroyed. To thwart the curse, Antonia had used her newfound powers to psychically destroy her own womb, rendering her barren. Since then, she had kept a sharp eye on Agatha, still despising her, but also recognizing her usefulness both in and out of the spirit realm. Their meetings afterward had been stiff, with Agatha attempting to control her distant relative every time. But Antonia had proven to be more than a match for her long-lost ancestor, and eventually the two women had reached an uneasy, arms-length truce.

That was a long time ago, Antonia thought. She had checked in on Agatha every so often, sometimes going years without calling her. During their past few conversations, she had noticed the elder Derlicht becoming less focused, if the term could be applied to a ball of light. While in the beginning Agatha had clung to her human form, sometime in the past half-century or so she had abandoned it for this aspect, to what end Antonia didn't know and didn't care.

I'm sure you have, großmutter, she said, using the archaic German term for her relative. Another thing Antonia tended to be during these conversations was all business.

There is no need for such a tone, child.

So you claim, Antonia replied.

The light ball shifted to a light green, a color Antonia associated with wistfulness. The tone of her relative's thoughts shifted to something approximating pensive. *How I have underestimated you,* enkelin, *from the very first time we spoke, and the choice you made. How I wish you had been my true daughter, instead of appearing so many years later—*

Why is everyone around me suddenly so nostalgic for the good old days? Antonia thought, then cut her great-great-great-great grandmother off. *Right. Your increased presence has me curious about many things, actually.*

The light that was Agatha turned turquoise, then shaded fully into blue. Antonia waited for the spectrum to run its course as her ancestor settled down. *Yes, much is happening in this dimension as well. You've felt the shocks, I presume?*

*Yes, but first things first. Benjamin Noir. Why have
you never told me about his existence?*

*My dear, I am not a social secretary. Spirits that do
not want to be found will not be. They have their ways,
after all. Not all are so—responsive to requests from their
grandchildren.*

Don't push me, Agatha, I am not in the mood, Antonia
said. *What else is happening there?*

*Much disturbance here—the psyches with a tenuous
hold on their reality are already slipping away...I expect
to join them soon.* Agatha flared bright pink, then toned
down into a subdued dusty rose.

*What are you talking about? You must be one of the
oldest psyches in existence,* Antonia said.

*The waves that you feel and we see are the end of our
existence, child,* Agatha replied. *As they grow in intensity,
they will wipe away our grip on this plane altogether,
sending us into the void for eternity.*

*Agatha, you've been disjointed before, but you're really
not making sense today,* Antonia said. *Do you mean that
all the psyches trapped on our material plane will be
gone?*

The ball of light froze for a second, its ever-shifting
pattern trapped in a kaleidoscopic burst of color. Then
it vanished completely, and Agatha as she had been in
life stood in its place, her imperious gaze turned on in
full-force, the gaunt, iron-haired woman stooped with
age, yet somehow still looking vital and strong, no matter
how impossible that was. Taken by surprise, Antonia
stepped back, then firmed her resolve and met Agatha's
stare with a burning one of her own.

For all your intelligence, child, you can be maddeningly obtuse, Agatha said. *What I'm talking about is the complete destruction of not only your world, but mine as well, such as it is. You can stop it, if you use the resources available to you.*

Antonia opened her mouth, but was cut off by her elder. *They will come to you; it is up to you to recognize them when they arrive. And one more piece of advice, cliché though it is: trust no one.*

What does that mean? Does Mason suspect something? I've kept watch over his office systems and found nothing, Antonia said, rattled by Agatha's sudden change in demeanor.

The elder Derlicht began to fade out from view, the last visible part being her cold gray eyes. *The answers are there, if you look in the right place.* The eyes flicked sideways, and Antonia saw an emotion she had never associated with Agatha in them—fear. *Another one is coming—so soon—*

Then she saw it herself, the manifestation of the next shock wave rushing towards her on her mental landscape, a boiling, roiling, storming wall of black nothingness. Forked bolts of silver electricity crackled through it, surrounding the wave in a glowing nimbus of angry energy. And the noise—an incredible, indescribable cacophony of sound accompanied it. Antonia just stood watching it approach, dumbfounded.

Get out now, or it will take you with it! Agatha's urgent cry sounded in her mind. With a start, Antonia began bringing herself out of the trance, but the white wall kept rushing towards her, obliterating the sky, the ground, everything around her, until it was the only thing she could see, towering over her, about to engulf her—

With a startled cry Antonia reared up to find herself on the floor next to the chaise lounge where she had apparently rolled in an effort to escape. Before she could make sense of her meeting with Agatha, the building shook even more than last time, actually swaying from the force of the shock wave passing through it.

Antonia steadied herself on the lounge, willing her heartbeat to return to normal. *I've never seen* anything *like that before,* she thought. *Could Agatha be right about this?* she pondered. *And if that's true, could Benjamin actually be telling the truth?*

Before Antonia could sort through the verbal web growing around her, the office wallscreen flashed amber, signaling an incoming priority message.

"Open," she said as she got to her feet.

Kar's face filled the screen. "Antonia, thank the Faces I got through to you. You'd better get up here. That last wave hit just as we were putting Mason under. We've got problems."

"I'm on my way," she said, sprinting across the office to the elevator. *Hold on, my dear,* she thought. *Nothing's going to happen to you.*

But even as she shot towards the lab, she couldn't quell a nagging thought: *What does Agatha know about all this? And even more important, what does Benjamin* really *know?*

CHAPTER SEVEN

At the top of a 750–story blockpartment, Shizume discovered she was having second thoughts about where she was going. Although she usually enjoyed "riding the roofs"—her term for when the Zippers traveled high on the buildings where there was less traffic—this time the view of Greater New York bathed in the rising sun was lost on her. Grandfather was absorbed in replying to his reader v-mail, and Fliv was uncharacteristically quiet, not even asking her to review the finer points of New York State laws on search and seizure. Instead of enjoying the silence, Shizume was left free to fill her head with increasingly doubtful musings about her current journey.

Maybe he's right, she thought. *I have one VR anomaly and one bad dream, and I'm ready to go charging off into Buddha knows what to find nothing? 'Cause that's what's going to be waiting for me down there, a big load of empty. I mean c'mon, it's more than 50 meters down, buried under who knows how many kilotons of earth sitting over it now, not to mention the ocean, eating away at it for the past century or so. This whole thing is just one big zipper circle. I can't believe I rushed into this; wait a minute, yes I can.*

Shizume shook her head and remembered her training yesterday. *Yeah, jumping into a situation without thinking it through, that sounds familiar.* She sat up as a sudden thought came to her. *Isn't that what I've been doing all my life? Jumping into school, jumping out, jumping into the police force, jump here, leap there, bound, bound, bound. And for what? Where has all of it gotten me?*

"Hey, Shizume, I think we're coming up on it," Payne said.

"Hmm—oh, yeah." And as she looked up at the building, what she saw there made her mouth drop open.

Emblazoned on the side of the stratoscraper, one hundred stories tall, was the face she had seen both in the simulation and in last night's dream.

"Stop right here," she said. Their vehicle slowed to a halt on the corner of a building, the other Zippers flowing smoothly around it. Shizume stared up at Jon Noir's face. He had the same hair, blond and tousled, the same chiseled features, but this time he sported a vague, bored look in those bright blue eyes. After several seconds the advirtisement blended into another, this one for Vapo-Dyne toothpaste (the cavity obliterator!). And still Shizume continued to stare at the building. *Then again, maybe I shouldn't be so hard on myself all the time,* she thought.

"Payne...Grandfather...tell me you saw that," she mumbled.

"Yeah, I certainly did," Payne said. "I'm tracking the model now."

"Model? What are you talking about? That was Jon himself!" she replied.

"Actually," Payne said as a small screen popped up in her left view quadrant, "that is Hanz, the latest trendy Euromodel to hit the East Coast. He's currently featured in the virtual model show for Jacobite Fashions Elite, with adverts on the Chrysler strato, the William Morris building *and* the Trident Tower, as well as the Amerimall. Rotating on the half-hour so consumers can see his pouty, laser-carved face whenever they want."

"You're psychin' me."

"No, although I'm tracing his family history right now—hmm, doesn't look like he has any relations on the Noir side—wait a flash, there were gossip column rumors of a bastard child born to the family in 2049, the father unknown Eurotrash, so that may be where he got his historical good looks from," Payne said. "Shi, are you rezzin' this? What are the odds that this guy would be Jon Noir's doppelganger?"

"There's no such thing as coincidence," Shizume said under her breath.

"So, let me get this straight. Because an ad agency took out space on that building, you're taking it as a sign to go forward?" Payne asked.

"That doesn't sound like the conspiracy-seeker I once knew," she teased.

"Well, perhaps, but my theories at least had a logical grain of connection linking them together. Like my almost-proven triangle linking NoirCorp with the recent alien landings and the Bermuda triangle. You see—"

"You can give me the run-down after this," Shizume said. "Let's go. Resume course to original destination."

The Zipper moved forward, accelerating off the building they had been resting on and soaring through the air until it was caught by the anti-gravity field of the next stratoscraper. One building later, and they whirred to a stop at the 100th floor of the building built over the site of Derlicht Manor.

Shizume and Fliv got out, and Shizume made sure her shock glove was fully charged, fitting it snugly around her hand.

"I trust you won't have to use that," Fliv said.

"I sure hope not, but I'd rather have it and not than have to and can't, rez?"

"Right. I suppose this will count as real-world training," her partner said.

"Does that mean you could charge my stunfinger?" Shizume asked.

"No, it doesn't."

Fliv led the way, floating in front of her as it scanned the hallway. Instead of the orderly neatness of Shizume's building, this one had seen better decades about fifty years ago. Although it looked very similar to the hallway she walked through every day to and from her apartment, this one exuded a general aura of hopelessness and despair. It was reasonably clean, but the floor was missing several tiles, the older kind that still could come loose from the floor. There was a long strip that looked as if it had once held a pedmover, but the parts and belt were long gone, leaving just a marginally brighter patch of flooring stretching off into the endless-seeming hallway, punctuated by the rows of doors on either side. Even at this early hour, at least a dozen people were moving towards or away from her along the hallway. Three caterwauling kids shattered the general stillness, engaged in some complex game that involved clomping up and down the corridor as fast as possible.

"Hey, Payne," Shizume subvocalized as they looked inside, "what was this building again?"

"*Now* you ask me," he replied. "Like I said, Grid C-8, block 41A, it's always been housing since its completion in 2062. Home to primarily middle- and lower-class skillworkers in manufacturing and industrial trades. Apparently the 'bots still haven't replaced everyone. Yet."

"Including smart-ass webporters like yourself," she said.

"Just bringing the truth to the people, my dear," he said. "Are you going to go in there or let your partner do all the work?"

"Watch it," Shizume said as she stepped into the hallway. "You can be turned off, you know."

"What, and miss you descending into GNYC's lower bowels? Forget it. I'm in for the full zip," Payne replied.

"Ok, just remember you said that," Shizume replied. "Keep your eyes rezzed, all right?"

"Don't you worry about that. If I could grow another pair out there, I'd do it."

"*I've located the elevator bank,*" Fliv informed them. "*We're about thirty minutes away from shift change here, when it would get really crowded, so we should move quickly."*

"Really, actual elevators? Psych, lead the way," Shizume said. As they walked down the hallway, she kept resisting the urge to stare at the other occupants of the floor. *I wonder if anyone here ever thinks about what their building was built over. Or if they even care.*

"We're here," Fliv said. *"These elevators are designed primarily to carry people between floors, but all blockpartments have several sublevels. We'll be able to access them through here, although I'm still unsure what you expect to find."*

"Um, not that it's my place to mention this, but—isn't that a violation of your programming to do go down there without probable cause?" Shizume asked.

"My records show that this building hasn't had a sublevel inspection in the past five years," Fliv said. *"As part of the Greater New York City Police, we are authorized to do just that."*

"And I thought only humans bent the law," Payne said with an admiring whistle. "Devious little floater, isn't he?"

"Yeah, apparently he's just full of surprises," Shizume replied, a little more uncertainly than she would have liked. Glancing around, she saw stillness in all directions. All of the hallway's earlier activity, including the rampaging kids, had suddenly disappeared.

The sound of working machinery echoed from somewhere high above them, and a noise of whirring plasteel pulleys and laboring plasticine cables got louder and louder. Shizume cast a nervous glance towards the doors.

"Shang, I can't believe people once did this every day," Payne remarked. With a final groan and clank, the elevator doors swung open, revealing a room large enough to hold thirty people. Like the rest of the building, it was technically clean but shabby and sad, a symbol of better times long gone.

As the three entered, Fliv floated over to the console that lined one entire wall of the elevator. This model predated chip-activated transportation, which would have scanned every one in the unit and automatically stopped at every floor each person lived on. Several dozen floor buttons were burned out, mostly near the downlevels. *"Here are the sublevels—strange, the circuits for the lower level's buttons have been disconnected. I'm running a bypass now."*

After a few seconds, the doors slid shut and the elevator began its slow descent. As she watched the numbers grow steadily smaller, Shizume came up with the one thing that had been bothering her. "Fliv, aren't all these buildings on the GNYC databases for scheduled repair, inspection, and maintenance?"

"You make an excellent point, Trainee Mader. I was just about to query precinct headquarters regarding the obvious disrepair."

"Um, I think what Shizume is saying actually goes a bit beyond that," Payne said. "If she and I are thinking along the same lightpaths, someone has gone to a lot of trouble to hide these levels, including fattening some city inspector's bank account to make sure—"

"Whatever *is* going in here isn't discovered," Shizume continued. "Once the building was removed from the record, it probably never was noticed again, which is hard to believe, given its size and all of the city departments that have to oversee maintenance and other upkeep."

"Unless someone is still making sure it stays off the records," said Fliv.

"Well, if that's true, why are we still going down there?" Payne asked. "I mean, it could be a body shop under here, or an army of floorsquats, who knows?"

"Good question, let's find out," Shizume said. "Fliv, stop the car and turn on my ultraural, please."

"Affirmative," it said. The familiar rush of noise burst in her ears as Shizume took in everything from the air currents whistling in the elevator shaft to the sounds of hundreds of people above her beginning their day.

"Ow, by the Buddha, cut off everything above me," she said. Fliv rose to the ceiling and began broadcasting white noise to cancel the sounds coming down from the hundreds of levels over them. "That's better. Now..." she leaned forward, listening.

"What is it?" Payne subvocalized, aware she'd hear him loud and clear.

After a few seconds Shizume straightened up. "Ultraural off."

"Well?" Payne asked.

"Uh—I'm not sure, I picked up humming, like the sound of a lot of power being used. I hear noises as well, voices, running, everyday stuff, that's the best way I can describe it."

"Okay, so what—or who—ever's down here is drawing a lot of current. So?" Payne asked.

"Fliv, do you smell that?" Shizume asked, sniffing near the doors. "Smells like—something rotten?"

"It's hard to miss, especially for me," Fliv replied. *"I'm analyzing content now."*

"So are we staying or going?" Payne asked.

"Pause yourself a moment," Shizume replied. "Fliv, do you have anything yet?"

"The odor in the air is emanating not from the next room but the one beyond it. It is primarily composed of human waste, various rotting things, including food and other items. I'm also sensing illegal pollutants, including the plant species Nictotiana Tabacum, *which hasn't been cultivated outside of a laboratory in more than sixty years,"* Fliv said.

"I'm not up on my ancient Latin. What does that mean?" Shizume asked.

"I think he's talking about that odious, and now illegal, habit of the 20th and 21st century: smoking tobacco," Payne replied.

"Tobacco—isn't that the plant that helped eradicate a lot of the diseases in the early 2020's by producing human enzymes and pharmaceuticals?" Shizume asked. "The one that put an end to the mutated Herpes VIII complexes in 2029 as well. But if they're burning it in there—oh no, you don't mean a squatcity, do you?" Shizume groaned.

"Most likely," Fliv replied.

Shizume made sure her shock glove was on and ready. "Only one way to find out." She hit the flickering open door button.

The room outside was long and narrow, extending

several meters on both sides of the elevator. Ahead was another large doorway, this one locked with a battered scanpad and a sign on the double doors that read OUT OF ORDER. Other than those two things, it was empty, except for the decaying smell, which was even stronger now, almost overwhelming. Shizume and Fliv approached the door.

"Hmm, that's a problem," Payne said.

"Not necessarily," Shizume said. "I'm sure Fliv can override the lock's circuitry."

"Yes, I could, if we had a properly executed search warrant and were here with the express purpose of looking for illegal floorsquatters," Fliv reminded her.

"You don't have to sound so snarky about it," she replied. "Doesn't that smell you analyzed count as probable cause?"

"No, as there is no definitive proof that anyone is in there," her partner replied. *"We could just be encountering residue from waste stored here many years ago. Or it could be a malfunctioning compactor unit. Hardly worth violating the law for."*

"Great," Shizume said. "Dead end."

"You mean that's it?" Payne said, caught up in the situation despite himself. "We have to stop here?"

"Yeah, as much as I hate to give it to him, Fliv's right, we're stuck," Shizume said. "I don't suppose there's any other way in?"

"Not without breaking several private property laws," Fliv said. *"This building is owned by someone, mind you."*

"Shang it!" Shizume said. "Probably just a wild zip-chase anyway. Come on."

She turned to go, only to find that the elevator doors had closed, the car long gone to another floor. "Even better, stuck down here for who knows how long," she said, stabbing the button and leaning against the wall.

"Taking this a bit hard, don't you think?" Payne said. "I mean, you were probably right, it doesn't mean anything."

"Yeah, but now I'll never know," she said. A chime sounded, and she heard the sound of a door opening. "Let's go."

But when Shizume looked up at the elevator doors, they were still closed. Her confusion was interrupted when a voice from behind her piped, "Who're you?"

Shizume turned to see a thin girl standing in the doorway, her smudged face partially obscured by a tangle of messy blonde hair. She was dressed in an adult jumpsuit that had been cut down, the legs rolled up and the sleeves hacked off. Shizume noted that the girl was looking at her with no trace of fear, just curiosity. Her body was slightly tensed, but whether she was prepared to flee or fight couldn't be discerned.

Best to start with the truth, she thought. "My name is Shizume. Who are you?"

"I don't know you." The girl's eyes narrowed, and one of her hands edged behind her back.

"I'm registering a threat rating of seventy-two percent," Fliv said on her optics. *"Stun is ready."*

"Don't do anything yet," Shizume subvocalized, then spoke up as she pointed back at the elevator. "They—up there, said I could get—you know—"

The girl's face brightened into a smile. "Oh, you came for stalk. Why'nt you say so in the first place?"

122

Shizume looked away. "I—I've never done this before."

"You got a personal floater?" the girl asked, peering at Fliv.

"Uh—yeah," Shizume said. "It carries my stuff, handy that way."

"Yes," Fliv said on her vision. *"Fortunately, the girl doesn't seem to be able to read, otherwise my markings would be a dead giveaway."*

"Doesn't appear to be a problem so far," Payne said.

"Until we come across someone who can," Fliv replied.

"I'm Flaya," the girl said, apparently deciding Shizume was completely trustworthy. "Come on, I'll light you up."

Shizume froze for a moment, until Payne's voice prodded her, "I think she means she'll get you 'stalk,' whatever that means."

Nodding, she walked forward. "Kay."

The girl led them into the next room, which, on first glance, was filled to the ceiling with five-meter tall piles of garbage. Her eyes watering, Shizume pinched her nose shut and attempted to breathe only through her mouth. She was even more surprised when Flaya walked to the nearest pile and began digging through it.

"What is she doing?" she muttered to Fliv.

"My reading of this pile, indeed, this whole room—" Fliv began as Flaya found what she was looking for and seemed to pull an entire section out of the pile *"—is that they are hollow shells, disguising something else."*

"C'mon," the girl said, heading into the darkness.

"Fliv, I think now is the time you call for backup," Shizume whispered as she followed the girl inside. "And if you could charge my stunfinger, it would be greatly appreciated."

"Your first request is granted, your second is not," Fliv said. *"I'm not reading any danger that would call for it yet. Your glove should suffice for now."*

"Thanks," she grumbled.

The first thing she noticed was that the smell was gone, replaced by a light, sweet scent. When they came out of the dark tunnel, they were in a much larger hall that stretched as far as she could see. The ceiling was at least four stories high, and the entire place was filled with tall, dark green plants about two meters tall, with broad, pointed leaves branching out from a central stalk and topped with white tubular blossoms. There were six rows of them that she could see, the ones above her head suspended from racks, their root systems exposed to the air. Above it all, bright heat lamps shone down over the entire area, bathing the plants and Shizume in an almost uncomfortable warmth. As she watched, a sprinkler system came on and showered the uppermost level in a mist of droplets that filtered down through the room. A shadow moved among the plants, then another. Shizume adjusted her optics to focus and magnify the shapes, and she saw several dozen people, many the same age as the young girl next to her, dressed in dirty, ill-fitting clothes, floating back and forth among the plants in an anti-gravity field, all intent on their various tasks of tending the huge crop.

Shizume just stared at it all for a moment. "Fliv, what have we stumbled into here?"

"An illegal hydroponic tobacco plantation, right in the middle of the city," her partner replied.

Virtual reality and smokeless, nonaddictive cigarettes had replaced the real thing before Shizume was born. She had thought the "vapor bars," places where people went to smoke real cigarettes that had been smuggled across the border, was just an urban myth. Her own eyes, however, now proved the fallacy of that belief. "So what do we do now?"

"First, close your mouth," Payne suggested.

"A Narcotix squad should be here in 6.5 minutes," Fliv said. *"I've informed them of our location. Just try to remain out of the way until they get– "*

"Hey–who are you? What are you doing here?" A young man was headed their way, dressed in a larger version of Flaya's clothes.

"Hoi, Pollas, got you a customer," Flaya's pride was obvious as she waved him over.

"You're not even supposed to be back yet, Flaya. And who is this–" his eyes widened as he recognized a police partner "–GNYCP–but, Carderas has already been paid this month–" He started toward Shizume, one hand reaching for her, the other going to a pouch at his side.

"Wait, sir!" Shizume raised her hands, intending only to stop the man from restraining her. Unfortunately, she grabbed for his wrist with her right hand, forgetting that she was wearing her charged shock glove on it. He stiffened then collapsed to the ground in a boneless heap.

"Tell me that wasn't what you were planning," Payne said, his mouth agape on her optics.

Flaya's reaction was more immediate. "What'd you do to him?"

"I—uh, he frightened me," Shizume said, aware of how false that sounded. Apparently, Flaya wasn't buying it either, for she took a few hesitant steps backward, then turned to run. She had only taken a step when she stumbled and slid to the ground as well.

"I'm afraid we cannot have her warning anyone else in here," Fliv said. *"No doubt the others will eventually notice us as well. I'm surprised they haven't already."*

"Well, there is a lot of foliage here," Shizume said. "What was that name he mentioned—Carderas?"

"My database lists one Alderwoman Hillary M. Carderas, most recently fighting charges of corruption and graft pertaining to less economically-viable areas of the city," Fliv said. *"It would appear that she has a hand in this little enterprise as well."*

"Oh, that's just what I need. Well, someone's palm would have to be greased—whatever that means—for this kind of thing to be going on. When is that Narc squad due?" Shizume asked.

"Squad will enter the building in 4.2 minutes," Fliv said. *"But what is more interesting is that I'm not reading a DNA neurochip on this man. Or the girl either, for that matter."*

After a twenty-year-long legal battle, in 2025 all citizens of the United States, including infants and host clone bodies, had been implanted with a subdermal biochip containing vital information on each person, including any allergies, the rare incurable chronic ailment, and the like, as well as being linked to thousands of businesses and urban systems in the city, such as the Zipper transit system. Of course, this also meant that the government could, if it wanted to, keep track of a family or an individual wherever they might go. Right-to-privacy protestors threw apoplectic fits, with the leading agitator against the bill, one Sherman Caralan, risking his life by using a scalpel to cut his chip out on the steps of Capitol Hill. But when the bill's primary proponent, an elderly senator named Alexander Walsh, pointed out that child abductions had dropped by fifty-three percent the following year and that chronic sex offenders, child-abducting parents, and criminals trying to evade parole could be easily tracked when they didn't register with the police, the protests lessened considerably. Despite the occasional outburst every few years, mostly by a new generation upset about the very technology that helped keep them safe, the chips had since become an accepted part of today's society.

Fifty years ago, NoirCorp had invented a way to synthesize the same ability using a person's DNA, making their own genetic material the trackable chip, in one of the first successful uses of living computers. They called it the neurochip, representing the body's ability to use genetic memory to store information. However, the nanobots that altered the signature DNA in a person's body had to be injected at a hospital, so if someone wasn't born there, they didn't always get the necessary shot. Not having a chip was a misdemeanor in Greater New York City, which meant that, theoretically, Shizume could arrest anyone here she found without one.

"That explains a lot," Shizume subvocalized back to

him. "Payne, can you give me that map. I need to see how far away we are from the site."

"I'm way ahead of you," Payne replied. "We have to go farther in, past this hall and into the next room. According to my calcs, we're still about thirty meters above it."

"All right, we'll just sit tight until—what is that?" Shizume said. The leaves of the plant nearest her were vibrating slightly in the windless room. Shizume leaned forward to examine it when the floor underneath her began vibrating, just a bit at first, then steadily growing more powerful.

"Get to the nearest wall," Fliv said, its voice as calm as ever. *"We appear to be experiencing some seismic activity."*

"When's the last time that happened?" Shizume asked.

"Whoa, I'm getting possible error messages too. I may not be able to stay linked with you," Payne said. "We haven't had anything like this since '13, but I thought it was taken care of since then."

"Apparently not completely," Shizume said, crouching down and hugging the wall. Looking up, she saw the men and women above her were scrambling along their rows, trying to reach the end of the room as well. The tremors increased, shaking several of the mounted racks of plants loose to drift around the room. The anti-grav generator hiccupped, causing everything in the room to drop several meters before reestablishing its field. Shizume covered her head as tobacco plants thudded to the ground around her. The tremors rumbled one last time then began trailing off.

"I think it's stopping," Shizume said as she rose to her

feet. "Grandfather? Are you there?" He had disappeared from her vision, and dialing him on her internal celplant got no answer. "I hope he's all right."

"I'm sure he is," Fliv replied.

"I'll try again when we get out of here, but we should get in there now. I can't have the Narcotix squad get here just yet. I won't be able to find Noir with them around."

"We should wait for their arrival, Trainee," Fliv said. *"I still don't know what you expect to find."*

"There could be people hurt in there," Shizume said. "We'll do a quick sweep and they should be here by the time we wrap up."

"Agreed," Fliv replied. Shizume picked her way between the toppled plants to the far side of the room and slipped through the half-open door.

The next room looked like a giant's fist had smashed through a huge house of cards. From what Shizume could tell, this hall had been partitioned into rooms using plasteel dividers and quick-fix ceramplast bonding agents. Apparently the dividers and bonding had been substandard because the tremors had torn through them like ancient cardboard, collapsing the multi-leveled structures into piles of walls, ceilings, and bodies. Smoke and dust layered everything in a gritty haze. Men and women dressed in ragged, patched together clothes scrabbled at the piles, screaming out names, calling for their children or relatives.

Once again Shizume's mouth hung open, this time at the devastation around her. Fliv's voice, sounding far away, called to her amidst the chaos. *"Trainee Mader, what are you going to do?"*

But under her partner's words, she now heard the whisper of another voice. *"Come to me...you are closer now...please..."* Its pull was insistent, hypnotic. Despite her best intentions, Shizume began walking though the ruins, somehow knowing exactly where she was going, ignoring Fliv's repeated queries. At the end of the row of broken living quarters were the remains of a cube, its walls leaning drunkenly against each other in a lopsided A-shape. Although it looked like it would collapse at any second, Shizume didn't hesitate, dropping to her knees and crawling inside. The plasteel around her shifted, and for a moment she thought the whole thing was going to come down on top of her.

"So close...I can...almost feel you," the voice said, a bit louder this time. *"Trapdoor...help me..."*

Shizume reached down and cleared away the personal effects of whomever had lived here; a holo-picture frame, now broken and derezzed, a still-folded blanket, a Kellie-Kiss morphdoll, its moppet face smiling and arms outstretched for a hug it would never receive. Shizume ignored all of it and found a recessed handle of the trapdoor. She pulled it up, revealing an even older tunnel carved into the earth and lined with climbing rungs, and slipped into the opening. Above her, she saw Fliv's shadow block out the light as it hesitated, then followed her down, still trying to make contact with her.

Shizume concentrated on the rungs in front of her, picking up and putting her hands and feet down over and over. After what seemed like a descent to the center of the earth itself, she hit the bottom, her boots impacting with a *chunk* that sounded dead in the oppressive silence. Her optics had adjusted to the lack of light, and she looked around.

The room she was in was small by modern standards, maybe ten meters long and five wide. Obsolete metal and plastic sheathed computer banks lined the wall, perhaps once used to run a smaller building, now useless and forgotten. The entire area looked abandoned, filled with the mingled smell of dusty metal and—

"Burned wood," Shizume said, even though there wasn't a sliver to be found. With a sensation akin to someone inserting a spoon into her ear and stirring her brain around for a second, she felt back in control of herself. "All right, whoever you are, show yourself."

"Who are you talking to?" Fliv asked. *"Trainee Mader, why did you come down here? There are injured people up there who could use—"*

"Shh," she said, waving her partner off. "If you want to help me, Fliv, give me some light." She addressed the room. "Show yourself. I know someone's down here."

Despite her improved vision, the optics program barely made out a human-shaped form standing a few meters in front of her. It was more like the thermal imaging registered the absence of heat in the shape of a man nearby.

"Forgive me...it has been...so long...since I've manifested on this plane," the voice said in her mind again. *"I...am not strong...here...as I once was...you can help me..."*

"What can I do?" Shizume asked.

The indistinct form wavered for a moment, then floated

hesitantly forward. *"Don't...move."* It moved closer toward her, then rushed at her, blotting out the rest of the room. Shizume threw up an arm to ward it off, but the figure passed right through her flesh, flowing into her body. As it flew into her, she had a brief glimpse of a face with sky-blue eyes and familiar blond hair...

"Jon?—what are you doing—Fliv, help me!" Shizume said, staring down at herself. She saw nothing different, but what was going on inside her head was something else entirely. Images whirled through her mind as if spun from the facets of a prism, dozens of them, each one as clear and real as if she was right there. A huge sprawling mansion, not the Derlicht Haus, this one shadowed and forbidding, aggressive in its sprawl, as if it contested every foot of land it sat on—a hillside view of a bucolic village below, surrounded by long gone foothills, with two mansions surveying everything they could, the first house, and a second one that Shizume recognized as the manse she had seen in the painting—a buxom blonde girl, her face the picture of innocence, looking at Shizume with concern. Behind her came others—a wizened old woman with wrinkled ebony skin sitting in a rocking chair by a roaring fire—another woman followed; this one, although white-haired, thin, and trembling almost imperceptibly, stared ahead with piercing eyes that had lost none of their intelligence over the decades—she was followed by a tall man with blazing eyes and strange stones woven in the great iron-gray beard that flowed from his jaw down over his chest—and last, a dark-haired young man with an insolent curl to his lip and a mocking yet haunted gleam in his eyes, with a face similar to the older man before him but dressed in finery that outshone the other—

The line of people faded away, replaced by a short man with dirty teeth and cropped hair with a wicked-looking blade in his hand—flames sprang up around him, consuming him—flames that came from below, came from everywhere—devouring everything—until a deluge of water came pouring down from above—

"For me to help you, I have to know where the threat is coming from," her partner said, hovering around her. *"Your temperature has risen three degrees, and your pulse is now 190 over 89—"*

"Quiet!" Shizume said. She regained her balance and stood in the center of the room, trying to recapture the flood of images and memories that had overwhelmed her for a moment.

"I am sorry, I had no idea what that would do to you," a quiet voice said in her mind.

Shizume looked around, but saw no sign of the human-shaped form in the room. As if answering her search, the voice spoke again, a hint of an unknown accent coloring his words. *"I must also apologize for this—intrusion. To allay your fears, yes, I am the spirit of Jon Noir, and a long, long, long-lost relative of yours."*

"Of—mine?" Shizume frowned.

"Well, as generations go, you most likely have only about one percent of Noir blood in you, but that is enough," Jon said. *"I sense that a part of you is surprised by this."*

"Yes—I mean, I knew I had a distant relation to the

Noir family, it's just—the manner of your introduction is what's really taken me by surprise," Shizume said.

"Again, I apologize," Jon said. *"My own father sired nineteen children, and of those, eleven, counting myself, lived to reach adulthood. With the theories running rampant in our family, my brother—"* was that a catch in his voice? *"—tried it as well, managing thirteen sons with seven wives, but the ritual didn't work for him either. One of his sons, Jacob, started the chain over again in 1880 and managed to have thirteen sons. The last one, James, began siring his brood in 1950, and, with the help of technology, managed to conceive thirteen as well, the final son being Mason Noir—"*

"Why are you telling me all this?—Jacob, James, I can barely keep them straight," Shizume said.

"The order or names of your ancestors isn't important. The point I'm trying to make is that with at least sixty male Noir children surviving through the centuries, the blood of our family has remained in Geistad for many years, spread among varied families here," Jonathan said. *"What I hadn't mentioned yet was the many Noir* females, *at least seventy, that were also born to our family, women who married and raised children who carried within them Noir blood, and perhaps a bit of the* heka, *or magic, as well, enough to enable me to contact you to come down here where we could finally speak."*

"Females, *heka,* I still don't understand any of this," Shizume replied.

"You will soon enough, but the important thing is that we have to get to the one person who can stop what is about to happen, and then find my brother."

"Stop, cut it, just cut it for a moment!" Shizume said. She walked back to the ladder, rubbing her temples, which now ached with a pulse that she knew was not her own. *I hope I'm not going insane,* she thought. "Okay, I've got to re-rez for a nano. You keep telling me I'll understand, but then you keep piling more on that I'm not. You either need to start from the beginning or give me the five-minute virt version."

"I'm afraid there is not that much time," Jon said. *"You have been feeling the shockwaves, yes?"*

"Shockwaves? How do you know about those?" she asked.

"Trapped in the earth, there are still things I can feel," he replied.

"Yes, trapped here—let's start with that," Shizume said, thankful for the darkness that prevented the blush on her face from being visible, even though there was no one around to see it. "What is this place?"

"Back in 1841 it was the attic space of the Derlicht Haus, before it was almost destroyed in a fire," Jon began. *"They rebuilt it—"*

"—and the house survived until 2061, I think, when it was flooded out with the rest of the town," Shizume said.

"Strange," Jon said, his voice holding a hint of amusement, *"I thought I was telling this. After all, I was there."*

"O-kay," Shizume said.

"Trainee Mader, to whom are you speaking?" Fliv asked. *"My sensors indicate no one else in this room, yet you persist in this one-sided conversation."*

"Fliv, you wouldn't believe me if I told you," Shizume

said. "I'm not one hundred percent sure I believe it. If it wasn't for the fact that I've seen him before, in the simulation *and* in the dream, I'd have thought I was losing my mind."

"If you did not have my blood flowing through your veins, believe me, that's exactly what might have happened," Jon replied. *"While other homes existed here, I've tried to enter those who lived in them, only to have unpleasant results. I didn't try for a long, long time—not until I felt the first shock. Then I knew I had to get out of here."*

"How were you planning to accomplish that?" Shizume asked.

"With your help," Jon said. *"Before the flooding, I was able to walk on the surface. But with the island submerged so long ago, I remained underwater, unable to interact with the world above. Even when the reclamation began, I remained trapped down here, cut off from the world above. When this site was excavated decades later, I was able to influence the engineers to excavate this area as a backup power system for the building that had existed here, now long gone. The site has been built on at least three more times, but access has always remained to this room, and the reason for it, you, is now standing here."*

"But that doesn't explain why you need me," Shizume said.

"The Noir family bloodline ties us together," Jon replied. *"Because of it, I am able to co-exist in your body, riding along, if you pardon the expression, as you leave. At least, that is what I hope will happen. One thing is*

for certain, you are the only person that I have been able to stay in for more than a few moments, and that gives me hope."

"How would I—if I wanted to—get you out?" Shizume asked.

"You would just have to ask," Jon said. *"Unlike some of my relatives, I do not seek power over others as they do. I can appreciate that this must not be pleasant for you, so I would understand. However, before you make that decision, you must hear me out, for the consequences of that could mean the complete destruction of your world."*

"Okay, I'll ride that line for a bit," Shizume said. "Uh, why don't we get topside? No doubt you'll want to see what happened to the world since you've been down here."

"Yes, perhaps I can explain on the way. Also, the increasing force of the tremors have weakened these walls, and I don't think they're going to hold much longer," Jon said.

As if proving his point, the earth shuddered around them, and a bank of computers shifted, leaning slightly towards Shizume. "Good idea. Fliv, let's get out of here."

"Affirmative, Trainee," Fliv said, then paused for a second. *"I'm registering some unusual fluctuations in your brain waves—almost like an echo."*

"Are you now? I'll make a believer out of you yet, you digitalized dispassionate floating hunk of ceramplast," Shizume said as she grabbed the ladder. As she put her foot on the lowermost rung, the room shook again, more powerfully this time, and she was nearly knocked away from the tunnel leading up.

"They're getting stronger—we'd better go now!" Jon said. Shizume didn't need any further inspiration, hauling herself up hand over hand, her feet scrambling to find the rungs before everything came crashing down around her.

The climb up was punctuated by aftershocks quaking the narrow passageway. Each one sent a shower of dust and crumbling, ancient concrete down with it. Although Fliv hovered above her to absorb as much as possible, Shizume learned after the first time to keep her head down and concentrate on nothing but the climb. Even though she had come down in less than two minutes, the return trip took much longer, with her muscles quivering with fatigue by the time she had pulled herself out of the tunnel into more darkness. Far below, she heard a rumble as the room collapsed in on itself, sending a plume of gray dust back up towards her. *Just what I need,* she thought, brushing off her face with shaking fingers.

"Hey, I got another one—with a Partner—what the hell?" an authoritative voice said from above her. "Hold on, let me get this off you."

The rickety walls above her were wrenched away, and Shizume looked up to see her eyes staring back at her dust-smudged face in a gleaming visor.

"Oh, thank the Universe," she said. "I have never been so happy to see you."

The man standing over her was encased in a matte-gray power suit covering him from head to toe. A bright patch on the shoulder of his suit read GNYSR, or Greater

New York Search and Rescue. From what Shizume remembered, the suit he wore gave him fifty times a normal man's strength and could be sealed against hostile environments, including underwater, for up to three days, relying on internal air and food supplies, if necessary. The cybernetic controls to its hands, arms, and legs were slaved to the controller, meaning that the suit reacted as its wearer did, down to the tiniest movement. They were used in situations exactly like this one, assisting in the event of a disaster, car accidents, fires, or even if the police encountered a situation they felt was beyond their own capabilities.

"What the hell were you doing down there?" he asked.

Shizume coughed out a plume of dust, then answered. "GNYCMP Trainee Shizume Mader. I called the Narcotix squad."

"Yeah, when they got here and saw all this, they gave up a light-up," the man said. "My suit says you're all right, just a bit dirty. You still haven't answered my question."

"What—oh, that. You won't believe this, but I thought I heard someone down there," Shizume said with a sheepish grin. "The room was empty when I got down there, however, and I hauled ass just before it collapsed."

"That was pretty ballsy, but maybe next time you should leave the rescuing to us," the S/R guy said, shaking his head. "The Narcotix guys are back in the plant room. You should probably let them know you're here and in one piece."

"Right, I'll let you get back to it. Um, one thing—did you find a girl about this tall—" Shizume indicated a height with her hand. "Dirty blonde hair, dirty face, dirty, well—everything, really."

"Yeah, she was still in the room back there, but there's lots more in here that need help. Now, if you'll excuse me." The Search and Rescue man moved on to the next pile of collapsed wallboards.

Suddenly exhausted, Shizume walked past the rescues going on around her, oblivious to the lives being saved at that moment. Although Jon Noir was mercifully remaining quiet, one sentence he had said kept running through her mind: *the complete destruction of her world.*

CHAPTER EIGHT

T he gravator didn't prevent Antonia from sensing the aftershocks jarring the building. Although she wasn't worried, she couldn't help glancing down the tube that stretched off into nothingness thousands of meters below her, wishing it would go faster. She felt the field slowing, and then she was at the laboratory doors.

Must remain calm. I'm in control now, she thought as she entered the lab. "Field on. Kar, give me a status check. What's the problem?"

"Don't you think—" Benjamin began from where he was, reading holo-monitors hovering in mid-air in front of him.

"Leave this to the people who know what they're doing," Antonia snapped. "Kar, report."

The lean biogeneticist didn't stop tracking the data scrolling in front of him as he replied. "We had just immersed him in the solution when the tremors began at cycle start plus one point four minutes. This wave wasn't just physical energy, it had some kind of neurological effect on him, like his brain spiked or something. I'm still trying to isolate it now."

"Damage?" Antonia asked, keeping a tight rein on her emotions. The last thing she could afford to show was indecisiveness or weakness now, especially in front of Benjamin, who she could feel watching her.

"Nothing that we can detect so far," Kar said, moving a 3-D model of Mason's brain, examining it from all sides. "Everything is functioning according to accepted parameters, but—wait—a flash, what's happening here?"

Mason's body had begun to shake and thrash, his mouth opening and closing. "I've got massive pulmonary emboli spontaneously forming in his lungs—this isn't possible, he was in perfect health presubmersion," Kar said.

"The psychic waves don't have to make sense," Benjamin said. "They will randomly destroy or create until the balance of the universe is restored."

"Give him 100 ccs of Altiplase-R44, inhaled directly into the lungs," Antonia said.

Kar introduced the anti-clotting agent into the liquid surrounding Mason. They watched as it moved through his airway and into his lungs, breaking up the deadly clots. Mason ceased struggling, his muscles relaxing with the inflow of liquid oxygen and medicine. Antonia, however, didn't rest just yet, her eyes never leaving her husband's face.

"Are the nanocells ready?" she asked Kar.

"Standing by as per Mason's orders," he replied.

"Inject 150ccs," she said. "I'd rather be ready if some other complication occurred then have to wait for them to travel. Even a few seconds can mean the difference."

Nanocells, yet another NoirCorp invention, were microscopic medical platforms designed to enter a human body. They could be programmed to perform certain duties, such as cleaning life-threatening plaque off arterial walls or patrolling for viruses, or an infinitesimally larger version could actually be controlled from the outside, to be sent where the doctor needed it, even into the brain if necessary.

Although Antonia had begun her studies in English and literature all those decades ago, her expanded lifetime had enabled her to collect degrees in business administration, law, and even more important as NoirCorp grew, medicine and biotechnology. *After all, a girl has to stay on top of technology in this day and age,* she had thought at the time. *Especially me.*

"Damn it, it's happening again! Blood clots—no, now we've got tumors growing in the lungs, both upper and lower lobes," Kar said.

"Where are the nanos?" Antonia asked.

"Entering the trachea now," a female tech said. "E.T.A. one minute."

"Tumors growing at a rate of one hundred percent every two point five minutes," Kar said. "I've never seen anything like this."

Absorbed in programming the nanos, Antonia almost didn't notice the first tremor. Only the flashing automatic warning in the corner of her floating monitor alerted her to the potential danger. "Kar, is that another seismic warning?"

"Confirmed, aftershocks of that first tremor. Coming in ten, nine, eight..."

"This will not be good," Benjamin said.

143

"Benjamin, if you can't contribute something useful to this situation, shut the hell up!" Antonia snapped.

At that point Antonia heard the faint stirring of a familiar voice in her head. *"He's right, you know. This can only bring the destruction of everything you hold dear."*

Antonia was proud of herself for not jumping or yelping for a second, then returned to the now three things she was doing. *This is not the time, Agatha.*

I must try. You are my only true flesh and blood, and yet you will not listen to reason, her ancestor replied.

"Kar, the nanos are primed. Give me a rez inside as they're doing it. I want to keep track of what's happening," Antonia said while carrying on her internal conversation.

What reason—yours? she thought. *Damn it, Agatha, you made me give up any chance of a family, only to find out I had to do it again when Mason perfected the cloning process! You can't imagine how much pain that was, to kill my own womb, my own eggs, not once, not twice, but three times, to destroy the life I could have created before it or I even had a chance! So, after all that, what reason could you possibly give to make me to believe anything you say?*

Because you are helping the Noirs at the expense of your own family, Agatha replied. *I cannot stand by and watch that happen.*

Unfortunately for you, that's exactly what you're going to do, Antonia said. *And don't even think about going against me; you know I'm stronger.* "Nanos have reached first tumor masses. Enable lasers."

144

On the screen, the tiny living artillery blasted away at the cancerous growths that had sprung up in Mason's body, drawing on his own bioelectrical field to power their minuscule weapons. Although the tumors attempted to keep growing, the tiny pulses of lights burned their cells away faster than they could grow back, and once a cell was fried, it was dead forever. Antonia kept her eyes on the screen, waiting to see if Agatha would dare try anything. The silence in her mind was answer enough.

"Tumor infestation at forty-three percent and dropping," Kar said. Just then another shock wave shook NoirCorp headquarters, and a piercing scream jolted through everyone.

"My arms—I can't move my arms!" The female tech assisting Kar backed against the wall, staring down at herself in horror. Her arms flopped limply at her sides, loose and distended somehow, as if the bones that had previously given them their shape had disappeared or become as soft as the flesh surrounding them.

"Get her out of here, and run a full scan on her," Antonia said.

"I'm surprised it took this long," Benjamin said at her elbow. "By the way, one of your little guncells in there is malfunctioning, drawing more power than it should. You should shut it down."

Antonia checked and sure enough, a nanocell was building up a dangerous overcharge of energy in Mason's body. She gave it the command to self-destruct, then looked at the elder Noir out of the corner of her eye. "What did you mean by your first statement?"

"Simply that as the waves increase in frequency and

power, their effects on humans will be more pronounced, more—dangerous," he replied.

"You sure know a *lot* about this process," Antonia said, the question evident in her tone.

"My access to other dimensions included more than just this one, " he replied.

"I'll bet it did," Antonia said, then turned to Kar. "How do you feel about earning some overtime?"

The wild-haired scientist shrugged. "You mean in addition to the twenty hours I'm already on the clock for? Don't worry, I'm not going anywhere. What did you have in mind?"

"I want to bio-seal the lab. It might prevent the temporal shocks from affecting us more strongly than that."

Kar looked at the door the female tech had been sent through. "If that's the first step, I don't want to see the next one. No problem. Why don't I set up a rotating field frequency to further confuse the issue? It can't hurt and might even help."

Antonia smiled, her first in many hours. "I can see why Mason keeps you around. Go ahead. And check on our back-up power systems. I want an entire system isolated for this lab if necessary."

Kar got busy, with Benjamin dividing his attention between the two humans left in the lab room. "You do realize that you're trying to stop the universe itself, and that your 'barrier' will do as much good as a twig trying to hold back a raging river?"

"I haven't gotten to where I am now by sitting back and just letting things happen," Antonia said. "My husband has more than nine and a half hours to go in there, and if anything you've said is true, then there's a lot worse to come, and I'm going to see him through it all, even if I have to get in there with him."

"Fair enough," Benjamin said with a nod. "Please know that if there is any way I can help, I am at your service."

Antonia appeared to ponder his offer for a few seconds. *Can I trust him?* she thought. *If Mason is his only chance to get into a body, he's surely not going to jeopardize that chance. Besides, if he's kept busy on something else, he'll be out of my hair.*

"Actually, there might be," she replied. "More than any of us, you seem to be more attuned to these waves, even more so than our equipment. When Kar's done, I would like the two of you to work together on a way to predict the pattern of the waves, then see if he can't come up with a way to record them. If I have something to work with, perhaps we can come up with a better way to block them."

"As you wish," he said, heading over to talk to Kar. Antonia finished bringing the nanocells out of Mason's body, then found herself with nothing to do for the moment. She stared at her husband for a long moment, watching the now-even rise and fall of his chest, gazing at his face, relaxed now. She leaned over and checked the progress of the bodyscan, which was holding steady at three percent. *Still a long way to go,* she thought, returning her gaze to Mason, *and I'll be there every step of the way, my love.*

CHAPTER NINE

S hizume punched the button of the elevator, Fliv close behind her. She had spent the last twenty minutes, with her partner corroborating her story, detailing what had happened to the sergeant of the Narcotix squad that was now busy shuttling members of the squat city uplevel. He had been impressed by her initiative, and although Shizume had endured a slightly longer lecture on waiting for backup before entering a situation like that, she could tell he had been pleased by her actions and had mentioned that she might get a citation added to her record. "Not bad for a day's work, even for a rookie. You ever want to work Narcotix after graduation, you let me know. I'm sure we could find a place for you," had been his parting words.

Right now, all I want is to sleep for about a week, she thought, leaning against a back corner of the elevator. She was riding up with a group of the squatters that had just had their lived turned upside-down, and she did her best to remain unnoticed by them. The two Narcotix officers were busy keeping an eye on their charges.

"Regrettably, that isn't an option," Jon's voice said in her head.

Ah, you are still in there, Shizume thought. *I was wondering if you had made it out with me.* Her thought was interrupted by a rough choking sound, and seconds later something wet splattered on her face. Shizume looked up to see Flaya, the little blonde squatter, her eyes bright with hatred, staring at her.

"You ruined everything! My family, my friends, everything we had is gone, and it's all your fault!" She lunged at Shizume, fingers outstretched, but the heavy hand of a Narcop hauled her back at the last second.

Wiping the saliva from her face, Shizume stared at her in shock. *Doesn't she know what happened to her family and friends in that room?*

"Apparently not," Jon said.

"You did the right thing," Fliv said.

"Did I?" Shizume asked. "After all, they were just trying to live their lives down here, like all of us here."

"All she knows is that you are the one who brought the police into her world and changed it forever."

"But they were living off of the society around them, not in accordance with it. They were not chipped, they did not pay taxes, and they were stealing space and power from those whom it rightfully belonged to," Fliv said. *"Wanting to live a free life isn't a crime, but living by taking from others, whether directly or indirectly, that is a crime in this city."*

"Your partner makes a good point," Jon said. *"Without laws, civilization does not exist. Even something as small as that back there is still part of a larger problem. Just*

*because a person does not agree with what the majority
of society has decreed does not give them the right to
make their own decisions regardless of others, especially
if those decisions are contrary to the laws already in
effect."*

"I didn't expect that from you, Jon. Wasn't there a lot
more freedom during your time?" Shizume asked.

*"Yes, and because of it my brother was able to murder
five people, including our father and myself, and get
away with it because there wasn't enough evidence to
convict him. I trust you can see why I am in favor of
laws and ordered society,"* Jon replied.

"I suppose so," Shizume said, keeping her eyes on the
young girl until they reached their floor. Flaya just stared
back at her like she was trying to burn holes in the older
woman's skull. The Narcops began hustling the small
group into the now packed corridor, filled with dozens
of men, women, and children, many of them carrying
suitcases or boxes as they filed by. No one was talking,
save for mothers comforting small children.

"What's going on?" Shizume asked one of the officers.

"These tremors have got a lot of people spooked, so
they're trying to leave the city. If this doesn't stop soon,
we'll have a full-fledged riotstate on our hands."

"Great. Are they pulling reserves up yet?" she asked.

"Just starting the lists right now, primarily to patrol
the buildings they live in and make sure everything is
orderly," the officer replied. "You should check in when
you get back. No doubt Central'll have something for
you as well."

"Thanks," Shizume said as she began struggling down

the packed corridor. "Fliv, can you re-establish contact with Payne? I need some more info on what's going on there."

"Sorry, Trainee, but all channels are restricted to essential communications only," Fliv replied.

"Any word on activating me?" she asked.

"The most recent report is that all officers, including off-duty and second year and above trainees, are to consider themselves on standby alert and have their partners with them at all times until the stand-down order has been given."

"All right, I'll contact Payne myself." Shizume activated her celplant, the small digital transmitter that had been inserted in her jaw for her sixteenth birthday. Another device powered by her body's electrical field, it allowed her to dial and speak with anyone, although for security reasons it could not be tied into her police optics, so she would have to make due with audio only. "Dial J. H. Payne."

Seconds later, Payne's voice was in her ear. "Shi, where the heck have you been? I was worried something had gone wrong."

"Thanks, Grandfather, but I'm fine," Shizume replied. "What's happening?"

"It's going crazy out here. I can barely keep up with the reports. Did you know an entire blockpartment is now speaking their own private language, and linguistics experts think it might be Eastern Abenaki, which has been extinct for more than one hundred fifty years."

"Well, if you like that, you're going to love this," Shizume said. "After we lost the connection, I ran into an old acquaintance of mine, Jon Noir."

"Ha ha, very funny, Shi—that *was* a joke, right?"

"Ask me a question only he would know, and I'll tell you in a minute," she replied.

"Okay, I'm game—let's see, how about the one billion dollar question—when his father's body was found, his heart was missing. What happened to it?"

"Payne, really—" Shizume said.

"No, it's all right, what's happening now is much more important that the shame of our family's history," Jon said. *"Tell him my father's heart had been buried in the large corpse flower in the glass house on our property, most likely by my brother. I believe it never left there, although Thomas may have removed and destroyed it later to prevent discovery by someone else, although I can't imagine who might have come to the house after all that."*

Shizume wished she could have seen the look on Payne's face when she told him what Jon had said. There was a long moment of silence, and then she heard her grandfather's awed voice. "You really are with him, aren't you?"

"More like he's with me," Shizume said. "I'm heading back home to check in, and you and I need to have a talk."

"Absolutely, and the sooner the better," her grandfather replied.

"All right, I'll keep my line clear, just in case," she replied. "I'll contact you once I'm home."

"I look forward to it," he said. "Talk to you soon." A slight click indicated the connection had been broken.

Indeed, I think your relative may be able to help us. I can fill you in on the way there, Jon said. Shizume just concentrated on getting to the Zipper ports. Struggling over to the packed waiting area, she was able to squeeze into one that was headed near her building.

"Okay, Jon," Shizume said once they were moving, "Since you can speak to me telepathically, can't you read my mind so I don't have to keep talking to you like this?"

"Regrettably, that isn't possible," Jon said. *"I'm only able to speak to you this way because of our bloodline. The communication is not two-way, I'm afraid."*

"And those images I saw when you—entered me, for lack of a better term?" she asked.

"Fragments of my consciousness integrating with yours," Jon said. *"It is a side effect of opening this connection. I'm sorry if it caused you distress."*

"Actually, it made it a little easier to understand what was going on," Shizume said, subvocalizing to avoid drawing unwanted attention. *Fortunately celplants are popular enough that the world won't notice one more woman talking to herself,* she thought. "Shang, I can't believe I just said that. Okay, what do we need to do?"

"In 2003, Mason Noir and Antonia Derlicht were married," Jon began.

"Yeah, 'Noir's Folly,' I think Payne called it," Shizume said, gazing out the Zipper window at the city around her, now packed with other Zippers scrambling everywhere. "So?"

"According to family legend, the joining of the Noir

153

and Derlicht families was supposed to cause our destruction, but once Mason and Antonia were united, nothing happened," Jon continued. *"Instead, it seems the opposite occurred. The Derlicht family gradually disappeared from the area, and the Noirs remained, consolidating their power for the past 150 years.*

"After our attempt to stop the wedding, Thomas and I went our separate ways in the spirit world, but I kept watch over what was happening here, well, as least as much as I was able to. The next forty-some years passed with relative quiet, at least in our realm. Mason and Antonia combined were a much greater force than either of them were separately. When Mason made his breakthrough on MIND-NET, his prototype neural downloading system, they founded NoirCorp together and never looked back.

"I kept watch over Geistad as well as I could, until the flood came and trapped me. But in all that time, I never saw them take any steps towards having a child and I feel that must have something to do with this, although I don't know what. I do know that our family has been obsessed with the idea of the 13th child and using them as a vessel for the future."

"Yeah, but Noir also invented cloning, so wouldn't that be not as important now?" Shizume asked. "I mean, the guy has a lock on immortality as it is, so what's the big deal?"

"I don't know, but there has rarely been a Noir family without offspring. It is expected, even today, I would think. If they haven't had children, there must be a reason for it."

"But what does all this have to do with me?" Shizume asked.

"*Recently I have been unable to sense my brother in the spirit world,*" Jon said. "*While he may have been destroyed in one of the psychic waves that have swept the area, I do not think that is what happened. Now that I am with you, I cannot feel him on this plane either, which leads me to surmise that he is caught between these two worlds somewhere, but if I know him, he will be working as hard as he can to gain a mortal body again. If it is the right body, the consequences could be even more unfortunate than what is happening right now.*"

"So we need to find your brother?" Shizume asked.

"*Yes, but not right away. There is someone else we need to locate first,*" Jon said. "*Throughout time, the Noirs and the Derlichts have been mortal enemies ever since we arrived in Geiststadt. Even the marriage couldn't dispel that animosity; instead it lifted one family while breaking the other. However, elements of the Derlicht family still exist in the area, and while I cannot locate my brother, I have felt the presence of a descendant of the Derlichts in Geistad that may be able to help us, a thirteenth generation child whose lineage reaches back to Agatha Derlicht herself.*

"*It won't be easy, though, as the marriage caused the Derlicht family to divide into two camps, those who saw the event as joining the enemy, and those who welcomed the chance for peace. I don't know anything about him or her, save that within this person is the potential to avert the disaster I know is coming.*"

"What do—oh, wait a minute," Shizume said, "we're here."

She got out of the still-stuffed Zipper and threaded her way back up the packed hallway, so much so that the pedmover had been shut off for safety. Reaching her door, she waited until the body scanner had verified that it was her waiting to enter, then opened the door and slipped inside.

Shrugging out of her clothes in the bathroom, she paused before signaling for the shower. "Uh, Jon?"

"Yes?"

"You can see what I see, right?"

"That is correct," he replied.

"Well, um, I'd like to clean up for a few minutes, so—if you don't mind—"

"Ah, of course," Jon said. *"What is the phrase—you won't even know I'm there."*

"Okay." *Of course, I hadn't known you were there earlier, either,* she thought. Still, Shizume took her fastest shower ever, setting the stall to produce billowing clouds of steam that obscured everything, even her hand in front of her face. When she was finished, she wrapped herself in a huge towel and wasted no time in getting dressed.

Sitting in a formchair in front of her wall screen, she saw a blinking light, indicating a message was waiting. Opening it revealed a message from her parents: "We've heard what's going on, and we hope you're okay, and we're wondering when you're getting out of that terrible place—" and similar concerns that went on for about five minutes.

Oh, shang it all, Shizume thought. She quickly recorded an answer; "Hi, I'm all right, but I'm on duty and can't talk right now. I'll call you when I can, but don't worry about me. I'll be all right, and besides, Grandfather's here too." She smiled as she said the last words; her mother and Payne had never seen eye to eye.

Shizume set the message to send only after she had left the apartment, then dialed her grandfather. When he answered, she heard resignation in his voice. "Shizume, it's good to hear from you."

"Hi, Grandfather. Can I come over?"

"Hey, the net's still free, last time I checked, and you know where I live."

Shizume faced the screen and visualized her grandfather's address. The room around her slowly faded out, replaced by verdant green prairie after a spring rain, at least that's what her grandfather had told her it was. "I always wanted to live on the prairie, where there weren't any skyscrapers or highways, and now I've got my wish," he had said. In the distance his log cabin sat at the top of a hill against the skyline, a simple weatherworn square building with a wood shingled roof. Smoke drifted from the large stone chimney at one end. The wind here was cool and soft and brought with it only the sounds of nature: running water from the creek that wound its way around his virtual property and the distant cry of a whippoorwill in the afternoon. Smiling, she walked up the dirt road to his house, Fliv floating close behind.

Payne was waiting for her on the porch, sitting on the front steps, dressed in a denim jacket he had worn when he was real, T-shirt, faded jeans, and cowboy boots. He watched her approach without a word, letting her come up and sit on the wooden steps just below him. They sat there for several long minutes, watching the wind ruffle patterns through the ocean of timothy grass surrounding his place.

"You're looking well, granddaughter," her grandfather said. "Is he—" he motioned vaguely at her.

Shizume tapped her temple. "Yeah, up here."

"Can Mr. Noir hear me?"

"Yes, and he says to please call him Jon."

"All right," Payne replied, leaning forward. "It is an honor to welcome both of—no, that's remiss, isn't it?—all three of you to my home. Why don't you, Jon, and Fliv come inside?"

He led them into the house. Shizume found herself in a room roughly the size of her apartment with sculptures and framed paintings floating near the walls, bathed in indirect light that seemed to come from all the walls at once. Gentle music drifted through the air, a symphony of instruments she had never heard before, a soft wash of strings behind a melancholy horn blowing rich mournful notes. She looked around, but Payne's avatar was nowhere to be seen.

"Grandfather?" she said, her voice echoing strangely in the room.

"Up here," his voice said

As she looked up, the darkness above her was banished by even more light, revealing a seemingly endless space stretching at least several stories above her. The entire room was a long vertical column. The prairie outside had vanished, replaced by the Greater New York skyline glowing against the dusky horizon through the wall-size window that formed one side of the room. And in the middle of it all floated her grandfather with a dozen holoscreens gliding around him, each tuned to a different channel, mostly news stations.

Shizume turned slowly around, trying to take it all in at once. The other three walls were dotted with various doors leading to other rooms, along with even more artwork, including a familiar painting.

"Hey, isn't that—" Shizume began.

"Cole's *The Burning of Derlicht Haus*," Payne supplied. "Yes, well, I liked it so much when I found it that I put a copy up on my wall here."

"You've certainly changed a few things around," she said, taking it all in.

"I like living the simple life now and then—" he waved his hand, and the room was replaced by a simply furnished cabin interior, down to the pine-log framed bed and enameled washbasin and pitcher on a tall table, "—but I can't give up the comforts of the city all the time." He waved again, and the room reverted back to its high-tech state. "Here, I get to have either, both, or any combination of the two.

"Now, let me get comfortable," Payne said, leaning back so it looked like he was reclining in mid-air. "And tell me everything that happened after we lost contact. Please, omit nothing, no matter how small."

Shizume filled him in on what had happened after they had lost contact, the squatcity, Jon's call to her, their conversation, the escape from the room, and their subsequent journey here. Payne didn't interrupt or ask questions; he just listened.

"So, Jon, do you have any idea what is behind these

energy waves that are flooding the city?" he asked when she had finished.

"As near as I can tell, they are a build-up of energy preceding a catalyst event that, depending on what it is, will either destroy or reshape the world as you all know it," Jon said, with Shizume relaying the information. *"Before my untimely death, I had managed to study enough to understand that the universe is in constant motion. During my time in the spirit world, I observed that if something occurs to interrupt that motion, then the universe takes steps to attempt to correct it. Unfortunately, if the 'event' is caused by one person, the unthinking universe takes rather broad steps to correct it, and woe to anyone who is caught in its way."*

"The universe doesn't care, as long as the anomaly is corrected," Shizume said.

"Correct," Both Payne and Jon said together.

"So why haven't I been affected yet?" Shizume asked. "What makes me so special?"

"Actually, nothing, I'm afraid," Jon replied. *"At its heart, the universe is random, and so are these waves. Eventually, they will affect you in some way. Everyone on the planet will be touched by it."*

"That's a cheery notion," she said, unable to stop the next thought that popped up. *What's going to happen to me?*

"Perhaps, but it certainly explains the high degree of impossibilities that we've been experiencing in Geistad and Greater New York City," Payne continued. "If I wasn't so concerned that the city is about to be wiped off the map, I'd have enough material to write columns for the rest of my life. However, my future career is of secondary importance. There are many more questions to answer, such as: what role does your brother play in all of this?"

"I am not sure yet," Jon replied. *"Given that my brother might be causing these waves, it would seem that he would be the one to stop the coming cataclysm. The truth is, I don't know. I only know he must be there."*

"Yes, that's another problem. Not only do we not know where he is, but we don't know what the catalyst event is, where it is, or what to do about it," Payne said. "All in all, it might be better to stick our proverbial heads between our legs and kiss our asses good bye."

"Grandfather, you don't really mean that," Shizume said.

"I suppose not, but answer me this, Jon: do you know where the missing Derlicht child is, or who it is?" Payne asked.

"No, I don't, although I believe he or she is somewhere in Geistad."

"Well, that's a start," Payne said, pulling one of his waiting array of screens to him. "I think I might be able to help a bit, but all of this is total conjecture, so bear with me."

The wall in front of Shizume and Jon blurred into a familiar map of the Geistad area. "I've been tracking the general reports of the unusual incidents in the area, as well as the surrounding boroughs," Payne said. "There is an interesting correlation between how these waves are impacting Geistad and—surprise, surprise, the headquarters of NoirCorp.

"This line—" a horizontal green line swept downward

through the map, leaving small green dots in certain areas where it passed, "—was the first one, on New Year's Eve. This—" a blue line moved over the buildings and streets, leaving a bit more blue dots than the first, "—was the second. You'll notice that the only area relatively untouched—"

"—is NoirCorp." Shizume said. "But isn't that coincidence?"

"It would be, except for the amazingly high statistical history the Noirs have of being involved in all of this weirdness throughout the centuries. They're a kind of lodestone for the strangeness, except now, when the strangeness is happening all around them, they seem incredibly immune to it. My theory is that perhaps they actually have something to do with all of this. That alone is worth investigating."

"If that's true, and, going along with it, if the Derlicht child is supposed to stop whatever's going on, shouldn't we find him first?" Shizume asked.

"Actually, that will be a bit easier," Payne said. "The Derlichts, being such an old family, have roots intertwined with Geistad back to the 18th century. Thank the Faces that Agatha or someone was such a meticulous record keeper because—" the beginning of a family tree sprouted on one side of the wall and spread across the wall, the generations spreading ever wider, the offspring flourishing in some eras, weakening or dying on in other truncated branches, "—just about all of their generations can be traced back to the original family in Geiststadt."

"There is a noticeable break circa the year 2003," Fliv noted.

"Fliv, I thought you weren't paying attention," Shizume said.

"*I always pay attention, even when the event in question is most assuredly outside my jurisdiction,*" Fliv replied. "*Given a statistical representation of the family, the break is fairly obvious.*"

"Your partner is quite right," Payne said. "The marriage of Mason Noir and Antonia Derlicht," he indicated the joining of the families with a flashing red dot, "marks the beginning of the Noirs' ascension and the Derlichts' decline. From here on the Derlicht line weakens, with daughters marrying into other families and taking their names. However, extrapolating through the generations, there are four thirteenth-level grandchildren still living in the area. There are others, but since you, Jon, can sense his or her presence still, we can assume they haven't left the city, for whatever reason.

"Now, one of them—wait a minute—that name looks familiar," Payne said, bringing another holoscreen down to him. "Well, let's hope its not Teralee Waysond."

"Why not?" Shizume asked.

"Because she was one of the most recent victims of the last wave," Payne said, showing them a news report with a strange vaguely human-shaped leafy picture above it. The caption read: LOCAL WOMAN TURNED INTO TROPICAL TREE.

"All right. You have whereabouts on the other three, right?" Shizume asked with a shudder.

"Addresses for all," Payne replied.

"*Actually, I can go you better than that,*" Fliv said. "*With my access to the neurochip tracking program, I can locate all three of these people's precise where-abouts."*

"So are you on the clock now?" Shizume asked with a sardonic grin.

"If these anomalies are disrupting the order of Greater New York City, then that is enough of a reason for me," Fliv replied.

"Okay, I'll buy that. Now, we can assume that Teralee isn't the presence, since the presence is still here. I mean, it *is* still here, right, Jon?" Shizume asked.

"Yes, I can still feel whoever it is," he replied.

"Okay, good, so they aren't dead yet," Shizume said. "Okay, this sounds relatively simple enough. I, Jon, and Fliv will head out to each location, and we see if Jon gets any stronger sense of this person at each one. When we get a better fix, Fliv homes in on him or her and wham, we've got him, or her."

"Although I cannot comment on your homing technique, if this 'Jon' exists, and can do what you say, the plan would be otherwise sound," Fliv said.

"Before you rush off, can I have a word with you, Shizume—in private, if possible?" her grandfather said.

"Sure. Fliv, would you mind?" she asked her partner.

"Not at all. I'll be over here if you need me." Fliv floated to the other side of the room.

"No need to ask me as well, Shizume, I understand," Jon said. *"When you are through, just keep repeating the word elephant, and I'll return."*

"Thanks, Jon."

Shizume gave him a few seconds, then turned to her grandfather. "Well, what do you think of all this?"

"I think the most important question is what do *you* think of all this? For someone with a tri-centuries old ancestor talking inside your head, you seem very calm about the whole thing," Payne replied.

Shizume tapped her temple. "Comes with being a cop, or an almost cop. Guess I'm more used to it, I suppose. Before I go running off to who knows where, do you think this is all on the level?"

"Right now, I'm only sure of three things," Payne replied. "First, something screwy is going on in the city, and it needs to be investigated. Second, the psyche, or spirit, or ghost, or whatever's in your head *is* Jon Noir."

"How do you know that?" she asked.

"The answer to the question he gave me," Payne said. "I've been trying to find out what happened to old Ben's heart for twenty-five years. Let me tell you, I got really good at separating the wheat from the chaff in what I found. He was telling the truth."

"Yeah, I got that impression as well," Shizume said. "So what was the third thing?"

Payne didn't speak for a moment and looked down at the ground before meeting her gaze again. "I don't want you getting hurt in all of this."

Shizume was caught off guard by his statement. "I–I don't know what to say. I mean, you didn't object when I joined the PD."

"I know, but there they partner you up–" Payne gestured at Fliv, "–and train you to handle whatever might come along. But what you're heading into in the unknown, not just some flaming firehead or dustjunkie. Me, Jon, you, none of us really know what's going to happen, and that's what worries me."

Shizume threw her arms around her grandfather, drawing him into her embrace. "I've got my head screwed on straight about this, Payne. It seems so strange, but—I feel better doing this than I have doing anything else, even the police training. I mean, that was good, like I was making a difference, but chasing down whatever we're going to find, facing it, for some reason that makes me feel more alive than ever."

"Great, my granddaughter is becoming a thrill junkie," Payne grumbled, drawing back to look at her with a rueful grin.

"No, its not that, its just the sense of being part of something bigger, bigger than the department, bigger than the city, bigger than anything I've ever known," Shizume said. "But don't you worry, I'll come back to you."

"You'd better," Payne replied, hugging her to him again. "Now, let's get you folks a Zipper. EWO maintains an account at an exclusive service. I know, I know, I'll never need it, but you'd be surprised what one can accomplish with a favor or two dropped in the right lap. Can your partner reestablish the link-up? I would like to accompany you, if I may, and hopefully can help out if necessary."

"Yes, please, Fliv. We're dealing with something much bigger than we know, and his help might just save all of us," Shizume said.

"I'm afraid that request is impossible, Mr. Payne, as all police channels are being used right now. My suggestion would be to continue with your voice only link," Fliv replied.

"Well, no harm in asking, I suppose," he said. "We'll

keep in touch by celplant until I can work something up. Just give me a few minutes. The car is on the way to your address right now. Good luck, and watch out for the next wave. It'll probably be along fairly soon, within the next hour at the outside. There's no telling what's going to happen when it hits," Payne said.

"Right," Shizume said as she reached the doorway, then turned to look back at her grandfather. "And thanks." Before he could reply, she bounded out the door.

"Elephant, elephant, elephant," she thought. "Jon?"

"*I'm here*," he replied.

"Great," she thought as the cabin and prairie faded out around them. "Now let's go find us a Derlicht."

CHAPTER TEN

Inside the nutrient chamber in the laboratory, Mason was encountering his own problems.

Normally a person undergoing a bodyscan would be sedated during the entire cycle so their active thought patterns wouldn't interrupt the process. But Kar and Mason had decided to give him only a light sedative to keep as much brain activity going as possible for transfer. Their initial studies had led them to believe that the more data they could retrieve from a person's mind with this program, the better chance they had of a successful clone.

However, there had been complications from the beginning. Mason had assumed he would be relatively unaware of anything going on during the scan, so it was quite a surprise to discover he was suddenly having problems breathing. The pains in his chest intensified, then as quickly as they had come, they subsided. Mason's ragged breaths became more even, as the liquid oxygen flowed into him. *Antonia—it must have been her,* he thought, a half-smile forming unbidden on his lips.

The kaleidoscope of colors that many patients reported dreaming about under the bodyscan whirled in front of him, bright swirls and shifts of every hue imaginable, flowing and blending into each other in a display such as he had never seen before, with no clash or jarring mix, lavender drifting into aquamarine deepening to sapphire blue turning to indigo that blended into pure jet, reminding Mason of his wife's raven hair. The cycle began again, blending into pastels of lemon, sky blue, and dusky pink. Now that the danger seemed to be over, he let his mind float along with the profusion of colors surrounding him. *I don't ever remember seeing anything like this when I first transferred,* he thought. *If this is what it's like, I'll have no trouble with the next eight hours.*

Amidst the rainbow of colors was a bright point of light, winking on and off. Mason pulled his scattered senses together and watched the dot. *I don't think anyone's ever mentioned that before.* The dot grew larger, shaded by the colors it passed right through.

"*Mason...Mason Noir...can you hear me?*"

For a moment Mason thought he had imagined the voice. Some patients had reported they thought they had heard vague noises during the scan but nothing as clear as this. The dot of light was even larger now, a glowing sphere of energy hovering in front of Mason.

"*Mason Noir, you are in danger,*" the voice said.

"*Who or what are you that is telling me this?*" he asked, focusing on this apparently intelligent talking ball.

"*Someone who does not wish harm to befall you or the ones you love,*" it replied.

"*If you can, assume a more normal form so we can*

169

converse more rationally," Mason said, figuring if he was having a conversation with himself, then the ball would take the form of someone familiar to him.

A woman of about seventy years formed in front of him, her steel-gray hair parted and bound in two smooth buns on either side of her head. She was clothed in a simple yet formal dress with slightly puffed shoulders and a laced bodice that outlined an almost boyish figure. Her face bore an expression that said she demanded respect, something that Mason wasn't in the mood to give right now. After his experiences during the wedding long ago, things like this didn't faze him anymore. And any spirit who had ever appeared to him, whether in the flesh or in this immaterial world, had always boded trouble.

"Well, you certainly know how to make an entrance, I'll give you that," he said.

"You do not know who I am, do you, young Noir?" she asked.

"No, you seem to have the advantage, Mrs.— "

The figure actually took a breath, as if steeling herself to continue. *"I am Agatha Derlicht, who lived during the time of your great-great-grandfather, Benjamin Noir."*

"Are you now?" Mason said. *"From what Antonia has told me, you caused enough trouble in your own time, why are you here now? And what did you mean by harm coming to me or my loved ones?"*

"I have come here to try to dissuade you from making a terrible error, one that will destroy your entire family and perhaps your world as well."

That got Mason's full attention. *"I'm listening."*

"You do not know your relative like I do," Agatha said. *"I lived with him for years, trying to exist side-by-side in Geiststadt during our lives. His singlemindedness nearly brought doom upon our entire community. His experiments brought evil into the town, and his son Thomas was no better. I could smell his rapaciousness, the lust for power, money, whatever he wanted."*

"While I appreciate your diatribes against my family mixed in with this history lesson, perhaps you could come to the point?" Mason said, watching the colors mix and eddy behind the old woman.

"And I see some of them in you, but hopefully not too much yet," Agatha said, her voice chill. *"You are already not inclined not to believe what I am saying, but you must. Whatever Benjamin is up to, it is not for your benefit, only his. He wants to live forever. It is a dream he has never given up on. It is why his psyche is so strong, why he has survived on our plane for so long. He will let nothing stand in his way to achieve his goals."*

"Funny, that's exactly why he's here, and that's exactly what we're doing," Mason replied. *"I'm not sure if you're aware of this, Agatha, but things have come a long way since your time of horse-drawn carriages and kerosene lanterns. I've conquered death, something he couldn't do—"*

"No, not without your help, he couldn't," Agatha replied, her voice almost lost in his.

"That's right, and he knows that," Mason said. *"In the end it was science that won out, not religion, not magic, not that ridiculous* heka, *but pure true science. Doctors and scientists unlocked the secrets of the body, and I took*

that knowledge to bring him back this far, and damn it, I'm going to finish it, and not you, not anyone is going to stop us!"

"Yes, your wife said much the same thing, only not in the same words," Agatha mused.

Her words brought Mason up short. *"You've spoken to my wife?"*

Agatha cocked her head. *"Why yes, I can't believe she didn't tell you. Her abilities in this realm are quite powerful, after all. We've spoken often over the years, ever since that unpleasantness on your wedding day. Most shocking behavior, I must say, and by your own family, too."*

Mason was on full alert now, the haziness and euphoria banished by the spinster's words. Whereas in the real world he would be calm and controlled during this conversation, this time there was the slightest tremor in his voice when he spoke. *"What would you two talk about?"*

"Oh, nothing of consequence," Agatha said. *"Your name never came up, if that's what you're wondering about."*

"Didn't it?" Mason said, pondering. Suddenly he knew. *It was this old bitch, twisting her against me from that day forward,* he thought. *And she went along with it, she wanted all of the power on her terms. It was all a lie, right from the beginning, and I was too enraptured to see it. All of it, nothing but lies, and me not figuring it out until now.*

"Mason, are you all right?" Agatha asked.

Mason looked up, a grim smile twisting his features.

"Your concern is touching, although I cannot see why you would care about what happened to me, now or ever."

Agatha shook her head. *"In my time spent here, I've seen much happen beyond my reach, out of my control. When my great-great-great-granddaughter married you, I thought all was lost for the Derlichts. Instead, the two of you have created an empire I could scarcely have dreamed of. And in the past decades, you have never lashed out at her, never lifted a hand to her in anger, not even when she could not give you children."*

Agatha's words twisted the knife already in Mason's heart, nearly tearing him in two. *"Yes, an heir, that is the one thing we could not achieve, no matter how hard we tried."*

"A lesser man would have been overcome with rage, suspecting something was amiss, but your patience has been incredible," Agatha continued.

"Well, we had always thought there eventually would be a way," Mason said. Until I discovered she had been plotting against me from the start, he thought. *"But as of yet, we haven't found anything that worked."*

"Now that is unfortunate, for if anyone out of your family deserved an heir, it would be you, Mason," Agatha said, her voice low, sounding every inch like the matronly grandmother she could appear to be. *"But I urge you not to follow through with providing Benjamin with a body—if that happens, he will take whatever he wants, and no one—not you, not your wife—would be safe."*

"Perhaps things will still work out," Mason replied. *"One thing I can promise you, however, is that you have not sidetracked me with all of your talk, woman. Nothing*

has changed. Benjamin Noir will receive his new body, I am certain of that."

Agatha looked at him for a long moment, and Mason couldn't read anything of what was going on in her mind. Finally she shook her head again. *"As am I, young Noir, as am I,"* she said, turning translucent as she began to fade away. *"If there is one thing I understand about your family, it is determination."*

"Good, then perhaps you'll leave me in peace, then," Mason snapped, turning away to brood while the colors whirled and burst around them.

"As you wish, Mason," Agatha said. Since Mason wasn't looking, he missed the triumphant look on her face as she dissolved into nothingness.

"Antonia, take a look at this," Kar said, not looking up from the monitors floating around him.

Antonia turned from where she had been watching Mason's motionless form. Since putting up the barrier around the room, they hadn't been bothered by the waves any more, but, as Benjamin was quick to point out, neither had the rest of Greater New York.

"What are you looking at?" she asked, walking over to him. Nearby, Benjamin was scrolling through a schematic of one of the machines, his absorption in what he was reading punctuated by an occasional "So that's how it's done" or "Of course, it's so simple."

"I've been keeping an eye on his brain activity, and I've just noticed a strange pattern—there it is again, see?"

Antonia looked just in time to see a spike in Mason's cerebrum wave which lasted for a moment, then subsided. "Okay?"

"Look at this activity over the last few minutes," Kar split the screen and scrolled the readout from before. Antonia read the ups and downs of the chart, frowning.

"So what do you think it is?" she asked.

Kar brought up a cutaway cross-section of the brain and highlighted two areas in the cerebrum, near the center and the cerebellum and occipital lobe. "The areas showing increased activity are—get this—his speech and listening centers."

"You think he's talking in there?" Antonia asked.

"If you've got a better theory, I'd love to hear it," Kar replied. "All we've ever seen is the light show. No one's ever reported auditory hallucinations yet, much less a response to them."

"Of course, no one's done extensive testing with this program and matrix either. Has it stopped yet?" she asked, rubbing the bridge of her nose while she examined the EKG.

"I'm not reading any activity other than the basic, so whatever stimulus he's reacting to seems to have stopped," Kar said. "I don't know if it's anything to be alarmed about. He could just be reacting to the vibrations from the electrical field on the chamber itself, or the resonance field."

Perhaps," Antonia said. *Then again, Mason does have some psychic ability,* she thought. *Maybe he is making contact with something.* "Stay rezzed on that monitor, and let me know if it happens again."

"Right." Kar bent to his task again.

Antonia turned to the glass, staring at Mason as if trying to see inside his head. *What is going on in there?*

she wondered, not for the first time. *First the attacks on his body, and now this...*

She looked around. Kar was watching three holo-screens at once, oblivious to her. Benjamin was equally distracted, scanning through diagrams of what looked like NoirCorp technology at a faster and faster rate. Antonia called up a chair and sat down facing the chamber containing her husband. She entered a small trance and sent out a call through the spirit world to summon Agatha.

But as hard as she tried, only silence answered her.

CHAPTER ELEVEN

D rumming her fingers with impatience, Shizume sat in the plush Zipper, unmindful of the luxuries around her. "Come on, come on," she muttered.

"As if that will help matters any," Fliv said.

"Well, I don't see you doing anything to help either," she said. "Here I am, sitting with the partner that could clear this all up, and you don't do a thing."

"Since you have presented me with no legal evidence that this—Ryan Darelight—has done anything illegal that would warrant clearing traffic for our passage, there is nothing I can do," Fliv replied with his now-often-infuriating logic.

"Well, he has to be the one. The other two didn't pan out at all," Payne said. He had visually linked up with Shizume by piggybacking on a government satellite in geosynchronous orbit over Greater New York City. "For research only," he had told her, making Shizume wonder just what else her grandfather was capable of in there. "Jon, you are still sensing him, aren't you?"

"Yes, I wish I could give you a more precise location,

but the residue of these waves appear to be interfering somehow," he replied. *"I'm sorry."*

"What are you talking about? Without you, we wouldn't even know where to look," Payne replied. "Especially since the chip tracker doesn't seem to be working properly. So please, don't apologize, just be ready to find this guy when we get closer."

One ear on the conversation inside her, Shizume flipped on the outside camera viewscreen again, trying to see past the rows and rows of Zippers lined up ahead, behind, and around her. The mission had been going well, with first one Derlicht descendant, then the other, checked out and eliminated. One had left town a week ago, and the next, a spry eighty-five-year-old living in a suburb with the macabre name of Gravesend, radiated no trace of the ability Jon had claimed he could sense.

On the way back, however, their problems had multiplied. First Fliv had claimed that he couldn't find a match for anyone named Ryan Darelight, the last possibility on their list. Then the private Zipper Shizume and Fliv were using to try and find him slowed, switched lanes, and came to a stop two thousand meters up on a stratoscraper's wall. A message Shizume had never heard before came over the loudspeaker. "Your attention please," the computer's male voice said. "There is an obstruction in the travel lanes ahead. It will be a few minutes before the lanes are cleared for passage."

That had been more than an hour ago, the message repeating every five minutes until Shizume had turned it off, and they hadn't budged yet. "What did they call this back in the 20th century, Payne?"

"I believe the term was a traffic jam, or in the cities, where this condition apparently could spread for many square miles, they referred to it as gridlock."

"Shang, it's a wonder they ever got anything done back then," Shizume replied. "What is going on up there? Fliv, please tell me what's on the police bands?"

"There's a bit more going on than you realize," Fliv said. *"These more powerful waves have caused an increase in mass crimes during the last few hours. All units are involved with policing for looting and dispersing riots, even in the blockpartments. Zipper lanes all across the city are filled to 103 percent capacity as people are trying to exit the area. They are calling up reserve units as well as S&R and fire departments as well, and there is a strong chance that you and the rest of the students will be mobilized as well."*

"What if they do summon you for duty, Shi?" Payne asked.

"What can I do? This is more important. What we're doing could mean the difference between the city's survival and its destruction," she replied.

"A not untrue analogy," Jon said. *"Everything rests on the shoulder of the one we're looking for."*

"Or trying to," Shizume said. As if the Zipper had heard her, it lurched forward, and they began moving, slowly at first, then gradually picking up speed. The computer's voice came on again. "The city of Greater New York thanks you for your patience and apologizes for any delay. The travel lanes are moving again, and you will soon be at your destination."

"I wonder what caused this—traffic jam," Shizume said, her mouth stumbling over the unfamiliar term.

"Judging by my report—although even I'm finding this really hard to believe—you should be seeing what caused it right—now," Payne said.

"Front and side camera on," Shizume said. She watched intently as they skimmed down the side of the building. Ahead of them and to the left, something large appeared to be jutting out of several floors of the building.

"Shizume, see if you can zoom in on that object, I need confirmation of it," Payne said. As they got closer, the protrusion grew larger until it filled the entire camera lens. Shizume saw what looked like knurled, thick, deeply striated tree bark, on a huge cylinder at least six meters in diameter.

"But that can't be—" Shizume said.

"Can't be, but it is," Payne replied.

"Can't be what—it is some kind of tree, correct?" Jon said.

"Yeah, that's the problem," Shizume said. "Fliv, what was that?"

"According to my data, that was the sequoia semper-virens, *otherwise known as the California redwood. Even more amazing, it looked to be alive,"* Fliv said.

"That's what I thought you were going to say, but no still-living example exists of the giant redwood since that West Coast sequoia blight seventy years ago," Payne said. "Great shots, by the way, Shi."

"Uh, thanks, I guess. Jon, what is going on here? How did a practically extinct species of tree end up growing from the side of a building fifteen hundred meters above the ground?"

"The temporal displacement is getting worse," Jon said. *"As the intensity of the waves increases, stranger things are going to keep happening—like a tree appearing in the side of a building—"*

"And? What is it?"

"I'm picking up the Derlicht descendent," Jon said. *"We're heading in the right direction—need to go further down."*

"No problem on that account," Shizume said, keeping an eye on the forward camera view, which showed them traveling lower and lower into the downlevels of the city.

"Trainee Mader, I have just received a bulletin from the Greater New York Metro Police," Fliv broke in. *"Recent events have caused the entire Greater New York area to be placed on city-wide riotstate alert. All trainees second year and higher are required to report into the neared precinct floor for assignment as backup to units citywide."*

"Fliv, you know I can't do that now. We may be a few minutes from finding this guy."

"Are you disobeying a direct order from your superior officer?" Fliv asked. *"Please understand that if you do, you will be brought up on disciplinary charges. Due to the severity of the insubordination, you most likely will face expulsion from the Academy. If you do not comply with your orders, I must shut down your cybernetic implants. Also, regardless of your decision, I must proceed to the nearest precinct and be reassigned if necessary. How do you respond, Trainee Mader?"*

Neither Jon nor Payne said a word, both knowing this was her decision alone. Shizume paused, thinking before giving her answer. Was she just running out on the police, like she had run out on being a student? The Metro PD was where she had felt the most at home, but now she was about to throw the last three years away on the strength of what? A faceless voice in her head? And yet what she had seen, and what Jon Noir had told her was all happening, just as he had claimed. *And, if that tree is any indication, it's about to get much, much worse,* she thought. *If I can stop that before it happens, then that's what I have to do.*

"Fliv, tell the precinct officer on duty that I am investigating a person who may have a connection to what is happening in the city, and I will report in as soon as possible but am unable to respond to their summons at this time."

"Very well, Trainee Mader, I am transmitting your message now." Fliv's voice was as toneless as ever. *"A formal notice will be served requesting that you to report to the Academy at a later date to answer the charges of insubordination and negligence that will be filed against you."*

The Zipper stopped for a moment, and Fliv paused before exiting through a hatch in the top. *"It is too bad that you have made this choice, Trainee Mader. In my opinion, you have all of the attributes required to be an excellent Metro Police Officer."*

"Thanks, Fliv. If we all survive this, the department can throw the data at me however they want, but I have to follow this up."

"So noted, Trainee," Fliv said, floating out of the access hatch and away from the Zipper. The portal automatically closed after it. Shizume looked down at herself, aware that the implants under her skin were now just inert hunks of ceramic, plastic and metalweave. *That's all right,* she thought, *I've gotten by without them in the past, and I can do the same now.*

"You did the right thing, you know," Jon said.

"Faces, I hope so," Shizume said. "Fliv told me that when we busted that tobacco garden, and I believed him, and you too, but that was doing the job. It's different when a decision you make affects you personally."

"But Shi, you've got to remember, this doesn't just affect you, but each one of the millions of people out there who are, right now, trying to all get out of the city," Payne said. "You've seen what's happening. Shang. It's happening to you right now, with Jon residing in your head. It's what I've been saying for the past decade, the events that have been building are coming to a head right now. As ridiculous as I know this sounds, we may be the only ones who can stop it before whatever happens, happens."

"Well, when you put it that way, what are we waiting for?" Shizume grinned.

"Stop the vehicle," Jon said.

"What—where?" Shizume asked.

"Stop the vehicle here, now!" Jon said. *"Ryan is somewhere on this floor."*

"Uh, where are you exactly, Shi?" Payne asked.

Shizume waited a moment before realizing that her

cyberware wasn't working. "Oh, shang, that's right. Um, we're—"

"Hold on, I can track the Zipper," Payne said. "Whoa, not a good part of town. Ozone Park, Grid G-7, Block-partment 12C, 56th floor. Geez, wherever this guy works, he sure likes taking his life in his own hands."

Like all metropolitan areas, Greater New York still had its slum areas, and Grid G-7 was one of the worst, a 15-by-15 block area carved up by rival drugbangers, rave-gangs and squatfamilies, all existing in a fragile peace balanced on the edge of a viblade. Violence was some-thing everyone grew up with here, and even the police didn't show up without heavy riot armor and multiple partners as backup. *And I'm about to go in here with a guy talking in my head and another on my phone and my partner out of the picture,* Shizume thought. *This does not rank as one of my brighter decisions.*

"Exit, please," she told the Zipper, which obliged by opening the door and revealing the unbroken wall of the building. "Oh, great, how are we supposed to get in?"

Squealing metal answered her rhetorical question, and a slab of the building slid aside, revealing a dark corridor that made the last blockpartment she had been in look downright inviting. Garbage littered the hallway, and for a moment she flashed back to the training mod-ule—had that only been yesterday?—and tensed, expecting a raving firehead to come lurching out of the shadows at her. People littered the hallway in sullen clumps sit-ting, rocking, or wandering aimlessly, the homeless, the mentally ill, the working poor wage-slaving for sixteen or eighteen hours a day trying to support their families

and the biohazarded wrecks that had destroyed themselves doing that as well. The stench wafting from the
passageway was unbelievable.

"Remember, I am not Metro PD anymore," Shizume
muttered, checking her shock glove one more time.

"Yes, I think that's a good idea for you to tell yourself
that about every fifty meters or so. It might actually keep
you alive," Payne said, his words as light as his tone was
deadly serious.

"Jon, talk to me. Where is he? The sooner we can find
him, the sooner we can try to get out of here," Shizume
said.

*"He's showing more brightly now. You should go down
this corridor for about fifty yards—I mean meters, then
turn right at the closest intersection,"* Jon replied. *"I'll
have to see what I see from there."*

"Okay, let's do it to it," Shizume said, squaring her
shoulders. "Payne, what do you want to do about the
Zipper?"

"If it's left alone it'll be stripped bare in under ten
minutes. I'll request that it circle the building, just in
case you need a quick exit. After all, it's not like there's
a lot of traffic over here," Payne said.

"Right." Shizume walked into the slumhall, keeping
an eye on three people at once in the landing. Only one
out of four of the public recessed lights were working,
casting the long corridor in eerie darkness punctuated
by irregular patches of dim illumination. Shizume waited
for her optics to switch to low light, only realizing that
nothing was going to happen after a few seconds.

"What are you waiting for?" Jon's voice prodded at her.

"Nothing," she replied, taking one hesitant step forward, then another. No one seemed to take the slightest notice of her there. One grizzled man carryied on an animated conversation with the air beside him, even offering his invisible companion a hit from a bottle containing a thick purple liquid that Shizume could smell from across the room. Everyone else was silent, caught in their own private miseries. The only noises seemed to come from the building itself, a shivering and groaning that set her teeth on edge. Shizume kept going, flitting from light to light across the patches of darkness. She made the mistake of looking back once to see the portal already a long, long way behind her, almost indistinguishable from the surrounding gloom.

"Ssspare a stalk or leaf?" a lisping voice said from the shadows as one of them detached from the pool of blackness and shambled towards her. Shizume whirled and brought up her glove, fingers clenched so that blue energy crackled between them in the darkness. The rail-thin beggar stumbled backward, pawing in his ragged clothes and coming up with a streetmade, cloth-wrapped blade, its edge nicked and dull. For a second the two just looked at each other, then Shizume relaxed a bit.

"Okay, I showed you mine, you showed me yours. Let's leave it at that, all right?"

The guy stared at her as if she had just asked him a Euclidean geometry problem. "Jug? Flake? Dust?"

Shizume looked around to see if they were attracting any attention. "I don't have anything," she said, still backing away. The man stepped back, his knife drooping down to his side. Shizume turned and trotted up the corridor, her gloved hand out in front of her.

"Nicely handled," Payne said.

"The next guy who tries that is just going to get 100,000 volts, no questions asked," Shizume replied. They came to the intersection, an eight-way hub with dark spokes radiating out in all directions.

"Which way, Jon?" Shizume asked in the silence.

"Just a moment," he said. *"Face each one in turn."*

Shizume did that while also trying to keep one eye on the corridor behind her. She noted a condom wrapper plastered on the wall where she had come out. *That looks vaguely familiar. At least I'll remember my way back,* she thought.

"Wait—take that one, the third tunnel. Can you hear it?"

Shizume listened, again lamenting the fact that Fliv was gone. She strained to hear over the sounds of the ancient building itself, and thought she caught a hint of movement—no—

"Well, what do you hear?" Payne asked.

"People, or a lot of something moving around," she said.

"The power is coming from right down there," Jon said. *"Ryan Darelight is in there somewhere."*

A noise from behind her made Shizume jump and whirl around, shock glolve crackling loud in the quiet. Two or three furtive figures shrank back into the darkness, but they were there, and getting bolder. "You better be right," she muttered, slipping into the dark corridor.

The noises grew louder the farther she walked, and

Shizume divided her attention between what she was coming up on and what might be coming down the tunnel after her. As she crept closer, the muted noise of what sounded like dozens of conversations, people walking, beds creaking, and even the smell of hot food all wafted toward her.

"Where are we going?" Shizume asked.

"I think I know—" Payne answered, but his answer was lost as Shizume came around a last corner to see bright light blazing in a doorway at the end of the corridor. Blinking back tears at the sudden intensity, she snuck up to the entrance and peeked inside.

She was standing at the end of a long rectangular room similar to the hydroponic farm. This one, however, had a row of beds all around the walls and three other rows that divided the large space into four broad aisles. Each bed was filled, some with a single person, ranging from underfed, sullen teens to suspicious-faced, hard-looking men and women. Several beds held families, all clustered around the mattress, facing inward as if they could construct invisible walls blocking out their neighbors. Everyone was dressed in government-issue gray jumpsuits, although no two were alike, some brand new, some filthy with encrusted sweat and grime, others modified by personal choice or long wear. Some people just stared blankly at nothing, others rocked back and forth, still others carried on their own conversations with invisible people or with their bunkmates next to them or just anyone who would listen. Half the room was eating off trays cradled on their laps or were tended to by a dozen people clad in olive-green jumpsuits with black and yellow armbands high on their sleeves. The smell in there was palpable, a living thing, comprised of equal parts food, dirt, sweat, confusion, and uncertainty. Off to one side, two rows of clean, groomed men and women were coming out of a set of double doors while another group of unkempt people exited through another door beside the first.

"Payne, what did you say?" Shizume asked when she could speak coherently.

"In poorer areas of the city there are privately-run shelters that help the 'displaced,' as it's so fashionably called, and mentally ill, because, of course, there aren't supposed to be any homeless in Greater New York. Looks like you're in the middle of one of them."

"Right," Shizume said, walking into the room. Her arrival drew the barest attention from the staff members and none from the bed inhabitants. For a moment she looked around, thinking somehow that the man she was looking for would suddenly appear before her, ready to go.

"He's in here somewhere. I can feel him," Jon said.

"End of the hall, you can be scanned and registered there, although there's a day's wait for a bed," a man with thinning red hair and dark bags under his eyes said as he trotted past with an armload of silvered heat-con-serving blankets.

"Actually," Shizume began, pulling alongside him as he headed down an aisle, "I'm looking for Ryan Darelight. Where can I find him?"

"Ryan's got about a thousand things to do right now. What's your business?" the man asked as he spun blankets to waiting downlevelers, many of whom clutched the artificial cloth to their chests like it was woven of platinum.

His question brought Shizume up short. *Well, the exact truth isn't going to work here, and since Fliv isn't with me anymore...* "I'm here from Greater New York Metro Police. It seems there's been reports of dangerous over-crowding exceeding the zoning ordinances on this level."

The man looked her up and down. "Geez, lady, don't you p-wonks have anything better to do than harass us?" the man asked. "Ever since these tremors have started we've been flooded with homeless and other indigents, and we're stretched to the limit as it is. Why don't you find someone else to harass with meaningless statutes and outdated laws?"

"Uh—yes, that's just what I usually do, but unlike most representatives of the government, perhaps I can help you," Shizume said. "I just need to speak with Mr. Dare-light about arranging an alternate source of funding, perhaps to expand your organization onto another floor in this building."

"You've got to be kidding me," he replied. "No GNYC employee, and especially no cop, would come here dressed like that."

Looking around, Shizume played a hunch. "Um, Alderwoman Carderas wanted me to send her regards. She thought this would, uh—work as a better disguise, to put you off guard. Look man, I'm just trying to do my job here."

"Oh, is it election time again, eh?" The young man relaxed at the magic words, a wry grin creasing his pinched features. "Good old Carderas, stumping for the indigent vote, eh? Well, why didn't you say so in the first place? Come on, he's still just as busy, but I'll see if he can squeeze you in."

The man, who introduced himself as Alex, finished distributing the load of blankets and escorted Shizume towards the back of the hall.

"That was pretty slick, but what are you going to tell Ryan when you see him?" Payne asked.

"I haven't the faintest idea," Shizume subvocalized. "I'll need you to patch into his wallscreen and give me a hand on this one."

"All right, but I'm not sure how having a netabloid editor along for this one is going to help you out, though."

"Between the two of us—"

"*Ahem,*" Jon said.

"Three—sorry—we should be able to persuade him—" Shizume trailed off as the absurdity of what she was about to say hit her. "Well, we'd better just start with the truth, and see where it goes from there."

"Well, that's one approach," Payne replied.

"It's bad enough I lied to this guy," Shizume said. "If Jon is correct, we need him too much for me to try and trick him into this. You and I believe Jon, and we have to make him believe in this too. I have to lay it all out and just try to convince him that he's a part of all of this."

"In for a kilo, in for a ton," Payne said.

"Did you say something?" Alex suddenly broke into her conversation.

"Me, no, not a thing," Shizume replied.

"All right, we're here. Ryan's office is through that door—you can hear him already," Alex said. The sound of a voice rising and falling came from the room beyond. "Oh—one more thing—Ryan hates polit-wonks, cop or otherwise."

Good thing I'm not sticking to that story, she thought. Aloud, she replied. "Thank you Alex. If you don't mind, I'll see myself in."

"No problem, I'd rather not enter when he's like this. Anyway, he's expecting you. Good luck." Alex turned and disappeared into the mass of people in the main room.

Shizume took a deep breath and knocked on the door. Instead of sliding open under its own power, the door jerked aside, and a hand motioned her to enter.

Shizume stepped inside and spoke to the back of the man who had ushered her in. "Mr. Darelight—"

"That's him," Jon said.

He whirled around on her, holding up a finger for silence, and continued his conversation with the air, pacing up and down the tiny office as he did so. "Look, I've told you every bed is taken here. I'd like to help, but I just don't have any more room—have you tried the G-3 level?...Kew Garden?...Woodhaven...G-1 even? Yes, I'm aware of its location, but they've got—all right, all right, I'll set up shifts in some of the outer halls—"

While he was talking, Shizume studied the man before her. There wasn't anything out of the ordinary about him, at least not that she could put her finger on at first. His hair was brown, with a touch of gray creeping in at the temples, even though he could have scarcely been thirty-five. His face was lean, drawn almost, with an aquiline, slightly crooked nose and cheekbones that all seemed to lead to his mouth, which chewed on the words he spoke then spit each one out. But it was his eyes that caught and held her attention. They burned with a determined light that she had never seen in anyone before, not in her grandfather, not in her parents, not in her friends, all of whom seemed very far away at this moment.

He really believes in what he's doing for these people, she thought.

Ryan Darelight glanced over at her and seemed to pause for a moment, looking her up and down as if evaluating her, but he never stopped talking. Shizume, on the other hand, as absurd as it seemed, felt like she was falling into those brown eyes of his, drawn down into that flame that burned deep inside of him. For an uncomfortable moment she flashed back to the dream of Jon Noir in the burned attic, only this time the man standing in front of her with his hand held out to her was this man in front of her, and—

"—you can send fifteen over, and give me families...it's safer for the children here." His strident voice cut through her thoughts like sunlight banishing morning fog. "Yeah, yeah, get me that funding for Q4, and we'll talk...right, we'll see them in half an hour. You got it. I've got to go, it seems I suddenly have an unscheduled meeting. Talk to you later."

He disconnected his call and held up his finger once more. "Just a sec, okay?" He cut in his celplant again. "Alex, prep the first row for a plus-fifteen cycle, four on, four off—Yes, I know we don't have the room, but it was either here or G-1...." Shizume thought she could almost hear Alex's reply in her own head. "I thought you'd see it that way...right, I know you will...thanks."

He discommed again and fell back into his chair, running a hand through his short hair.

"Alex seems like a good man to have here," Shizume said.

"He's the best man to have here," Ryan replied. "This place wouldn't function without him." He looked up again, almost as if seeing Shizume for the first time. "I'm sorry, just another 20 hour day in the trenches. You are again—?"

"Shizume Mader," she replied. "I am with the Greater New York Metro Police Department, and I need to talk to you."

"Yes, Alex mentioned something about financing. I'm impressed that the GNYCMP would take an interest in our operation here. Perhaps you can give me a rundown on what your contribution would entail—"

"Actually, that wasn't the kind of assistance I came here for, Mr. Darelight." Shizume took a deep breath. "In fact, I came here to ask for *your* help."

He didn't laugh or sneer at her, but his brow furrowed a bit. "I don't understand."

"Payne, get ready," Shizume subvocalized, then raised her voice again. "If I could just access your wallscreen, I could explain this a whole lot better. Uh, where is it?"

He looked around the office, which held a battered desk that looked to be at least fifty years old, the chair he was sitting on, and nothing else. "Officer Mader, as you can tell, our budget isn't really geared for things like wallscreens. We prefer to deal with the more practical aspects of helping the homeless, such as food, shelter, and whatever medicine we can get our hands on. Now, if you cannot help me, I don't possibly see how I can help you. So, if you'll excuse me—"

"Your celplant," Shizume said. "You do have one, otherwise you were just talking to the air just now."

He smiled at that. "Yes I do, why?"

"I need to conference in someone that we can both talk to. Between the two of us we can explain what we need, and how you come into it. Please, it could affect everything you're doing here."

He looked at her again, and Shizume was struck by how his gaze seemed to penetrate right through her. "You've got five minutes, and please, please, whatever you do, don't try to sell me something."

Not exactly, we won't, Shizume thought, then said. "Payne, are you there?"

"As always," he replied.

"Dial the number I'm about to give you and patch me in, too," she said. Ryan rattled off his access and Payne linked up. "Are we all here?"

"I am. Who am I speaking with?" Ryan asked.

"Sir, my name is J. H. Payne, you may recognize the moniker from a newsweb called "Eyes Wide Open.""

"I don't read the tabs. What is this all about?" he replied.

"This is an interesting story, which, in the interest of time, I am going to give you the condensed version of," Payne said. "Back in the early 1840s—"

Ryan looked over at Shizume, who nodded and smiled, hoping she wasn't coming across as a complete mind-freak. As Payne launched into the story, his brow furrowed even more.

"*Are you both sure this is the right way to go about this?*" Jon asked.

"If you've got a better idea, I'm listening," she said. "Payne's pretty persuasive. I'll let him have his shot and we'll see what his reaction is." *And pray all the while that he doesn't throw us out on our ear when grandfather is finished,* she thought.

CHAPTER TWELVE

O pening her eyes, Antonia slumped forward, drained by the exertion of trying—and failing—to summon Agatha. Her head throbbed with the effort, but the elder Derlicht was gone, and no matter how hard or wide she had looked, the spirit was nowhere to be found.

"Just two hours to go," Kar said. "Mason's doing really well in there, this is the best scan we've ever gotten, even with the earlier difficulties."

"No other anomalies since, either. That's odd," Antonia said.

"Not really. There hasn't been a wave since that last one three hours ago. That in itself is odd," Benjamin said behind a three dimensional model of some kind of complicated molecule chain. "From all of the previous data, I had expected the waves to increase both in frequency and intensity, yet it hasn't happened."

"Perhaps we're in the eye of the storm," Kar mused.

"What did you say?" Antonia asked, her head whipping around to look at him.

"Huh? I just said maybe we're in the eye of the storm,"

Kar replied. "I've been thinking about it during the past hour. Perhaps these waves aren't originating from one fixed point across this plane of reality but are part of some kind of vast cycle radiating around a central point. And, like hurricanes, perhaps there's a central calm part, or eye of the storm, that exists, and right now we're in the center of it."

Antonia mulled that idea over a bit then lifted her eyes and actually took a look around. Other than the silent operation of the computers and machines that made up the lab's equipment, it was still, much too still. Usually NoirCorp's headquarters had a presence of life always about it, thousands of men and women bustling to and fro around the massive building, but that had been replaced by a pervading sense of emptiness and abandonment.

That's impossible, Antonia thought. *There's no way everyone has left this building but the four of us.* And although she could have requested and received a scan of the building and located every employee in a second, she did not call up the data. For the first time, she was afraid of what she might find.

Antonia walked over to the glasteel separating her from the chamber where Mason's body lay. She pressed her fingers hard against the barrier, as if trying to will them through the wall and into the cylinder where her husband lay. For a frantic moment she was overwhelmed by the sudden fear that this was as close as she would ever get to touching him again, that she would never feel his arms around her again—

Stop it! she ordered. Still, the feeling of impending doom wouldn't leave, and Antonia couldn't help thinking that she should have been up here when Mason was prepped, she should have been the last person he saw before going under, and that she might never have that chance again.

But it doesn't have to be that way. No sooner had she thought it than she tried to reach out to Mason with her mind, questing to touch his consciousness, to tell him what she had wanted to say but had put off in favor of interrogating Agatha. She had never purposefully touched Mason's mind before, considering it a gross violation of everything she held dear, but the worry consuming her blotted out everything else but speaking to him, no matter what the consequences.

Kar, Benjamin, the laboratory, everything took on a dreamy, surreal appearance, cast in a shimmering light that made their normally clear definitions turn golden and hazy. Having never used her powers outside of a meditative state, Antonia was unprepared for the sensory change. She found it not unpleasant, like viewing her surroundings through several meters of sun-dappled water. Everyone seemed frozen in time, Kar forever reaching out to push a holoscreen aside in favor of the one behind it, the hologram of Benjamin bent over yet another model, this one of what appeared to be a DNA helix. If it had been silent before, the lab was remarkable now for its complete absence of noise, as if sound could not even be created in this new reality she was in.

Reaching out, Antonia watched her hand pass through the invisible energy barrier surrounding her. She kept going, penetrating the glasteel window in front of her. Her arm followed, and then her rest of her body, flowing through the barricades as if they weren't even there.

Looking down, she was not surprised to see that she was floating a few inches off the ground. She looked back to see her physical body immobilized outside of time as well, her hand pressed against the window, eyes open but unseeing, bathed in that strange golden light that emanated from nowhere, yet illuminated everything. But Antonia only looked back for a moment. All of her attention was on the man held in the fluid-filled container before her. She reached out with her psyche again, saw her spectral hand contact the outer edge of the tube, passing through it with ease like everything else. The viscous liquid inside was no obstacle either. Antonia pushed into the goo, coming ever closer to Mason, seeing his chest rise and fall with each breath. The light was with him as well, surrounding him in a sunlit halo. Antonia let her ethereal hands roam over his body, just millimeters away from touching him, not yet daring to disturb the moment. All the love she had borne for him over the long years and decades threatened to overwhelm her, so she reached into him, reached for his mind—

—the shock she encountered was so sudden that Antonia recoiled before she even knew what was happening. She found herself hanging beside him in the chamber, the light around him pulsing in time with the pulsing pain behind her eyes. Antonia reached out again, more carefully this time, and found an impenetrable barrier blocking Mason's psyche, a whirling, shifting wall of light that she could not even see past. It stretched up beyond where his head would be in the material world, a column of brightness that made her eyes ache. For a moment Antonia considered trying to force her way through it, but she did not know what effect that might have on her husband and the scan, and she could not stand having him trapped in this prison for a second longer than necessary. *I'm being foolish,* she thought, even though a part of her was still deeply concerned, she tried to dismiss it. *There will be plenty of time to talk to him once this is over with, I shouldn't disturb him now.*

She soared back out and flowed into her body again, feeling the strange dislocation as she resettled herself behind her true eyes. The world blurred around her for a moment, that unique golden light fading into nothingness.

"Antonia, you'd better brace yourself. I think we have another one coming," Benjamin said.

Both she and Kar looked at him. "How do you know?" she asked.

"There are some things the dead know better than the living, and this is one of them. It's going to be a bad one," he replied.

Antonia exchanged glances with Kar, then both looked back at Benjamin. Tensing, she waited for the effects, bracing herself against the tremors that would shake the building. "Do you know when?" she asked.

"Any second now," he said.

There was no concussion, no earth-shaking shockwave. Instead, all at once, the lights and all power in the room went out, plunging them into darkness.

"Kar, why aren't the backup generators online?" Antonia asked after a few seconds, her face demonic-looking in the crimson battery-powered emergency lights. "Does the bodyform lab still have power? If the clone is interrupted now, it's over."

"I'm scrambling maintenance teams and checking that

right now," Kar said. "If this is widespread, it means the fusions at Perth Amboy, Bayonne, and Valley Stream have scrammed or gone offline. The lab's battery backups are still functioning, but I don't know if they'll have enough power to finish the scan. I'm shutting down all non-essential systems to conserve energy. What about Benjamin?"

"What about him?"

"Shall I reinstate the hologram?"

That decision was no decision at all. "No, not until we restore power," Antonia said. "If this scan isn't completed, he's got no chance anyway. I'm sure he'd understand."

"Affirmative, the teams are working on the generators now. They report that the online electromagnetic wave generators have been fused. They're no longer drawing power."

"Fastpower the reactor. I want it online in twenty minutes," Antonia ordered. With the perfection of hydrogen fuel cells, many stratoscrapers kept those kinds of systems available as backups. Kar opened his mouth, then looked at the expression on her face and quickly shut it again. "Reactor warm-up—I don't believe this."

"What is it?" Antonia asked.

"The reactor team is reporting in, Mrs. Noir. They say all of the core systems are gone—vanished like they never existed. The hydrocells are just a big block of inert compounds."

"Damn it, how can I be in the middle of the 22nd century with no power!" Antonia said. "How much time for the scan to complete compared to the energy we've got left."

"Estimated scan time remaining...forty-three minutes. Battery power remaining for this floor...twenty-seven minutes."

"Damn, where am I going to find those sixteen minutes? What about draining the stored charges of the Zippers on the building?"

Kar began to nod, then his expression changed to one of horror. "Oh my God, if the fusions are off, and the backups didn't activate—Antonia, there's no Zippers left on the buildings—hundreds of thousands—maybe millions—are dead."

"Yes, but we're not yet, and the one man who can stop all of this is still in here," she said, pointing at Mason. "We can't afford to grieve for them now, we may be the only ones who can prevent more people from dying." She paced the floor, thinking out loud, "Main power gone, backups inoperable, hydrocells—disappeared." Her erratic walk took her close to the window, where a cloud was slowly drifting by below their floor. "At least the wind hasn't stopped blowing."

"What—what did you say?" Kar asked, trying to pull himself together.

"Kar, scramble the best repair team you've got to the roof. I want them to divert the power from the windmills to this floor. The building systems may be shot, but they can jury-rig some way of getting that power back in here. They've got twenty minutes to do it, or they might as well take the express elevator off the side home tonight."

As large as Greater New York was, fusion power wasn't the only source of energy used. Tens of thousands of massive windmills constantly sculpted ambient wind energy from the air, while thousands of tide generators converted energy from the ceaseless ocean tides that flowed back and forth around the bases of the strato-scrapers. When the technology had first been implemented, it was strictly regulated for public use only and controlled solely by the city government. Tampering with either form of power generation was punishable by huge fines and several years in prison.

"Yes, ma'am," Kar said, sending the orders out. Antonia stopped her pacing by the glasteel, watching Mason's face, barely lit by the emergency lighting. She set her beautiful features into a grim mask of determination. *The universe may be trying to stop this,* she thought, *but it's going to have to go through me first.*

CHAPTER THIRTEEN

"...and that is why we've come to you, sir," Payne said. "As a direct descendant of the Derlicht line, the only direct thirteenth generation descendant left here, you are truly the only one who can help us right now."

Shizume had watched Ryan closely during Payne's explanation of why they were there, taking him from what had happened three centuries ago to yesterday and everything in between. His expression hadn't changed during the whole of it, not showing shock, disbelief, or any emotion in between. He just listened and didn't interrupt once, didn't ask a single question, didn't make a single noise or agreement or denial. She had no idea what he was thinking.

Ryan leaned back in his chair, rubbing his hands over his face for several moments. When he began speaking, his tone was calm and measured. "Ms. Mader, Mr. Payne, I don't know what to say—"

"The best thing to say is that you will help us," Shizume said, leaning forward in her eagerness. "There is no one else—"

"As flattering as it is that you have chosen me to ply

your story on, I really do not have the time for this," he continued as if she hadn't spoken. "I have more than three hundred people out there who need my help right now, with more on the way. Even if I did believe you, I would hardly go with you to who knows where—"

"Touch him," Jon whispered in her mind.

"—and I'm certainly not going to abandon my responsibilities here. We're chronically understaffed as it is. Normally I would suggest several outpatient treatment centers for both of you, but, despite the solidity of your story—which is very well thought out, mind you—I think you can both find someone in the private sector to help you both, as, in my layperson's opinion, you are both suffering from some kind of dementia, perhaps a specialized psychosis affecting just the two of you. I don't know, it's really not my field of expertise—"

"Reach out," Jon said. *"I can prove it to him."*

As much as she wanted to follow his advice, and not just for Jon's reasons, Shizume tried one last time to reason with him. "Mr. Darelight—I know this story sounds far-fetched, well, more than far-fetched—"

"That's the first believable thing you've said so far," he said with a smile.

"Yes, however, just because it is far-fetched doesn't mean it's not true," Shizume said. "I mean, you must have heard of the strange events happening all over the city. Surely it can't be that impossible that these are not random occurrences, that there is something more behind these events. If you care at all about this city, about these people—" Shizume saw him stiffen a bit at those words, "—then you owe it to them, if not yourself, to try and do something."

"Take his hand," Jon said.

"First of all, I am doing everything I can for these people, and to insinuate that I should suddenly drop everything here and go with you to God knows where is insulting in its own right," Ryan shot back. "As I recall, neither of you know what this 'thing' is, where it is, or what we could do about it. Given your massive lack of supporting evidence, I am quite confident that I am making the right choice by staying here and helping those people that I know need my help."

"No one is saying that isn't a wise course of action," Payne began, "but if we cannot convince you to come with us, hundreds of thousands of lives will be lost—"

His voice was interrupted by a far-off dull rumbling. "Not another wave!" Ryan was out of his chair in a flash. "Damn it, not now! This is the last thing we need!" He skirted the corner of the desk and headed for the door. The lights flickered and dimmed, then went out, plunging the room into darkness.

"What, another tremor? The buildings can withstand that," Shizume said, her face shaded by the reddish glow of the emergency lights.

"No, it's what the tremors bring with them," Ryan replied. "I don't suppose you have any medical training?"

"I was a third year Metro PD student before—" Shizume began.

"Close enough. Come on." Taking her by the sleeve, he drew her up out of the chair and headed towards the main room of the shelter. "I don't know what to expect out there, so be ready for anything. Oh, and by the way, we have literally nothing in the way of serious medical supplies, so you'll have to improvise."

"Improvise for what? Why don't you call the paramedics, or the S&R team?"

"Where have you been for the last twelve hours? These—waves—for lack of a better term, have got every hospital, firefighter, and other civil servant up to their eyebrows in caseload. We're way down on the priority list. Here we go."

They entered the dimly lit main hall, which was buzzing with activity. Ryan took Shizume to the first knot of people. "What's going on here?" he asked, gently but firmly shouldering people aside to find Alex kneeling next to a women who looked like she had just come out of a ten-year coma. Dressed in the standard shelter jumpsuit, she only had eyes for the year-old child she was cradling in her arms. The people around her were patting her, congratulating her, one was even on his knees praying over them.

Alex couldn't tear his gaze away from her. His normally narrowed eyes were as round as dinner plates. "Ryan, look. If I hadn't seen it, I wouldn't have believed it."

"What? What is so special about this?" Shizume asked.

"May-Lin lost her daughter four years ago. She was killed by her abusive husband. She carried a doll wrapped in rags around wherever she went. I—I saw the doll. It was one of those kind that closed its eyes when you lay it down. I don't know, it must have been her grandmother's. Anyway, that black hair and blue eyes are all she would ever talk about. She was catatonic otherwise. But that's—"

"Impossible?" Shizume said. "You should have been with me earlier today—"

"Take his hand now," Jon said. *"Grab it, let me talk to him."*

"What?" Shizume asked, but she was drowned out by a piercing scream a few meters away. Ryan was on the move again, and Shizume trailed behind him to another bed, this one clattering on the floor from the spasms of its occupant.

"Ryan—you gotta help me—I burn—burning up inside—" the teen-age boy said, his teeth chattering as he writhed on the bed. The red emergency lights lent a demonic glow to the drawn planes of his face.

Now Ryan dropped to his knees, clasping the boy's hand. "Tamil, I thought you weren't using any more?"

"I'm not, Ryan, I swear—I didn't break my prom-ise—*Madre de Dios*—but I feel like I just came down from a killer fireride, and I'm in serious ash here, man—please, on my mother's grave I swear I'm not using again."

"Fireduster," Shizume said, not quite succeeding in hiding the contempt in her voice.

"Former fireduster. Tamil's been clean for six months. His nails are fine," Ryan said. "Hold on, *amigo*, we're going to get you some help. Tell Alex to get me a hypo of Quarinth LD-4—"

"Ryaaaaaan!" the former addict reached, his fingers clutching Ryan's shoulder as a seizure arched his back off the bed. "Don't leave meeee—" As they watched, black sores erupted all over his body, his flesh and muscle wasting away around his arms and legs, leaving pale sticks that thrashed helplessly. The skin over his chest contracted, showing each rib in prominent detail as he labored for breath. He tried to keep gripping Ryan's shoulder, but his weakened hands slipped off, the oozing and broken fingernails sloughing off his uncoordinated fingers. His formerly smooth cheeks hollowed, his wildly dilating and contracting eyes searching for a last minute salvation in the faces of the two people above him.

"I—I don't wanna die," he said around a mouthful of suddenly rotting, crumbling teeth. He looked as though he had aged eighty years in less than a minute. Before Ryan could say another word, he collapsed back onto the bed, his last breath rattling through protesting lungs. When that was gone, his ravaged body relaxed into the stillness of death, his jaundiced eyes rolling back into his head.

"Damn it, I had promised him he was going to be all right," Ryan said, still holding Tamil's now-shrunken and lifeless hand. He closed the boy's eyes and laid his hands on his sunken chest. It was like he had just gone through the effects of a twenty-year fireride in two minutes.

Shizume looked around only to see other strange effects happening across the room. In one corner a young woman was taking off a gravity cast, saying her leg was as good as new, and in the bed next to her were two young children with wild eyes clutching two screaming babies that were now swimming in jumpsuits that had fit their previous adult frames moments before. Two beds down a woman stared down at her body like she had never seen it before. Hesitantly she reached up and poked at a swelling breast, then took her hand away like she had been burned. Shizume heard one of the staff ask, "Patrick?" Not everyone had been altered by this latest wave, but Shizume had never seen so many changes at one time. Men and women everywhere were trying to keep order, and many were glancing anxiously at Ryan, who was still kneeling beside Tamil's bed.

"*Take his hand* now," Jon said, his tone so commanding that Shizume's body reacted before her mind did. She reached down and took Ryan's hand, her dusty, sweaty fingers curling around his.

The feeling was akin to grasping a live electrical wire. Shizume's legs buckled, unable to support her. She collapsed on the tile floor next to Ryan, who had galvanized at her touch, his limbs stiffening into immobility. The room, the people, everything swirled away from her, fading into grayness as Ryan and Shizume were thrust into a different world.

—*It was summer, a hot summer, long ago. They were in a small village, lorded over by two large manor houses and populated everywhere by men and women clad in ancient dress, all buckles and knee breeches and voluminous skirts. They zoomed into one of the houses, which was on fire, smoke and flames licking up the walls into the attic, where two men desperately struggled for control of a long dagger while a white-haired woman watched from a corner, her face contorted in pain. The smaller one twisted it free and stabbed the blond headed one in the side. The younger man grunted and grabbed the knife fighter by the throat...*

The scene changed again, and two men—one older and dressed in fine clothes, the other younger and not—stood in front of a young dark-haired man seated at a desk. They threw a knife down in front of the sitting man—the same knife from the fight—Shizume thought, watching the point stick in the top of the oaken desk. The seated

211

man shook his head, then one of the standing men said something that caused his face to flush with anger before the two men stalked out.

The scene changed yet again, to an altogether different time. Men and women dressed differently, in fitting blue pants and multi-colored shirts, some in matching suit jackets and slacks with antiquated neckties. Shizume saw a young man who looked much like the previous one in a dark room that appeared to have been carved out of stone. He was bent over a strange-looking machine connected to a bank of computers. The scene blurred again, and he was shown talking to a dark-haired beautiful woman at a café, then the two of them were shown in horribly out-of-date wedding clothes in a church. The two men from before, the seated one and the blond-haired one, were both there, swirling around the couple, while behind them loomed the specter of the same white-haired woman that had been in the burning attic, now ghostly translucent and beaming a frightening smile.

The scene seemed to fast-forward, and Shizume was taken on a blurred ride of what appeared to be a family history, faces of men and women passing by along with the decades. There were entire generations that she didn't recognize, and she had no idea why she was seeing them. With an effort, she looked over at Ryan, and saw him staring at the procession in ve, a rapt look on his face.

The scene changed again, and now Shizume saw the familiar skyline of Greater New York. The man and woman they had seen before, looking more or less unchanged since the last time, were now on a top floor *of a stratoscraper that bore a well-known symbol often seen in the city—*

NoirCorp, she thought. *The couple looked down on the cityscape spread out below them, and still another man she didn't recognize stood beside them, dressed in a strange amalgam of ancient and new clothes, with what looked like rocks braided in his beard.*

Then a blinding flash of incredibly bright light devastated everything it touched, destroying buildings, disintegrating people, laying waste to the boroughs of Greater New York, Geistad, Queens, Manhattan, Long Island, Staten Island. Everything was gone, even the land itself, leaving nothing but a black, empty void, with even the vast ocean swallowed into nothingness—

Opening her eyes, Shizume wrenched back to the present, finding herself crumpled on the floor, holding Ryan Darelight's hand in a death grip. His eyes were open but unseeing, and she jostled him gently. "Ryan?"

He quivered and looked at her. "Shizume? That was real, wasn't it?"

"I—" She paused, unsure of what to say. "It was as real as anything I've seen lately."

"Who was that?—came into my mind—I couldn't do anything except watch—" Ryan said, the struggle of trying to fit the illogical into his decreasingly logical world showing on his face.

"Um, that was Jon Noir, the tri-centuries dead ghost of one of the brothers, the blond one you saw wrestling for the knife."

"Wait, you saw that too?" he asked. When Shizume nodded, his voice grew a bit stronger, drawing back from

213

insanity. "So you saw the fire, and the marriage, and the old woman, and the three in the strato, and—everything—gone—"

His voice trailed off again, and Shizume feared she was going to lose him again. "Ryan?"

"No—no, I'm all right—or all right as one can be after something like that," he said, attempting a grin that came out as a wry crooking of his lips. "It kind of takes the breath out of you, you rez?"

In spite of herself, Shizume had to smile back. "Tell me about it. I had to put up with Jon all by myself at first."

"Now that's hardly fair—" Jon began, but neither one was listening.

"I saw my family—generations upon generations—all leading back to that old woman," Ryan said, almost as if he hadn't heard her either. "My father tried to tell me our blood reached back to the first families that had settled in this area, but I never listened, thinking he was looking backward when we needed to look forward, to the problems right here, right now. But he was right, he was right all the time, and I hadn't listened. But why me? Why am I important in all of this?"

"From what Jon told me, and what we saw, the Noirs and Derlichts have always been enemies since the Noirs arrived in Geiststadt all those centuries ago," Shizume said. "The only thing I can think of is that the ghosts are up to something again, but whatever they're planning, you can stop, just like Agatha did to the Noirs on that wedding day. Whatever the brothers were planning to do, she prevented it, isn't that right, Jon?"

"You have the truth of it, Shizume," Jon replied.

"Whatever abilities she was able to bring to that ceremony were stronger than anything my brother or I could counter. I can only hope that you, Ryan, can muster that same power now."

"I—I can hear you, in my head," Ryan said, his fingers going to his temple.

"Yes, and that is a good sign, for it means you will be strong enough for what lies ahead," Jon said. *"We have a long way to go and hardly any time to do it in."*

"All right, then," Ryan looked around as if seeing where he was for the first time.

Alex came running over to him. "Ryan, what are you doing? I need your help. The entire Manning family has disappeared, right out of their clothes, and the Oneald children are trying to take care of two babies they swear were their parents five minutes ago—"

"Alex," Ryan said, silencing the other man with that one word, "I have to go. I know you won't understand, but I have to leave right now, and I don't know if I'm going to see you again. The shelter is yours now. Take care of everyone here, do the best job you can, the one I know you can do."

"What? Where are you—" Alex's voice almost cracked as Ryan's words sank in. "What the hell are you talking about?"

"If I'm lucky, you'll know when nothing happens at all," Ryan said. His nervous energy was still now, his attention entirely focused on the task ahead. "You'll have to explain to the staff. Shizume and I have to leave immediately."

"I—" Alex's words died off as he stared at the face of

his boss. His mouth opened, closed, opened again, and in the end there was only one thing to say. "All right."

Ryan embraced him hard for a moment, then turned to Shizume. "Let's go."

Both of them walked out of the hall, brushing by the men and women who were giving and receiving help there. A new group plodded into the hall, and Ryan and Shizume mingled with them, weaving their way though before anyone could accost them. Neither one looked back.

Once outside, Ryan began striding through the hallways, the darkness no impediment to him.

"Um, I have a Zipper waiting outside—" Shizume began.

"No, with these waves getting more powerful I don't trust them," Ryan replied. They reached the corridor hub and he turned down a completely different path. "I've got another way out of here."

"Okay," Shizume lengthened her stride to keep up with him, casting wary glances around them, every nerve still jangling from what she had witnessed both in this world and the other.

"So, how do I bring about this 'power' of mine?" Ryan said.

"Hm—oh, I'm sorry, I really have no idea," Shizume said. "Jon, maybe you can help with that. I need to talk to my grandfather. He must have some information for us."

"I'll do what I can," Jon said. *"Ryan, have you ever heard of a concept called heka?"*

"Can't say that I have," the other man replied.

Shizume pushed their conversation to the back of her

mind, such as it was, and redialed her grandfather, hoping that the satellites hadn't been knocked out of orbit, or even worse, transformed into trees or asteroids or something as equally useless. After several rings, his familiar voice reverberated in her head. "Shizume, are you all right?"

"Grandfather, I'm all right, and I've got Ryan with me. We're leaving the shelter now."

"Did the tremor change his mind?"

"That and the fact that Jon—talked to him," Shizume said. "We'll discuss that later. The important thing is we need to figure out where we're supposed to go, and also how we're supposed to get there. I have an idea on the first one but am not at all sure about the second."

"I know exactly where you're supposed to go, but I have no idea how you're going to get there," Payne interrupted. "That last shockwave has caused panic all over the city. Power is out almost everywhere; the whole city is down. The entire Zipper system is gone. Even the backups to my system almost went out—"

"Oh, my God," she said. "Are you all right?"

"Yes. I'm running on batteries now, in a very bare room, but don't you worry about me now. I've lived long enough. Whoever—whatever's behind this, they cannot be allowed to do whatever it is they're doing. I will do whatever I can, whatever you need, to help, and there will be no discussion on the point."

"It won't come to that, Grandfather," Shizume said. "We'll find a way. But now I do need you. Jon has convinced Ryan of his role in all this, but we have no idea what he's supposed to do."

"Oh, boy. I'm not sure what I can do, but I'll try," he

said. "I may have to cancel the connection to conserve power for research. I'll call you if I come up with something,"

"Thanks, Grandfather. I love you, you know," Shizume said.

"Child, I've always known," Payne said, the smile evident in his voice. "One more thing: when you get out, look to the NoirCorp building. You'll see what I mean. Now get going. I'll be in touch."

"Okay," Shizume broke the connection without saying goodbye, not wanting to think about never seeing him again. She tuned into the ongoing conversation between Jon and Ryan.

"—reach deep down inside yourself and bring it up, like, I don't know, reaching into your soul and using that power. Can you feel anything?"

"That soul analogy is a bit weak, Jon, since I was never sure I had one or not."

"I would hope that our conversation right now might strengthen your position on the matter," Jon said. *"Trust me, humans exist past your mortal plane. I'm proof enough of that. Now concentrate, for the universe's sake."*

"Nothing like putting the pressure on," Ryan replied. "All right..."

"Sorry to interrupt, but where are we going?" Shizume asked, looking around the unfamiliar hallway. "None of this looks familiar."

"We're going down to the ocean levels," Ryan said. "Several years ago we suffered a power failure—I doubt you ever heard of it—but since then we've taken precautions." He pushed open a metal door that led to an inky black stairwell. There was a rustle of clothes, and Ryan's suit began to glow, the white stripes down his arms and legs giving off enough light to see by. "Forty floors down there's a powercraft we can use to get out of here."

"You know, even if the power failed again, the gravators would still be working," Shizume said. "They aren't on the same power grid as the rest of the city."

"I know," Ryan replied. "But they would be crammed full of people. It's better—and safer—this way."

They began the eerie descent, lit by Jon's glowing limbs, which cast unearthly moving shadows as they walked down the stairs. "So, I know the story your grandfather told me, but what's your stake in all this?" Ryan asked.

"I was a third-year student at Metro PD, like I told you earlier," she said. "When I started seeing Jon, first in the simulator, then in my dream, it just fit too well with things my grandfather had been telling me about Geistad's past. I went to the site of the Derlichts' old mansion, found Jon, and you know the rest."

"Yes, but you haven't answered my question," Ryan said. "Why are you doing this?"

"I don't think I had any choice in the matter," Shizume said. "Ever since I found the building this morning—was it only this morning?—I've been sort of blindly moving forward, just doing because—"

Shizume paused for a minute, thinking about her answer carefully. Reassuring her grandfather was one thing, but answering the question for herself was something else. *And yet what I told him is true,* she thought. *Doing this helps me feel more alive than I ever have been.* Put that way, there was only one answer to give.

"—it has to be done, and I was the only one who could, until we found you."

"I understand," Ryan replied, nodding. "I understand that completely. What about you, Jon?"

"Me?" The voice in their heads seemed taken off guard. *"What do you mean?"*

"Why are you able to contact Shizume now, after all these decades? After all, she's lived here—let me guess—all your life?" he asked, glancing at her to see a confirming nod.

"Ah, that," Jon replied. *"I don't know if they told you, but I had tried to contact other descendents of our family before, but it always went wrong. The waves must have changed—reality, for lack of a better word—enough to allow me to reach out, but even that was limited. Fortunately Shizume retained the Noir intelligence—or an indefinable something—and came looking for me. However, we should really keep trying to bring out your power, Ryan."*

"Not now, these stairs aren't something to lose your concentration on," Ryan said. "We can try again at the bottom."

"Very well."

For her part, Shizume also concentrated on putting one foot in front of the other. She made the mistake of looking up the narrow gap between the floors only to see the deep narrow chimney of plasteel and ceramic, framed by seemingly endless rows of stairs. Shuddering, she returned her gaze to the steps in front of her, leading down, always down. The smell of salt water and oil, faint at first, grew stronger with each downward level. She cocked her head for a moment, listening. "Hold up a flash," she said.

"What?"

"I don't know, the echo sounded wrong, like there was more than just us in here," Shizume whispered, listening to their steps die away. She peered up again, unable to see anything beyond the dim light of Ryan's clothes. "I wish my partner was here. He could tell me for sure." She listened for a few more seconds. "Just my imagination, I guess."

"I cannot sense anyone around, but then again, my abilities are limited in this world," Jon said. *"It is as if everything is hidden behind a veil to me. Only Ryan shows clearly in here."*

"Everything plays tricks on you in this building," Ryan said, keeping his voice low. "Don't worry about it."

"Ryan, don't you want to call anyone, warn them about what you're doing?" she asked.

He smiled, his teeth white in the gloom. "I'm surprised you hadn't noticed by now, but my chosen career doesn't leave too much time for outside interests—like a wife and family. My parents are gone, and my relationships never survived my leaving at all hours of the night to bring in a family or just one person. It's probably better that way. I'm sort of independent anyway. It'd take someone with a lot of patience to put up with that."

"Oh," she replied.

"What about you?"

"Who, me? Uh, actually the same. I mean, my grandfather is always around, but I've pretty much thrown everything into the academy, until today..." she trailed off as she thought of the door she had closed off earlier.

"That's right, you were called up, weren't you? Every-one would have been," Ryan said. "I'm not surprised at your choice, given what you know."

"Just like I'm not surprised by yours," she said.

He stopped and looked at her closely for a moment, then continued down. "Maybe so, but I still needed a bit more convincing."

"The important thing is that you were able to keep an open mind. Not many people can do that today," Shizume said.

"The one person I wish I could tell about this is my father. He was always wondering when I was going to give up on 'helping people' and get a real job. Who knows, maybe we'll run into him on the way," he said, forcing a smile. "Well, let's not start congratulating ourselves just yet. We're here."

The stairway ended in a small flat platform with an old, unpowered steel door operated by a wheel in the middle. Ryan put his weight on it, spun the wheel clockwise until they both heard a clunking noise, and the metal slab popped open.

"It's right outside," Ryan said. "Come on."

"Is there someone waiting for us?" Jon asked. *"I think—"*

Ryan was already pulling the door towards him. He turned to usher Shizume through, but before she got there, a pair of hands reached in and grabbed him, jerking his body through the opening.

"Ryan!" she cried, heading for the doorway. She heard grunts and the sounds of scuffle on the other side. Leaping through, she found two dirty, rag-clad men hauling him down the concrete platform while a third

222

kept watch. Off to the side, a small, squat five-meter boat rocked in the gentle swells.

"Damn it, get his hand and let's get out of here," the watchman hissed as he spied Shizume.

"Let him go, and you can all walk out of here," she said, her eyes shifting from the wicked-looking blade in his hand to the squinting leader.

"No go, girlie," he said, taking one step toward her, then another, his blade seeming to float in his hand. "We need his hand to start the boat, it's our ticket outta here."

"Shizume, get away, get out of here!" Ryan said, trying to keep the two men holding him off balance as he struggled to get free.

"That's not going to happen," she said, stepping forward as well and flexing the fingers of her shock glove. Instead of sparking off each other, the weapon remained dark and silent. Glancing at it, Shizume saw it was completely drained of power. "Okay, we'll do this the hard way."

The leader's eyes widened in his blackened face, then he flashed rotting teeth and waved the knife in front of him, its point thrusting downward to cut or stab. "Makes no difference to me, girl."

Shizume didn't answer but kept her eyes locked on his, waiting. The man blinked then moved, swiftly slashing the blade in a diagonal arc that would have opened her from hip to shoulder. Shizume leaned backward as the dagger hissed by, then grabbed his wrist with her right hand and drove her left forearm into his elbow. The snap as the joint broke was audible even above the dirty water lapping at the crude concrete jetty. Her opponent gurgled in pain, his arm bent twenty degrees the wrong way. Whirling inside his guard, she backfisted him across the face, dropping him to the pavement.

Meanwhile, Ryan had wrested an arm free and elbowed one of his captors in the nose, sending him staggering backward off the platform to splash into the water. He grabbed the other man's greasy hair and wrenched him backward, distracting him from trying to saw his left hand off. Shizume was on him in a second, driving the heel of her palm into his face with the crack of splintering bone. The scruffy man forgot about the hand, the boat, everything, and clasped both hands to his broken, bloody nose.

Shizume shoved him away and grabbed Ryan. "Let's get out of here!"

"No need to tell me twice," he said. "Cast the line off. I'll get it started."

He leaped aboard as Shizume looked at the twists and loops of the knot around the metal bollard on the platform. Scooping up a dropped knife, she tried slashing through the rope, only to watch the knife bounce off the braided silver strands.

"It's Tyvek-nylon. You can't cut it. That knot's a Carrick bend, you'll have to untie it, just push one end out and follow it through," Ryan said.

"Great, now you tell me," she said, puzzling through the unfamiliar twists. "How'd they know you were coming here?"

Before he could reply, the echo of boots pounding down the stairs and a shout from the doorway answered her question. "Shizume, get aboard!" Ryan said.

"Almost got it," she said, untangling the rope at last and standing up.

"Kill those fugs!" the still-bleeding man screamed. Shizume lashed out with her foot, catching him the in jaw and sending him sprawling against the wall just as three more men burst through the doorway.

"Shizume, let's go!" Ryan called from the boat's controls.

"Coming, coming," she said, throwing the rope into the boat and jumping after it. Ryan placed his left hand on a touch screen and the boat began moving away from the platform, but not fast enough. All three of the men leaped for the moving vessel as well. Two made it on board, one at the bow and one in the cockpit. The third one didn't, clawing in vain at the gunwale as he slid into the murky sea.

The small boat rocked as the thieves' weight overbalanced it, sending it heeling dangerously close to the water. Shizume hadn't recovered from her jump before the men came aboard and found herself half in and half out of the boat, her face just inches from the ocean. The boat turned sharply to the right, and she was thrown back into the small cockpit, rolling into one of the men, who had just gotten his hands on Ryan. Shizume's impact made him lose his grip and sent them both to the deck. The boat heeled over again, and the Shizume and her opponent skidded across the boards again to thud into the boat's sidewall. The impact knocked Shizume's breath out of her for a second, but she retained enough presence of mind to keep gripping the man on top of her. He freed himself first and locked both hands around her throat. Before he could strangle her, she snaked her arm in between both of his and clamped her hand on his right arm. Swinging her forearm upward, she broke the grip of his left hand then lashed out with her nails, raking him across the eyes. Screaming, he clapped his hands to his face and pushed away from her. Shizume sucked in a breath of fetid air and hauled herself to her feet, bracing herself against the boat's erratic movement.

The man had recovered enough to be ready for her, and the two squared off for a moment. Shizume flicked her eyes towards Ryan and saw why the boat was moving so crazily. The second thug on the bow of the watercraft was trying to reach the cockpit, and every time he got up, Ryan would turn the boat sharply, sending him back to the deck rather than risk getting thrown overboard. He had learned from the last turn, however, and was inching his way towards the cockpit in a slow crawl, a rag-handled knife clenched between his teeth.

Shizume looked back, hoping the man had been fooled by her perceived distraction, and was not disappointed. He stepped in and launched a right jab at her nose, powering his fist from the shoulder. Shizume watched the blow coming as if it was in slow motion, then ducked away and let it sail past her head, following it with her eyes. Crouching, she whirled around so her right shoulder was underneath his elbow and she was facing away from him, then grabbed his wrist and pulled his arm downward while lunging up with her entire body, bending his limb over her shoulder. Much like her first opponent, his elbow joint fractured under stresses it was never made to absorb, bending at a crazy angle, the ends of the bone pushing through the skin in a spray of blood. For a moment, all was frozen, with Shizume gathering herself for her next move, feeling warm wetness on her head. She heard a whimper from behind her, then a weight suddenly slumped against her back. Shizume released his limp hand and turned around to see the prostrate form of her attacker, his arm impossibly bent, unconscious. Just to make sure, she kicked him at the base of the jaw, snapping his head back, then looked up to see how Ryan was faring. Her eyes widened, and she tried to scream a warning, but it was too late.

"Look out!"

The second man leaped over the windshield right at Ryan. He looked up just in time to see the man plummeting toward him, dagger held out to spear his victim in the chest. Ryan threw up his arm to keep the knife from impaling him, but the man knocked him away from the controls to the back of the boat. Both of them rolled towards Shizume, who tried to leap over them. Her leg was caught by one of the men, and she fell as well.

"Shizume, the boat!" Jon's frantic cry snapped her head up in time to see the boat heading back towards the wall of the building they had just come from. Rising to her feet, she evaded a wild swing from Ryan and made for the control panel. The wall loomed larger, and she knew she wasn't going to make it in time. Just as she reached the controls, the massive wall of the building no more than thirty meters away, a red light flashed, and the autopilot gently steered the craft away from the obstacle back into an open waterway.

Oh, thank the Faces, she thought, then turned back to untangle the two fighting men. Ryan had ended up on top and was knocking the thief's head into the gunwale over and over, until she managed to restrain him.

"I think you got him," she yelled in his ear. He whirled on her, and Shizume kept her hands up and took a step back. Ryan took a deep breath and let the man's head thump against the gunwale. He got to his feet and looked at the other one, motionless at the bottom of the boat.

"What the hell did you do to him?" he asked, spying the oddly bent arm.

"A little infighting trick we learned at the academy," Shizume said, trying not to smile at her first successful real hand-to-hand combat.

"Some trick. Remind me not to get you angry at me," he replied.

"Shouldn't you be steering the boat?" she asked.

He jerked a thumb towards the controls. "I forgot it had autopilot. What can I say, I haven't piloted it in a long time. What are we going to do about these guys?" he asked.

"I don't think they're going anywhere right now," Shizume replied. "But I'll stay back here and keep an eye on them anyway."

"I'm on it," Ryan said, trying to spring to the controls, but wincing as he did so. "Ow. That guy must have knocked into me harder than I thought." He resumed his position and took the vessel off autopilot. "Where we going, by the way?"

"Look up," Shizume said, pointing to a building that towered above the rest, piercing the night sky like an eternal monolith, existing outside of time itself. Emergency hazard lights blinked on several levels of the stratoscraper, when all around was dark. High up, almost lost in the dimness, a floor was lit up with bright white light.

"NoirCorp, that's where," she said.

"Hmm, I wonder why they have power when everyone

else doesn't," Ryan mused as he steered a course for the black tower.

"When we get there, I'll be sure to ask them," Shizume said.

CHAPTER FOURTEEN

Kar died just as the scan ticked off its final minutes. It wasn't loud, or explosive, or even messy. One moment Antonia was staring at the numbers on the countdown clock draw closer to the sacred moment when she could hold Mason again, Kar muttering to himself behind her, the next there had been—a *ripple* would be the best way she could describe it—in the world around her. Antonia had actually seen the ceiling, walls, computer systems, and chamber with Mason inside physically bulge and snap back to its present reality.

Along with it came the most disturbing sensation, a sense of being overwritten, canceled out, erased. This one was stronger than any previous wave, and Antonia felt its power as the universe tried to right the wrongness it felt. Even stranger was the overwhelming temptation to give in to this feeling, to succumb to the new order the cosmos was attempting to imprint on this dimension. If she thought about it for more than a moment, she would have been lost. But Antonia mustered all of her flagging powers to erect a barrier against this sudden assault, and for a moment she wasn't sure she would be able to fend off the inexorable invisible weight pressing on her psyche from all sides. The force was intolerable, and Antonia drew on reserves deep inside of her, feeling something crack and splinter in her mind.

Then it was gone, as quickly as it had come, the wave stopped. Antonia slumped against the wall, uncaring that her energy shield was gone, exhausted by her efforts. She looked back at Kar, the question forming in her mouth before she saw anything:

"Are you—"

Where Kar had been now stood a perfect likeness of him, exact in every single way, down to his jumpsuit and labcoat, the horizontally striped haircut, every wrinkle, every eyelash. The only difference is that he was composed entirely of granules of a black, powdery substance. It looked familiar to Antonia, so common that she almost overanalyzed it at first, then it came to her.

"Carbon," she whispered. "Pure carbon. You poor man."

Kar had been transformed in the act of reaching for a holoscreen, which now floated forever out of reach. Antonia just stood and stared at him, stunned, until a soft chime and computer voice spoke three words she had been waiting to hear for what seemed like eternity.

"Genetic bodyscan completed."

At that exact moment, the lights in the lab flickered back on. Antonia ran over to a flashing holoscreen, signifying an incoming message from the tech crew on the roof. "Begin subject drain and revival," she ordered the computer as she slapped at the screen. "This is Antonia Noir, go."

"Mrs. Noir, Tech Janssen, night crew!" the indistinct

shape of a man's helmeted and enviro-suited head yelled back at her. "Sorry for the volume, but the wind up here rips through the mufflers in our helmets. Damnedest thing—"

"Understood," she replied. "Report."

"We've patched you in to the mills, but I can't tell you how long it's going to hold, and I've already lost two men to the wind and the shit that's been happening up here is something you wouldn't believe."

"Janssen, I'll pay each man who stays up there five years' salary to keep that power flowing for the next two hours. Do you understand?"

Her connection was muted for a moment while Janssen conferred with his team. Antonia could have eavesdropped but didn't waste her time; she already knew the outcome. "Affirmative, we'll remain here for one-two-zero minutes. Janssen out."

Antonia turned and watched the last of the fluid sluice down from the sides of the chamber, rendering her husband's body clearly visible. The entire tube declined until it was horizontal, then the main glasteel plate slid open. For a moment, nothing moved in the entire chamber.

"Anti-gravity field, bring subject out," Antonia commanded. The lights dimmed as the power was redistributed into the scanning room. Long seconds passed, then Mason's body, hairless and dripping, floated out of the tube and over to the cleansing room. His head was already moving, eyes fluttering with sticky liquid. Antonia tracked his movements on a nearby holoscreen, and Mason was scanned for potential post-scan problems, injected with a tailored cocktail of drugs designed to assist his body in recovering from the scan, washed, dried, and clothed. Antonia watched it all, her foot tapping on the floor the only sign of her impatience.

After a few minutes, Mason appeared at the door of the laboratory, his scrubbed skin shiny under the lights. He was moving under his own power, clad in a silver heat-containing robe that clung to his body. Taking a step, he put a hand on the wall to steady himself.

"Mason," Antonia breathed, waiting for him to come closer.

"What—what has happened while I was under? I don't see Benjamin, and the lights—why does the power seem to be fluctuating so erratically?"

"That, my love, is a very long story," Antonia replied. "Why don't you sit until you've regained some of your strength?"

"Not until I see how successful the scan was," Mason said. He walked unsteadily into the room, spying the remains of Kar as he did so. His smooth brow raised in surprise. "What happened to him?"

"The last wave—affected him," Antonia said. "I was reviewing the scan in the final minutes and—when I looked back, he was like that."

Mason looked at the sculpture's features. "That *is* too bad. Shouldn't we block that off with a field to prevent contamination?"

"Mason, I don't know if the windmills will be able to produce that much power. The grid is off all over the city—the Zippers all fell. They were drained of their power—no one ever thought something would take all of the systems off line."

"Still, we can't have anything contaminating the lab," Mason said, still looking at the motionless form of his chief assistant. "Sheath—carbon mass, isn't it?—in the center of the room." And then, almost casually, "And pinion Antonia Noir as well."

Just like that, the energy sheath flashed on around Antonia, but instead of moving with her, this one immobilized her, wrenching her arms down next to her body, holding her standing perfectly upright, clamping down on her jaw before she could say anything. Antonia could breathe, blink, see, and hear but couldn't talk or move.

Mason pulled several holoscreens to him, studied their contents, then smiled. "Poor Kar, he certainly deserved better than this. Perhaps I'll name a Euro-Combine facility after him. He will be missed."

"Establish sound link with Benjamin Noir," Mason continued, his eyes now on Antonia, who struggled to make some kind of intelligent noise. In desperation she reached out with her mind, expending the last of her psychic energy in an attempt to reach Mason. All she encountered was that same wall of mental noise. He was only across the room, but he might as well been across the continent for all it mattered. *Mason, please, give me a chance to explain,* she thought, directing her words at him even though she knew it was hopeless. *All of the time we spent together must mean more to you than this...*

"Mason, what is the meaning of this? I'm watching your scan and the next thing I know I'm trapped back in the computer mainframe?" Benjamin's voice echoed around them. "What is going on? Why couldn't I access my body? Did Antonia have something to do with this?"

"There was a power outage, Benjamin, and we can't

afford to give you that body right now. And yes, Antonia has everything to do with this," Mason said.

"What do you mean?" his ancestor asked.

Mason walked over to Antonia, his face right in front of hers. "It means that while she has seen a Noir cheated, successful, angered, triumphant, exhausted, and over-joyed, she has never seen a Noir wronged—until now."

At that moment, Antonia discovered she could do one other thing. A tear brimmed in her eye and dripped down her cheek, followed by another. *Please, Mason, please talk to me, not at me.* Mason saw it and leaned closer, as if inspecting it.

"A masterful performance, my dear," Mason said, "calculated, I'm sure, to make me doubt my intentions, and who knows, perhaps even free you from this prison to tell me how wrong I am," Mason said. "But no, I'm going to give you the same chance you gave me—the same choice, arbitrarily made by you, without consulting me, without even discussing it with me."

Mason, I did it for you, Antonia thought. *I did it for us, to save us.*

"What are you talking about, Mason?" Benjamin asked.

"I'm talking about her betrayal of me, of everything we held dear for each other," Mason said. "Antonia lied to me from the beginning. She knew what exactly had happened at the wedding, she remained in contact with Agatha Derlicht, and most importantly, she denied me my heirs."

"You mean that business with her inability to con-ceive?" Benjamin asked.

"That's precisely what I mean," Mason said, a flush creeping over his features. "I had the most interesting chat with a relative of hers while I was under. Agatha Derlicht—who had come to gloat over me, over the fact that I have no children."

If Antonia's mouth could have dropped open, it would have. *Oh my God, she couldn't get to me, so she got to him instead,* she thought. *Mason, don't you see, she's playing you for a fool, and you're falling right into her trap. What is she really planning? AGATHA!"* she screamed in her mind. *"AGATHA, WHERE ARE YOU?!"*

Mason resumed pacing the room while he continued, "That crone was behind this from the beginning, but I never suspected. My own ancestors could come back, why couldn't hers, their wills would certainly be strong enough. She took my wife away from me, she took my children away from me, now I'm going to take the one thing she could still hold dear—her beloved great-great granddaughter."

When she heard that, Antonia tried to break free of the implacable energy sheath surrounding her. She screamed with all her remaining energy at Mason, trying to break through, trying any way she could to reach out to him. Everything she tried, focusing her love, focusing her hate on him, had no effect whatsoever. He continued walking and talking, outlining his plans for her.

"You see, Benjamin, one thing we didn't tell you is that it is possible to directly overlay a person's memories and personality on another living human being's psyche. This aspect of memory transferal, when discovered, was outlawed almost immediately. It's too bad, really, as the neural pathways of a living person are actually easier to download, many of the thought processes are already mapped out, so to speak."

"What happens to the original person's psyche?" Benjamin asked.

"Well, it's kind of like overwriting a datacomp," Mason said, stopping in front of Antonia so she heard every word. "The original person's memories and personality everything that made him or her who they were, is gone forever. For a while there was talk of using this method as capital punishment, you know, terminal people who couldn't afford clones downloaded into criminal's bodies, wiping out the original personality. But the public wouldn't stand for it. But I guess there will be one more experiment with it before we delegate it to the mothballs."

"You're going to kill your own wife?" Benjamin asked.

"I'm going to—erase her," Mason said. "But first she'll have the pleasure of knowing that the most hated enemy of her family will be inhabiting her body—just for a few minutes, mind you, while your bodyform is prepared. Then, once you've obliterated her, we'll transfer you to your new body." He tapped another datascreen. "Power levels are stable for both here and the bodyform laboratory. We can begin whenever you're ready, Benjamin."

"Mason, how do you know this is going to work? It certainly isn't what I had in mind—"

"I don't care what you had in mind, Benjamin! This is her punishment, and it's going to happen with or without you!" Mason said. "Now if you don't want to be involved, I'll wipe her mind clean with someone else, but I would have thought you'd want to stick it to Agatha Derlicht, because wherever that bitch is, I'm sure she's watching."

"Not that the idea doesn't appeal to me, mind you, but—you've been with her for more than a century. How does that fall by the wayside so easily?"

"When a foundation is built upon lies, it doesn't matter how long it has existed, it cannot hold when those lies come to light," Mason replied. "Besides, as I recall, you didn't have a problem removing your wives when the time came for another."

"They passed naturally," Benjamin replied, a strange gleam in his eye. "Not like what you have in mind."

"You're the last person I would have thought to be squeamish about this sort of thing, considering what you had planned for your own son," Mason snapped.

Antonia watched as the two argued over her life. Her rage and helplessness had dissipated, replaced by an exhausted, sad resignation. Despite what Mason had accused her of, tears still coursed down her cheeks. *Where is the man I fell in love with so long ago? Have we both changed that much? If only I had told him sooner, we could have tried to find a way to change this, but he won't even let me talk to him now.* She returned her attention to the conversation, not caring one way or the other how it turned out. *It's over, no matter what happens, it's all over.*

"What if something should go wrong?" Benjamin asked.

"Nothing will go wrong. I'll be guiding you every step of the way," Mason replied. "Look, time is running out. I can do this without you, but I'd rather do it with you. Now what's it going to be?"

Antonia held her breath, such as it was, hoping

Mason's ancestor wouldn't go through with this savagery. There was a long silence as Benjamin pondered his options. When he spoke again, the last remnants of hope died within Antonia's soul.

"You truly are a Noir, Mason," Benjamin said, his smile just as cruel as her husband's. "Your company has been most enjoyable, Antonia. I regret that you will not be around to see me when I regain my body, but I have been without one for *so* very, very long."

Triumphant, Mason turned away from her, busying himself with preparing the chamber for transferal. Antonia heard Benjamin mutter something that sounded almost like, "And in a few minutes, it won't matter one way or the other anyway."

A flashing holoscreen attracted Mason's attention. "Security, report?"

The computer itself replied. "Intruders approaching the main lobby, sir."

"And no staff on duty? Where are the guards?"

"They are not at their station, sir."

"Fire them all," Mason said. "Show me who they are."

A corner of the screen enlarged to show a man and a woman entering the NoirCorp headquarters through a punched out window section of the lobby.

"Now how did they do that without us noticing?" Mason asked.

"Th—that bastard—Jon!" Benjamin hissed.

"What are you talking about?" Mason asked. It's just a man and woman, probably refugees from the disaster zone I'm sure the city has become by now."

"You don't understand, my—the spirit of my son is down there, in this very building," Benjamin said. "They mean to stop us, at any cost. He's always been against me, from the very beginning."

"Is that so?" Mason said, a wolfish grin creasing his features. His fingers flew over the holoscreen for the building controls. "Then we should prepare a suitable reception for them. Adam?"

The answer came instantly. "Yes, sir?"

There will be two people coming up to the office on my private gravator. They will not be leaving. Disable the gravator to this floor and wait for their arrival."

"Understood, sir."

"Is he—?" Benjamin asked.

"No, he's going to carry out his orders as I gave them—he will prevent them from leaving the office. If they attack him, he will respond appropriately, including the use of appropriate force. They won't be disturbing us."

Trapped in her golden prison, Antonia could see no way to disagree with him.

CHAPTER FIFTEEN

S hizume first noticed a mass covering the water all around them as the boat approached NoirCorp headquarters. "What are those?" she asked, watching the ocean around them.

"Look up," Ryan replied, his tone grim. Shizume did, and for a moment didn't understand what he was talking about. Then she saw it

"By the Faces..."

All around them stood the stratoscrapers, blockpartments, the buildings that made up Greater New York. What was missing were the normally ever present swarms of zippers that sped up and down their sides, twenty-four hours a day. They were all gone, the walls of the towering structures as bare as when they had first been built. Now that she noticed it, Shizume also realized that their sound was gone as well, the constant humming and whooshing as they zoomed up and down, across from building to building, all day, all night. Now the city was deathly silent and dark, no advirtisements, no sirens, no humming, no life. In the distance she could see plumes of black smoke from what appeared to be burning buildings, with no firecrews coming to battle the blazes.

She looked around wildly, seeing the wreckage floating everywhere, the twisted and pulverized plasteel of thousands of Zippers that had impacted the water or each other at terminal velocity. The boat slowed as Ryan navigated through the ocean of debris, the hull pushing mangled remains out of the way. Even the water wasn't as black anymore. It was ruddy maroon, as if the blood from all the victims of the latest wave had dyed the water. The entire city now felt like—

"A tomb," she said. "A huge, underwater tomb. Thousands—hundreds of thousands—millions—all dead."

Engrossed in getting them to the destination, Ryan hadn't heard her. "My father once told me that there were four separate fail-safe systems built into the Zipper system to prevent this kind of thing. And that included the separate backup systems contained in each building. For the past twenty years there hasn't been a failure of a single Zipper, not one loss of life. But I don't think the city ever planned on anything like this happening."

Shizume stared at him. "How can you be so calm about all this? We've failed already," she said, sinking to the floor of the boat, her trembling arms wrapped around her knees. "Look around you, they're dead—they're all dead!"

At that moment the boat nudged against the side of the monolithic NoirCorp building. Ryan turned to her. "At my—well, it wasn't mine, it was all of ours—at the shelter, we lost people every single day. Not as many as this, but they came and went, or we learned almost every week that someone who had stayed with us for a while had died. But the one thing we always knew—always—is that there would be someone else coming in. We mourned those who had passed on, but that didn't make us any less sensitive to the new people who needed our help."

"What's your point?" she said, tears streaming down her face.

"My point is that yes, hundreds of thousands, perhaps millions of people have died, but there are still millions out there. But this time, if we don't help them, no one will. You told me that if I cared about the people of this city at all, then I had to do something." He knelt beside her. "Well, I do care, and I know you do as well. And we are doing something, right now, for those who are left. I can't do this without you. And I don't want to either. We will grieve for everyone in our own time, but we're not finished here yet."

"Ryan is right," Jon said. *"When I was alive, I couldn't prevent the killings that happened in Geiststadt, but even as I was dying I was able to prevent the rest of the town from going up in flames. That didn't bring anyone who had been killed back, but it did save the rest of them. This is a tragedy on a much vaster scale, but there are still people who need our help, and we cannot lose sight of that, even for a moment."*

Shizume wiped at her teary face. "I can't even wallow in despair for a minute before you two have to go and remind me why we're here?"

"Only because I know you would do the same for me,"

Ryan replied. "And, unfortunately, we don't have a minute to spare."

"I know, I know. Uh, one question," she asked as she got up on shaky legs and stared at the endless expanse of electroglass and plasteel, "how are we going to get in?"

"I've got an idea," Ryan said, taking a fist-sized plastic bundle and, holding on to a rope trailing from it, threw it overboard. The package inflated with a pop and a hiss as soon as it hit the water, expanding into a four-person raft with collapsible paddles. Meanwhile, Ryan was busy at the controls, overriding the autopilot and programming a new course for the boat. He turned it around and headed about two hundred meters away from the building, then turned the boat around again and idled it.

"You're not—" Shizume asked.

"I sure am. Always wanted to do this to them, smug monopolist bastards," Ryan said.

"You know, that is my very extended family you're talking about," she replied, trying to look stern.

"Oh—no offense," he said with a grin. "It's going to go in about a ninety seconds, so we'd best get off while we can."

"What about them?" she asked, nodding to the two unconscious men in the bottom of the boat.

"Well, I'm not a total brainfry. We'd better take them with us. It'll be crowded, but I think we'll all fit."

They managed to offload the would-be hijackers and disembark in the small raft with a relative minimum of difficulty, only soaking Shizume's leg to the knee and both of Ryan's arms when he pushed off the boat and overbalanced for a moment, almost tipping them into the murky water. They concentrated on getting away from the speedboat, making clumsy progress with the unfamiliar paddles.

"Five...four...three...two—" the boat spat water as it leapt forward, heading right for the side of the NoirCorp building. Shizume and Ryan watched it in a kind of dreadful fascination, simultaneously fearing and hoping for what might happen. The boat gathered even more speed as it drew closer to the huge building, then blasted right into it. Even without the electrostatic barrier, the electroglass was very strong, strong enough to withstand the boat's impact. The frame it was in, however, was not, and the prow of the boat punched the entire pane into the building's interior. The sounds of the boat and the pane of glass careening across the floor of the building could be heard fading into the distance, then all was quiet again.

"*Wow*," Shizume, Ryan, and Jon all said together. Shizume and Jon paddled towards the dim hole in the side of the building. Beaching the raft on the lip of the lobby, they stepped out carefully, walking with exaggerated care on the now-slippery marble floor.

"I've never been in this building, have you?" Ryan asked.

Shizume shook her head, just looking around in the gloom. The NoirCorp lobby was huge, easily five stories tall, and built of all natural materials at what must have been an exorbitant cost. A double row of malachite columns stretched toward a large, circular, deserted desk, with the rear end of the boat sticking out of its shattered body like some bizarre new age sculpture. On the wall above it, mounted on what looked like a smooth polished expanse of now-extinct mahogany, was a huge map of the world forged out of what looked like platinum, with winking diamond dots portraying NoirCorp holdings or subsidiaries. As the two walked closer, they could see just how much of the world NoirCorp had under its control, directly or indirectly.

"I thought they had a hologram of this rendered for everyone to see when they came in," Ryan whispered.

"Well, the power is off, you know," Shizume said.

The chime of a gravator door answered her comment, echoing in the cavernous room.

"You were saying?" Ryan asked, heading for the desk and what looked like a hallway beyond. "Remember what you told me in the stairwell about the gravators operating on a different energy source? They run on geothermal power, completely separate from the electrical grid—one of the bright things the city did after the Night of 2044."

Shizume followed, a bit more wary. "Yeah, I remember the stories about the blackout. It's also what powers the A-G fields in these new offices as well. Let's not be hasty, Ryan, after all, we don't even know what we're looking for," she said.

"Take the elevator—gravator—whatever you call it now—up," Jon said to her. *"We're very close now."*

"Can you feel anything?" she asked.

"Oh, yes," Jon replied. *"He's very close now. They're also very close to completing whatever it is that they're about to do, so we must hurry."*

"Shizume, what's the hold-up? The gravator's working just fine," Ryan said. "It's a bit small, though, must be a private one."

"Just a minute, I want to see if I can call my grandfather," Shizume said, activating her celplant. The annoying tone reverberated in her head. *"We're sorry, but the number you have called is not accessible at this time. Please try your call later."*

"Something must be wrong with the satellites. I can't get through. I hope he's all right," she said, tiptoeing through the broken glass towards the dozens of gravator tubes.

"Over here," Ryan said, his face lit by the interior light in the tube. Shizume walked over, frowning.

"You don't think both of us are going to fit in there, do you?" she asked.

"Don't think we've got much choice," he said. "And I'm certainly not letting you go up by yourself or wait down here until this thing is clear."

"Yeah, I was just thinking the same thing about you," she said. "All right, move over."

"Looks like this only goes up to the 425th floor," Ryan said. "Shall we?"

"Uh—yeah, ready when you are," Shizume said. Even with their mingled aromas of sweat, dirt, and brackish ocean water filling the chamber, she was suddenly aware of Ryan's nearness to her in the enclosed space. *I must look a total mess,* she thought, then shook her head. *Why am I even wondering about that when we're heading into God knows what?*

"Don't worry about it, you'll do fine," Jon said.

"It's not later I'm worried about, it's right now," she replied under her breath.

"Did you, uh, say something?" Ryan asked.

"Who me?—no, nothing," Shizume replied, feeling her skin flush.

"Oh, I thought you had, that's all," he said. She noticed that he had adopted the "male elevator posture": looking only at the flashing numbers on the walls they passed by, avoiding any eye contact but trying to look casual about it.

"Oh, my God, he's as embarrassed as I am," she mumbled, looking down to hide her grin.

"Yes, but he's managing to hide it well, I think," Jon said.

"Hey, you stay out of this," she said.

"Are you sure you didn't say anything, because I thought—" Ryan began.

"Oh look, we're here," she said as they slowed to a stop. The numerals 425 glowed on the panel before them, then the recessed doors opened.

"Look at this place," Ryan said as they walked into the sumptuous office. "I think that chair's made of real leather."

"Yuck," Shizume replied. "It's certainly big enough. This room's larger than my entire apartment. Is that real furniture? And look at those paintings on the wall. Well, where do we go from here?"

"Nowhere, I'm afraid," said a neutral voice at the other end of the room. Shizume and Ryan both turned to see an average-looking man with short hair and gray eyes walk towards them. He was dressed in a long sleeve shirt and fashionably slash-creased pants and looked completely at ease. *No,* Shizume thought after a moment. *He looks totally emotionless.*

"Is there someone else in here?" Jon asked.

"Sure, can't you see him?" Shizume muttered.

"I can hear a voice, but I don't sense another life here," Jon replied. *"Something is wrong."*

"What?" Shizume asked.

"I don't know. Just be careful," Jon said.

"Tell Ryan that, too," she said.

Ryan was already moving forward, putting his hand out in that ingrained male act of non-aggression. "Are you Mr. Noir?"

The man looked at his outthrust hand in silence for several seconds until Ryan cleared his throat and dropped it. "No, my name is Adam."

No one said anything for a few moments after that, then Ryan tried again. "We're here to see Mr. Noir. Can you take us to him?"

Again that flat, almost inhuman gaze. "That is not possible."

"Can you tell me how to get to Mr. Noir?" Ryan asked.

The man nodded his head towards a paneled wall across the room. "Access to the laboratory is through there."

"But you can't take us to him?" Shizume asked.

"I'm afraid my orders do not permit that."

"What do your 'orders' permit?" Ryan said, crossing his arms.

"They are very specific," the man said. "Neither of you is to leave this room."

"Well, I fail to see how you plan to stop both of us," Ryan said.

"Um, Ryan—" Shizume began.

"No, you just go that way, and I'll make sure—Adam,

was it?—doesn't do anything he might regret," Ryan said, not in a boastful way, but simply stating a fact.

"I wouldn't attempt that," the man said, even more tonelessly than before, if possible.

"Go, Shizume," Ryan said, not taking his eyes off the man in front of him. He uncrossed his arms, letting them hang at his sides. "I can handle this."

"I'm not so sure—"

"Go," I said, Ryan replied, tensing.

Shizume took one step towards the panel. The instant her foot hit the floor, the man blurred into action, interposing himself between her and the gravator before Ryan could even lay a finger on him.

"Whoa, what the hell was that?" Ryan asked, flummoxed.

"Didn't Jon tell you something isn't right with this guy?" she asked.

"Yeah, but until he did that he looked perfectly normal," Ryan replied. "Okay, so he can move a little faster than the average flunkie. You take the left, I'll take the right."

"I don't think that's a good idea," Jon said.

"I don't either, but I don't have a better one," Shizume said, backing off from the man and waiting for Ryan to catch up with her. "Whenever you want."

The man's gaze swept over both of them impassively. "Just try to get around him," Ryan said. *"Now."*

They both moved as one, Shizume balanced and flowing around him to the left, Ryan trying to remain out of his reach as he passed on the right. The man seemed to freeze for a moment, then moved faster than they could follow. With one stiff arm he shoved Ryan in the chest so hard that he stumbled backwards to the floor. While Ryan was still tripping through the air, the man repositioned himself in front of Shizume, who hadn't been able to take more than two steps towards the panel. The man held up his finger and waggled it at her.

"I am really not—Ryan—no!" Shizume said, seeing what he was planning.

Righting himself, Ryan was already running at the man, intending to tackle him. When she cried out, he pivoted, grabbed Ryan by his jumpsuited front and turned, using his momentum and throwing him across the desk several meters away. The anti-gravity field the desktop floated on managed to absorb the sudden impact, but swayed under his weight, tipping him off.

"Oh my God," she said, running to him. "Are you all right?"

"How in the—how did he do that?" he asked, rubbing his head. "I'm okay, just got the pride knocked out of me, that's all." He pushed himself to his knees and groaned again. "Ow, that flight didn't help my side any, that's for sure. What are you going to do?"

Shizume poked her head up, looking for the man, who was still standing in front of the panel. "All right, let me try this time. You," she said, tapping the leather chair with her palm, "be ready."

Ryan's eyes widened as he comprehended her plan. "Ouch."

"Hopefully," she said, standing back up.

"Hey," he said, getting to his feet and gripping the chair back, "Be careful. I'd hate to see your face get pushed in."

"So would I," she said, turning towards their opponent.

251

Raising her arms, she took a cautious step forward, then another. The man didn't move, but his eyes followed her every motion.

"What is happening?" Jon asked. *"Why did Ryan suddenly leap through the air?"*

"NoirCorp's security system is activated," Shizume said, then attacked, lashing out with a front snap kick aimed at the man's groin. He stepped to the left even before her leg had begun to extend horizontally. Shizume moved right, trying to make him put his side or back to Ryan and the chair. Amazingly, he did so, facing her completely, his entire back to the desk and everything behind it.

Ryan didn't need an invitation. With a grunt he hoisted the chair above his head, then stepped around the desk and brought the unwieldy bludgeon down on the man, the heavy metal and brass frame crushing his head and sending him unconscious to the floor. Or at least that's what should have happened.

The legs and stalk of the chair *thunk*ed into the man's head and neck and stopped dead, not even knocking him over or bending his head to one side. One of the radial arms had lain open a gash near his temple, but the dripping redness didn't appear to inconvenience him in the slightest. He picked up the chair with one hand and tossed it off him like someone would remove a wet towel from their shoulder. The chair flew the length of the office and cracked against the paneled far wall,

Shizume and Ryan exchanged shocked looks. "What the hell is this guy?" she asked.

Ryan held his hands out and shrugged in the universal

damned if I know gesture. "More importantly, how are we supposed to get around him?"

"Ryan, you have the power to stop him," Jon said.

"Maybe so, but that doesn't mean I know how to use it," he replied. "Our lessons have been slight at best."

"Still, you have the best chance. You just have to open yourself up to the ability," Jon said.

"If you can't give me anything better that this psycho-spiritual new age crap, Jon, just keep your mouth shut, all right?" Ryan said.

While Ryan argued with Jon, Shizume was studying their opponent. At that same time, a snippet of advice from Fliv came back to her: *"There will always be someone who is faster, stronger, or tougher that you. When that happens, your only recourse is to outthink your opponent."*

Good advice, Fliv, but I never thought we'd find a guy who's all three at once, she thought. *Still—* "Ryan, I've got an idea."

"Really, what?"

"Just hang on a nano, and I'll let you know," she replied, walking away from the gravator wall to the floating desk that hovered in front of the windows. Waving her hand over its surface, she saw a password requirement to access any NoirCorp files, but in one corner was an innocuous little square marked MANUAL SETTINGS.

Right, she thought, hitting it and opening up a menu. "Come here and give me a hand with this," she told Ryan.

"What are you doing?" he asked.

"Getting you away from him and over here," she said,

her fingers dancing over the board. "When I give you the signal, head for those far doors along the way, partly as a distraction and partly to see what he does. I've got an idea that should get us out of here...okay, go...now."

Throwing her a quizzical look, he began sidling along the wall, glancing at the motionless man watching them both. Ryan kept going, passing the halfway point, each step taking him closer to the door. The man still didn't move.

Why isn't he going after him? Shizume wondered. *He'll be at the door soon.* A flashing square on the desktop caught her attention. DOOR LOCK/UNLOCK it said. She stabbed the button with her thumb. The double doors at the end clicked and began to swing open.

Now the man moved, so fast he almost caught Shizume by surprise. As she had hoped; he headed straight across the middle of the floor, angling to intercept Ryan before he could get to the doors. She hit the button and looked up.

As he was running, the man suddenly levitated into the air, as if he was climbing invisible steps. His inertia would have kept him going, but he encountered another invisible wall that stopped his forward movement cold. As soon as he was completely off the ground Shizume canceled the anti-gravity field emanating from the wall, preventing their opponent from using it for leverage. The man was trapped, floating in mid-air, slowly spinning in space.

"Stick to the edge of the wall and come back around to me," Shizume said.

"Not bad, not bad at all," he said, careful to stay far

out of reach of the suspended man. Adam kept watching the both of them as he drifted round and round, always moving his head to keep them in view. His eerily calm expression still hadn't changed.

"How'd you know about that?" Ryan asked as he reached her.

"The desk itself tipped me off," she said, taking his arm and steering him towards the wall. "We learned at the academy that rooms like this have the A-G projectors built into the floors, ceilings and walls, so the owners can set up floating desks, or shelves, or display areas wherever they like. Now, let's find that gravator and get out of here."

When she looked over, she saw a blur of movement next to him. Ryan was jerked away from her and flung across the room again, this time into a painting on the wall, which dropped off when he did, crashing down on top of him. Shizume turned to run but was caught by plasteel-hard fingers gripping the back of her neck. Adam actually threw her into his other hand, then lifted her off the floor with ease, cutting off her air supply. She kicked and flailed, but her feet bounced off his abdomen without doing any appreciable damage, while her arms weren't long enough to reach his eyes or nose. She tried wrenching at his fingers, but they were locked around her throat, and she couldn't get a grip on them. Desperate, she dug in with her fingernails as hard as she could, but she might as well have been digging into sand, for all the good it did.

"You are not to leave," Adam said, his voice as empty of inflection as it had been the first time he spoke. Shizume couldn't think, even to call for help. *Jon, where are you?* she thought weakly, but there was no answer.

"Hey!" Through her oxygen-starved haze Shizume saw someone that looked a lot like Ryan pick himself off the floor and stride towards her. *But that can't be Ryan,* her foggy mind thought. *He's never looked that—radiant.*

There really wasn't a better term for it. The Ryan walking towards her was—brighter somehow, his face glowing from within, almost luminous. Before he had walked favoring his injured side; now he looked like he had never been hurt. The look in his eye was the strangest of all; it was as if he had become attuned to everything around him, as if he knew his place in the universe, and that it extended beyond the shelter, his life, the city. He walked like he knew something that no one else knew, and whatever that was gave him an overwhelming edge over anything he faced.

Adam kept hold of Shizume with one hand and watched Ryan approach, his other hand still at his side. When Ryan got close enough, his arm shot out, planning to grab the other man around the throat like he had Shizume.

This time, however, it was Ryan that blurred into motion, snatching Adam's arm and pulling him off balance. Adam dropped Shizume as he staggered into the middle of the room. Ryan kept holding him, whipping him around faster and faster, then releasing him, sending him spinning towards the main doors. The man caught himself and faced Ryan, who stood in the middle of the room.

Shizume collapsed against the far wall and Adam took a step towards her. When he did, Ryan stepped into his path, blocking him from her. The man took another step, as did Ryan.

"No way," he said. "You're going to have to go through me first."

The man looked at Shizume, then at Ryan. When he moved, it was with that same preternatural speed. But this time Ryan matched him movement for movement, step for step, the two men shifting and evading, each trying to gain the upper hand, with Adam trying to get back to Shizume and Ryan constantly distracting him and making him veer off. Strangely, the man still didn't attack Ryan. He just kept trying to get between Shizume and the gravator door.

Sucking air into her empty lungs, Shizume began crawling to the desk again, ducking as a large plant-filled vase sailed through the air above her and shattered against the wall, showering her with dirt. She kept on and reached the floating platform, hauling herself to her feet again and hoping she wouldn't see Ryan's broken body on the floor when she did.

The sight that greeted her, however, was quite the opposite. The man was now chasing Ryan around the room, as fast as ever, but every time he tried to lay a hand on his opponent, Ryan blurred into motion for a moment and evaded him, ending up on the other side of the room, leaping off the wall or hurdling furniture.

Ryan saw Shizume as he went by and called out to her, "I'm not sure how much longer I can keep this up, so you'd better come up with something."

"I have," she gasped. "Just keep him busy." She attacked the desk again, laying out a vertical anti-gravity field behind her that stretched from floor to ceiling, then created another one, horizontal this time, that she extended to the glasteel pane behind her, focusing all of the projector's power on one tiny point. The metal-glass alloy was strong, but it was no match for the force of gravity. The pane buckled then spider-webbed all over. Held in an unbreakable weave, it didn't shatter, but like the one they had hit on the ground floor, the frame couldn't take the pressure and the entire gigantic sheet popped out with a squeal of tortured metal and sailed into the atmosphere. A howling wind ripped through the office suite, cutting right through Shizume, chilling her to the bone.

She screamed over the roar while stabbing buttons on the desktop. "Ryan! Get him over by the window! Move when I tell you to!" *God, Buddha, anybody, please let me time this right,* she thought.

Ryan nodded, leading his pursuer closer to her. Adam was only a half step behind him, occasionally appearing to lay a hand on Ryan, but he always managed to escape his pursuer's grasp. The pair reached the corner of the room where they had first come in, then Ryan turned and ran past the back wall, directly in front of the break in the windows.

"Jump!" she screamed when he was halfway across the window. Ryan did so, leaping up almost to the ceiling. At the same time Shizume hit the last button on the desk, sending the horseshoe-shaped top hurtling on one more anti-gravity field straight towards Adam. The U-shaped ceramic slab caught him right around the waist, knocking him off his feet. Even as fast as it happened, the man still clambered on top of the desk, running up its side as the entire thing slid into the nothingness outside the building. Just as the rounded edge of the desk toppled over the edge of the window frame, Adam leaped off, soaring back into the room directly at Shizume.

Ryan had reached the top of his leap and was now coming back down. He saw Adam jump back into the room and let himself fall, timing his attack to the second. As he came back down, Ryan lashed out with his foot, catching the man square in the chest and driving him backward. Adam's hand snapped out and caught Ryan's foot, pulling him toward the open window.

"Ryan!" Shizume darted around the vertical anti-grav wall and dove towards him, grabbing the collar of his jumpsuit as he headed towards the empty sky. Her weight stopped him and brought Ryan crashing down to the floor, Adam still hanging on to his right foot. Ryan's left leg pistoned out and hit the man again in the chest while he arched his right foot, letting the laceless shoe he was wearing slip off.

Adam's face finally showed an emotion—surprise. He clutched at the shoe as he overbalanced, his arms pinwheeling as he tried to overcome gravity's incessant pull. Without a word, without a sound, he toppled backwards out of the empty frame, falling silently more than four hundred stories to the unforgiving ocean far below.

Ryan rolled over and crawled to Shizume, who had fallen to her knees. "Hey, are you all right?"

She looked up at him, her throat bruised, and gestured him to bend down to her. He did so, cupping his ear to hear what she was going to say.

"What the hell," she said. Before he could react, Shizume grabbed both his cheeks in her hands, brought his face down to hers, and kissed him with abandon.

CHAPTER SIXTEEN

Mason strode around the room, regaining more
strength with each movement. Antonia watched
him make the preparations from behind the
transfer chamber wall. She had no more tears left. He
had floated her, energy sheath and all, into the next
room, then placed her into the unbreakable chamber,
sealing her in. At least he had canceled the energy sheath,
so she could move a bit in her transparent prison.

She watched him as he pulled holoscreens around
himself, readying everything for the transfer that would
end her life. Benjamin had been restored to holographic
form now, and he alternated between talking to Mason
and watching Antonia, an inscrutable expression on his
face.

A wild spark of an idea came to her in that instant.
Summoning the last reserves of her power, she reached
out, past the chamber, past the room, aiming past Mason,
trying to contact another nearby mind.

Benjamin, can you hear me? she thought. For a
moment she thought she saw the hologram look up, as
if catching something in the air. But he bent back to the

screen he had been perusing before, and Antonia slumped backward, exhausted, knowing her last chance was gone.

She raised her head to see Benjamin wink out of existence back into the computer. Mason was sitting on a high chair he had formed in the room, holoscreens floating around him like mute servants. His arms blurred and she saw a constant stream of commands issuing from his mouth to the computer system.

...*Grote dochter*... the voice in her head was faint, an echoing shadow of the power it once commanded.

Antonia cast around with her psychic senses. *Agatha? Is that you?*

Yes, child, it is, the voice grew stronger, more confident. *You seem to be in a bit of a spot right now.*

Yes, one that you helped put me in, damn you! Antonia replied. *Why did you have to contact Mason? Were you trying to stop him too?*

Agatha chucked, a low sibilant hissing in Antonia's mind. *Oh, my dear, you are clever, but not clever enough. I had done my part to ensure that you would continue with the experiment, to ensure Noir would be encapsulated in a body, but I feared that Mason might become—distracted from his mission as well, so I thought I'd reinforce his decision. Granted, I did not think he would go this far, but sacrifices have to be made. A nudge in the right direction regarding your sad lack of children put him firmly on the right path.*

You told him...Agatha, how could you– Antonia's thoughts failed her at her ancestor's betrayal.

How could I? Very simply! The elder Derlicht's words stung with venom. *The accursed Noirs nearly destroyed*

261

our family, our very lineage, you fool! Then, when I finally have one of mine poised to bring their family down forever, she turns against her own family, for love, she claims!

That war was yours, always yours, never mine! Antonia snapped. *Mason had nothing to do with whatever happened all those centuries ago. Why can't you let this go and let Mason and I live in peace?*

Peace? You expect peace when Mason is bringing that vile monster back into this world? Agatha asked. *Do you honestly expect the Noirs to sit back on their laurels and let everything continue as it has been? You are even more of a silly, prattling girl than I ever imagined.*

Fortunately, your precious love is an emotion I am not saddled with. Honor, yes, duty, yes, but love has no place in what I must do. You, I, anyone is expendable as long as the Noirs are destroyed. Mason has already set that chain of events in motion, and I stayed to ensure its completion.

I saw your distrust of Benjamin from the beginning—and you were right not to believe him, but you still wouldn't disappoint your darling husband—and I thought you of all people might be able to persuade him not to bring Benjamin back. When you couldn't, I had to make sure you could not interfere any further.

You're not making any sense, Antonia said. *First you say bringing back Benjamin will be bad, then you want him alive again?*

Of course I want him alive, then I can destroy him forever, she replied. *He is protected by that vervloekt computer. I cannot touch him now, but once he is in a human body again, he is—what is the phrase—fair game? Then, at long last, my revenge shall be complete.*

Is that why you have clung on in the spirit world for so long—revenge? Antonia asked. *You are a contemptible excuse for a human being. If you ever knew what it was like to love, that emotion must have died when you did, old woman. Now leave me in peace. If I am going to die, I'll do it without your eyes watching. Go, before I banish you!*

Grote dochter, *you are already dead to me,* Agatha said. *My only regret is that you will not be around to see the destruction of the Noirs, once Benjamin has had his way with you. From what I understand, it isn't pleasant. I leave you to think about that as you await him. I have my own preparations to make.*

Get out. If I ever find you in the spirit world, I'll destroy you forever, Antonia said. Only silence answered her last threat. She clenched her fists in frustration, then relaxed. A cool wetness tickled her toes, and she looked down to see the nutrient fluid flowing into the chamber, enveloping her feet and rising towards her knees. She looked up to see Mason regarding her, stoic calm on his face. *Not even going to sedate me for this, are you?* she thought, shaking her head. Leaning forward as the glutinous liquid swirled around her hips, Antonia placed both hands on the glass, making sure he saw her face. *I love you,* she mouthed clearly. He did not react, did not even blink, but just watched the fluid climb past her chest, her neck and eventually to her face. Antonia didn't take her eyes off her husband. Even when the liquid rose above her head, she kept them open, trying to see Mason through the opaque goo. She choked and spluttered a bit when the liquid coursed down her throat and entered her windpipe, but then her lungs began to extract the oxygen out of the fluid, and she could breathe again.

Antonia was so distracted by the immersion that the initial engram download caught her by surprise. She arched her head back as the superimposed memories surged through her, trying to impose themselves on her synaptic patterns. Antonia felt her own mind begin to fragment and cascade away, the memories of her own life disappearing under the mental onslaught. And underneath all of it was a repeating mantra: *Don't resist...don't resist...don't resist...*

No! You will not have this mind so easily! Caught unaware at first, she almost didn't realize what was happening, but Antonia struggled to bring order out of the chaos that her brain was becoming. Frantic, she grasped the strongest memory she could think of, that of her wedding day, the church...the battle with the spirits...Mason cradling her in his arms as she passed into unconsciousness. She felt the flow of implanted memories slow, as if buffered by her own thoughts. Heartened by this, she kept thinking of her life over the past centuries, anniversaries, business ventures, incorporations, vacations Mason and she had taken over the decades, even arguments she had fought with her husband.

Still, as Antonia battled to preserve her sanity, other images began flashing into her mind—the walls of a room carved out of stone, seeing—Benjamin?—looking at a circle of people, including a tall, older man with a long braided beard, and a young, simply-dressed man with blond hair and blue eyes, all examining another desecrated body—bending over the pot of a towering, bulbous plant with another wiry man with dark, cold eyes as they dug a small hole and buried a small leather bag fastened with a leather thong—sitting behind a large desk as two men point accusing fingers at him, a quivering dagger embedded in the desktop between them—the wedding day from above, with a ghostly white spirit swooping down to seek entry into her body—

"Antonia, it will go so much easier it you do not resist me," a new voice said in her head. *"I know you have no reason to trust me, but I truly do not wish you harm."*

Benjamin, you cannot do this, Antonia said, weakening more and more every second. *I beg of you,* she thought, hating the words even as she thought them. *For your great-grandson, for me, please, you mustn't.*

"Shh," he soothed. *"Everything is going to be fine. It's not you I want, after all."*

What? she asked. *What do you mean?*

And, as if bound together by invisible cords, her mind was rejoined and whole again, every memory intact and in place. Antonia felt at peace and together, and Benjamin was just a fading presence in her mind. He called to her as he passed out of her mind. *"For me to truly live, I have to be in a Noir, and the best vessel is just a few meters away."*

What are you talking about? she asked. *The cloneform isn't ready yet.*

His last words to her, however, froze the very blood in her veins. *"I know,"* he replied. *"That's not where I'm going. Thank you, Antonia, for enabling me to live again."*

Horror overcame her as she comprehended his words. Antonia opened her mouth, but her burbling scream was caught in the sticky fluid all around her. She screamed anyway, hoping that somehow, her beloved would hear her, and knowing deep down that it was just as impossible.

"MASON!"

CHAPTER SEVENTEEN

How did you do that, with Adam, I mean?" Shizume asked Ryan. They were standing in front of the gravator panel, now pried open, with Ryan providing most of the muscle during the effort.

"After that guy threw me across the room, I got back to my feet, and all I saw was him strangling you. I'm not sure what happened after that, uh, I just remember getting really angry, and—then Jon kind of took over, I guess, and, I don't know, the best way to describe it would be he gave my brain a quarter-turn to the right."

"Let's just say I opened Ryan's mind to the possibilities," Jon said.

"I want to hear his side of it, thank you," Shizume said.

"Sorry," Jon replied, his tone of voice making it clear he wasn't.

"Actually, there's not much more to tell," Ryan said. "I can feel the difference in me now, but it's impossible to put it into words. The best way to put it is that instead of using the normal twelve percent of my brain like everyone else, I feel like I'm using all of it now. I can *feel* every aspect of my body, and how I relate to the universe, and how the universe works, I suppose, and what I can control and what I cannot. Is this what it felt like when you called that storm down on Derlicht Haus, Jon?"

"What? Oh, yes, a bit like that, however, I didn't have the chance to experience it much longer after that," the spirit replied. *"We need to keep moving. I have a feeling that whatever is coming is about to happen."*

"Okay, but how are we supposed to get up there?" Shizume asked. "This gravator doesn't seem to be working."

"Well, they can be turned off, which is what someone must have done. But I think I can help," Ryan said, his face flushing. "You'll, uh, have to hold on to me."

Shizume tried to keep her face neutral as well, although she felt the heat rise in her cheeks. After their kiss, which Ryan had not resisted in the slightest, they had broken apart and just stared at each other for several long seconds. Ryan had muttered something about getting to the gravator, and they hadn't said anything remotely connected to the incident until now. Despite only a few minutes passing, Shizume knew that their relationship had changed, all because of her one impulsive gesture to celebrate their both surviving those previous few minutes.

The one thing I hadn't expected would be that he would be so good at it, she thought. *I wonder what he's thinking—*

"I could tell you—" Jon began.

No, *thank you, I got myself into this mess, and I'll get myself out,* she thought. *But how?*

Before she could frame a reply, Ryan smiled and spoke first. "Don't worry, I won't take any liberties unless I'm sure I can get away with them."

Shizume grinned back, his expression telling her everything she needed to know. "All right, Mr. All-powerful, let's go," she said, wrapping her arms around his neck.

Ryan picked her up with ease and stepped over to the gravator tube. "Well, I wouldn't say that, but I can do this." He stepped out into the middle of the silent tube. They dipped a bit, causing Shizume to lock her arms a bit tighter around his neck.

"It won't help if you're strangling me too," he gasped.

"Sorry, I'm just used to gravity being at my command, not someone else's," she said, burying her face in his shoulder to avoid looking down at 250 floors of nothing. *Ryan's got me. He won't let me fall,* she thought.

Ryan concentrated for a moment, and they began to rise, just the two of them, slowly at first, then faster.

"I'm sensing him about twenty-five floors up," Jon said

"Do you have any idea what's up there?" Shizume asked.

"I'm afraid not," Jon replied. *"I am a lot more confident that we will be able to handle whatever we encounter, however."*

"That makes me feel a bit better," Ryan said.

"Hey, don't make me laugh," Shizume said, trying to stifle the inappropriate fit of giggles that came over her.

"On the contrary, I think a good laugh is what we all need right about now," Ryan replied through his own chuckles. "Hey, I think we're here."

They had slowed to the 465th floor, hovering in the void. Shizume was about to tell Ryan to open the door when her celplant rang. "Wait a minute," she whispered. "Grandfather's calling, I think." She opened the connection. "Hello? Grandfather?"

A burst of static knifed through her head, then Payne's voice came through in scattered bursts. "S h i – m e – r e s e a r – a n c ... t – m a g i c – b l o o d rituals–pos–ssion–some–to do...with taking bod–"

The connection suddenly cut out. "Payne? Grandfather? I lost him," she said. "I hope he's all right."

"GNYC is probably working around the clock to get everything back in order," Ryan said. "I'm sure he'll be fine."

"Besides, I'm afraid we have our own problems to deal with right now, and the quicker the better," Jon said to both of them.

"Yes, yes, you don't have to remind me," Shizume said. "Ryan, can you open those doors?"

"I think so," Ryan said. Bracing himself, he took hold of the doors and wrenched both open with a loud crash. "Oops, guess I don't know my own strength yet."

Ryan let Shizume exit first, then followed her into the room. As soon as they were inside, both were immediately encased in a shimmering field of golden energy that rendered them unable to move.

The man facing them in the middle of the laboratory was tall, black-haired; and had a look of utterly mad glee on his face. Behind him, separated by a row of transparent glasteel windows, Shizume saw what looked like a woman struggling in a two-meter tall chamber filled with a thick, semi-clear liquid. The rest of the laboratory was spotless, with sleek supracomputer banks, many of them dark and unused, built into the walls. The only exception was a strange, six-foot-tall black sculpture of a man with one arm outstretched in the center of the room.

"Ah, brother, it is so good to see you." The man's smile was a manic display of teeth, so wide Shizume had the absurd thought that if he smiled any more his head would split in two. "You of everyone—well, everyone left alive, that is—will appreciate this moment the most."

"What happened to Mason?" Jon's voice could now be heard in the room itself.

The man straightened up and tugged at his disheveled bodysheath. "Oh, he did put up a good fight, but in the end, my will won."

Everyone heard a loud *thump* from the liquid-filled chamber, audible even through the windows. The man's smile didn't waver as he looked behind him, then turned back. "Ah, the little wife. I wonder how she'll like her husband now. Not as if it matters."

"You know I cannot allow whatever you're going to do, don't you?" Jon said, his voice calm and low.

The man's reaction was not what anyone had expected. His smile slipped a bit, then a chuckle escaped his lips, followed by a snort, then a laugh, then a full-blown guffaw. He howled with derision, his glee echoing around the sterile chamber. When he finally got himself back

under control, he wiped his tear-filled eyes and took a
deep breath.

"That is the funniest thing I've heard in the past three
centuries, you know that? Especially coming from you.
'Whatever I'm going to do,' indeed. You have no idea
what I'm planning, and that scares you, doesn't it? You
were pathetic during your entire life, and you're just as
pathetic now. Served you right to rot in Geiststadt all
those years, stuck, just as I was.

"I see you've found two new patsies to dance to your
tune. What story did you feed them? I hardly had to do
anything, and Mason was eating out of my hand. His
wife didn't succumb to my charms, but soon it won't
matter anyway. I didn't even take her life, although
Mason wanted me to."

It sounded like Jon was about to say something else,
but the black-haired man held up his hand. "NO! You
will listen to me, with none of your whining."

With a visible show of self-control, the stranger in
Mason's body continued. "You see, this—all this, the
buildings, the people, the hectic pace you people call life
today," he said, gesturing around. "For more than three
hundred years I've watched this city grow, growing,
expanding, swelling, and always I was helpless to do
anything but watch. Never able to grasp a piece of it, to
claim what was rightfully mine, not while I was alive,
and even more so once I was dead. Everyone else took
what they wanted, power, money, status, fame, and I
was always on the outside, looking in. You never
understood either, too wrapped up in your own petty
concerns to see the big picture."

"People can change, brother," Jon said.

"Yes, people can change, that's good, that's very good, I see you have learned something in all those decades of imprisonment," the man said.

"What's he talking about, Jon?" Shizume asked. "Who is that?"

Jon didn't reply, but the man did. Her question sent him into peals of hysterical laughter once more. Ryan and Shizume had no choice but to stand motionless in their energy prisons and listen to him cackle. Although Shizume tried to contact Ryan, she couldn't speak to him at all. Jon's next words, however, commanded her full attention.

"Shizume, Ryan, I would like to introduce you both to my brother, Thomas Noir."

CHAPTER EIGHTEEN

O h, the secret's out!" Thomas said, clapping his hands as he strode closer to the frozen pair. "And when I discovered that this energy field blocks everything *inside* it as well as out, the trap I could set was just too perfect.

"The blood in the canopic jar that Mason so lovingly safeguarded all these years was *mine*, Thomas, not our dearly departed father's," Thomas continued. "Callie had been taking blood from both of us, on Father's orders. I found his jars after his—untimely death, and I filled it with my own blood, so when poor Mason read the will, he thought he would be bringing Benjamin back. He got quite a surprise.

"But now, besides the delicious thrill of actually *being* in a body again, especially one as well cared for as this one," he paused, stretching both arms high above his head. "I had forgotten how wonderful that feels. Where was I? Ah yes, my plans have worked out perfectly. I'm the most powerful man in the world, I have a gorgeous wife—" he looked back over his shoulder, the expression on his face truly evil when he turned back "—whom I'm looking forward to getting to know intimately, and I'm in control of the largest company in the world.

"Obviously I've got a lot of catching up to do, but I'm looking forward to continuing the work my great-great grandson started," Thomas said. "He's got a lot of the planet under his thumb, and I intend to finish what he's started. And since I can clone myself, I've got all the time in the world to do it.

"There just remains the matter of what to do with you two," Thomas said, his wolfish smile now a terrible sight to behold. "I think a terrible, terrible accident is going to occur, and in all this destruction, who's going to notice two more bodies—"

"NO!" The scream in Shizume's mind was psyche-shattering, but she still couldn't move, couldn't scream, couldn't do anything in response. All she could do was cry at the incredible pain knifing through her body. Every nerve, ever synapse in her body was on fire from the deepest emotional pain she had ever experienced. There was a wrench in her mind, and Shizume watched as a stream of misty white vapor coalesced from her eyes and mouth in front of her, passing through the energy barrier unimpeded.

"Oh, Jon, I seem to have hit a nerve, didn't I?" Thomas said. "Apparently that barrier doesn't hold *everything* in. Well, what are you going to do about it?"

In answer, the white mist streamed towards Mason/Thomas's body, swirling around him. Thomas watched as a vaporous tendril reached out and touched him, then began flowing into his body.

The expression on Mason/Thomas's face changed from

arrogance to shock to fear. "Jon—what are you—wait, you—you can't—you can't do this—YOU CAN'T!—"

Mason's body fell to its knees, his mouth locked open in a silent rictus of agony as the two Noir brothers battled for control inside him. Fingers curled into talons clawed at his head, as if trying to scrape whatever was going on his mind out. He stiffened, his back arching in one huge convulsive shock, then toppled over, several drops of blood dripping from his nose.

"Ryan? Cn U heer me?" Shizume said as loudly as she could through her frozen lips. There was still no answer. She was about to try again when she saw something that made her effort trail off before she had even begun.

Mason's body twitched, then rolled over onto its back. His arms flopped around, the fingers twitching as they scrabbled against the floor. He pushed himself up and raised his head, the scratch marks and bloody nose at odds with the calm look on his face. He stared at his arms and hands as if he had never seen them before, then touched his face, running his fingers over his features, testing their solidity.

"Oh, Go—oh, God, the feeling of a body again," said a voice that wasn't Thomas's. "He should have remembered that I was always stronger."

Jon? Shizume thought.

He turned to look at her, his eyes shining with concentrated power. "Oh, Shizume, I had forgotten what is was like just to breathe again."

Something about the tone of his voice made Shizume uneasy. *That—that's great, Jon. Can you get us out of here?*

Mason/Jon put a finger to his lips, as if thinking about

her request. Shizume frowned. *What's to think about?* she wondered.

"I—I'm sorry, Shizume, I appreciate all you've done for me, but I'm afraid I cannot do that," Jon said.

What! Shizume thought. *Why not?*

"Because you aren't going to like what I have to do, and I'm afraid I might have to hurt you if you tried to stop me," Jon said.

"You see, this—all this, the buildings, the people, the wanton destruction you people call life today," he said, gesturing at the windows and the rows of buildings surrounding them. "For more than three hundred years I've had to watch this—plague of a city grow like a cancer, spill over its banks time and time again, expanding, swelling, consuming, destroying, and always I was helpless to do anything about it but watch. My home, flooded and built over, buried like it never existed, then built up more and more, always people building, like ants, creating mindlessly, with no real concept, no thought of what they were doing. Just like you, I'm afraid. You see, my brother never understood either, he was too wrapped up in his own petty concerns to see the 'big picture,' as he called it."

Jon turned back from the window, his voice flat. "After all those centuries, all that time watching all of you, I've come to the realization that there must be a change. The world must be set on a different course. And I alone have the ability to do that. Now that I have the body of a 13th generation Noir, I'm going to use it to the fullest," Jon said.

Jon, you can't mean this— Shizume began. *What about*

what we've been through together—how we fought to get here?

"You're right, Shizume, and I will always remember you for the ultimate sacrifice you made for this world," Jon replied. "Don't think I haven't thought this through, but there has to be sacrifice made to save the rest of the world as well. You and Ryan did better than I ever could have imagined—you got me here, now I'm going to take care of the rest.

"I've got the chance to set things right, from the very beginning," Jon continued. "I'm going back to the start of it all, that June day in 1842, the day of our birth. They thought that snowstorm was something, well wait until they get a load of me. Once there, I'll ensure that *I'm* born first. I'll be the thirteenth son, the *true* thirteenth son, in name as well as order, and then I'll learn everything I can from Father, but he won't get me like he thought he was going to do with Thomas. No, I'll sire my thirteen sons afterward and live forever. I'll be the one in control, first Geistad, then New York, then America itself.

"And all *this*—" Jon said, throwing his arms wide to encompass the Greater New York skyline "—waste, this pollution, this overcrowding, this unthinking human expansion—all of it will be controlled. There won't be the pitiful ghettos, the poverty, the rampant violence, the races turned against each other, all of that will be gone as well. *I* will rewrite history and reshape the world as it should be, not the pathetic squandering of this land's glorious natural resources that has gone unchecked for the past centuries."

Jon—is that even possible? Shizume asked, still numbed by the announcement that the person she had put her faith in from the beginning had been deceiving her with every word he said.

"Possible? Possible!" Jon said. "You're all going to find out it is more than possible, it is going to happen. My powers will protect all of us, and you'll have a front row seat to the reshaping of history."

Shizume tried to turn her head, but the field held her tight in its invisible grip. In the background she heard a faint voice she thought might have been Thomas (*Ryan?*) trying to reason with his brother, but it was like he was speaking with his mouth stuffed full of cotton. Time itself seemed to slow, with Mason/Jon's frenetic pacing and gestures now sluggish, drawn-out. Shizume looked past Jon's face and locked eyes with the woman trapped in the fluid-filled chamber on the far side of the room. Through the clear gel she saw the woman's eyes widen, and heard one thought:

It's coming.

Before Shizume could ask *What's coming?*, she felt the floor shift under her, just a fraction, and then she knew.

Oh, God. Another wave.

The tremor hit the building like a cosmic bowling ball hurled right down the middle of Greater New York City, and cracks immediately sprouted across the walls and ceiling. Jon reacted first, throwing out his arm as if to stop the damage and shouting "No!"

The NoirCorp building had been constructed of the strongest, highest-tensile materials known to man in the

22nd century. Earthquake and tidal wave-proof, the composite layers of plasteel and ceramic-bonded beams and framework could even serve as a radiation shelter at a mile from ground zero if needed. But the forces arrayed against it this time were space and time incarnate, against which nothing can stand forever. To its architects' and engineers' credit, however, it did last long enough for Jon to stabilize his floor and the rest of the building below.

The cracks in the laboratory walls widened, the room splitting in half diagonally. But it wasn't just the room, Shizume realized—

—*it's the entire building,* she thought.

For the next few seconds, the shrieks of overstressed girders and tearing of molecular bonds was all that could be heard as the top portion of the building groaned and shifted, slipping off its underpinnings, grinding fractured plasteel against glasteel windows, which bucked and spider-webbed, transforming into opaque sculptures of disaster. There was little debris; the materials used in the building's construction weren't designed to splinter or crumble. Once joined, they hadn't really been designed to come apart at all.

Through all of this Shizume watched, still encased in her damnable prison. She saw Jon throw his arms up, and the top portion of the building actually *moved* when he did, rising off the lower portion of the stratoscraper for a moment, then settling back. Behind him she saw the chamber holding the woman pop open, spilling her and the liquid onto the floor. A wordless shriek from Jon brought her attention back to him, and she saw him, quivering and enraged, actually *push* the top section of the building off the bottom, tipping it like a person would pop open a chugpak top to pour out the liquid inside. Only Jon simply pushed the top away, sending it plummeting down to the ocean far below. As it flipped end over end, she caught a glimpse of tiny exposure-suited men flung into the atmosphere with it, next to a flash of whirling energy windmills, still beating the air as if they were trying to propel the top floor of the building back to its rightful place.

The bright afternoon sun flooded the now ceilingless laboratory, and Shizume saw the damage the wave had wreaked on the other buildings surrounding them, twisting and bending them like plastic toys assaulted by a demented giant five-year-old. The building they had seen that male model on just that morning was now a grotesque parody of architecture, the ravaged remains of the Trident Tower stretched and bent into an unrecognizable mass. The top fifty floors of another building she didn't recognize slowly topped over, its middle section squeezed into a solid cylinder of ceramic, plasteel, and plasglass, unable to support the upper floors.

The wind roared into the uncovered lab, howling everywhere and sending the temperature plunging one hundred degrees in a matter of seconds. Jon stood only a few feet away from the jagged edge of the building's end, his arms outstretched again, soaking it all in. Try as she might, Shizume couldn't help but shiver as the gusts tore at her clothes and skin. It was only then that she realized what had changed.

I'm not held anymore, she thought. *The power must be off, and with it the energy field.*

"Appropriate, don't you think?" Jon screamed, his voice knifing through the gale. "Just like a certain birthday a long time ago."

Shizume risked edging her head to the left so she could look at Ryan, who still looked frozen. *Oh, come on, if you're not free, I can't stop him by myself,* she thought.

Jon walked over to Ryan's still form. "I'm so glad you can see this, brother. Everything you've strived for all these centuries ends today." He swung a fist, ready to knock Ryan off the building.

Shaking her head, Shizume saw a gust of white vapor eddy around Ryan's still-frozen form. At the same time, his hand flashed up and caught Jon's descending fist. "All those times you tried to stop me in the past," he said, his voice an eerie blend of Thomas's and his own, "And now I must stop you."

"You cannot stop this, fool," Jon rasped, twisting out of Ryan's grasp. "Look around you, it has already begun."

As soon as the words were out of his mouth, the wind died around them, and the clouds flashed by them, accelerated like Jon had pressed fast forward on a worldwide remote control. But the clouds weren't growing, they were shrinking, and the sun, the brilliant sun—

The sun is going backward, Shizume thought, watching the golden orb settled toward the eastern horizon. The red and gold fingers of dawn receded over the edge of the ocean, plunging the ruined city into darkness. Seconds later the sun popped up in the west and arced across the sky again, moving faster and faster, light and dark alternating until time was flowing by so fast that day and night were indistinguishable, blending into a pale gray.

The weather changed as well, with thunderheads reforming out of flashes of bridging rainbows and rain flowing back up into the sky, swelling the dark gray cloud systems even further. Lightning surged across the sky in brilliant strobes, casting its own brief flashes of silver light against the grayness. Occasionally streaks of pale or deep blue sky could be seen as summers passed in blinks of an eye. Alternately, winters appeared in an instant, layering the city in deep, pillowy mantles of snow, turning the streets and buildings of Greater New York into a white-blanketed wonderland for several seconds until the season passed. Throughout it all, flocks of sub-orbital aircraft soared backwards, returning to their starting points either coming into or climbing away from the city.

Most shocking of all was how the city itself began to change, unraveling before her eyes. Much like the holographic projection she had watched with her grandfather, but instead of building, the city started shrinking, construction hovercraft removing bits and pieces of the stratoscrapers and blockpartments a bit at a time, constant swarms of machinery tearing the buildings down instead of building them up. Around them all were hundreds of thousands of Zippers, resurrected to do what they had done for decades, carry the millions of people living, loving, working, fighting, dying, surviving in the city every day. As she watched, a stratoscraper grew shorter and shorter, slowly disintegrating from the relentless assault of builders unbuilding, of plasteel beams and electroglass windows and supplies removed instead of installed, leaving instead of arriving.

Do they have any idea what is happening to them right

now? Shizume wondered. *Do they know that their lives are being unwritten day by day, minute by minute?*

"Shizume, is that your name?" a new voice asked in her head.

Who's there? she replied, looking around. Jon was gone. She couldn't feel his presence at all anymore. When she saw the other woman looking at her while struggling to crawl around the sheared off glasteel barrier of the lab, she knew who was speaking. Shizume threw a glance at Jon and Ryan/Thomas to find them frozen in time, struggling with each other in silence, muscles straining as each sought to overcome his opponent.

"Please, hurry, there isn't much time," the woman said. *"I—am Antonia Derlicht. You must help me stop them."*

Stop both of them? Shizume replied, scrambling to help her around the barrier. *Isn't Jon the danger now?*

"The danger lies in both of them," Antonia said. *"Thomas says he wants to stop Jon, and I'm sure he does, but he will grab that power just as quickly if Jon is vanquished. No matter who wins, either one would create the world they want the most, and I'm afraid that this reality would be destroyed in the process. Now that Mason is—is—"*

I'm sorry, Shizume said. *Is there any way I can help?*

"We have to find a way to stop both of them," Antonia replied. *"And I think I know how to do it—but I'll need to use your power. I'm sorry, this might be a little uncomfortable—"*

Shizume suddenly saw herself from where Antonia was sitting on the floor, superimposed over her view of

Antonia below her, the two images blurring together. Startled for a moment, she blinked and looked away, but that just made it worse, the walls tilting crazily around her from two different viewpoints and who knew how many dimensions.

"Try to relax—that's better—it might help to close your eyes," Antonia said.

Shizume did, and found she was now just seeing the other woman's viewpoint. *Yes, that is better. Now what?*

"Now I have to call on an old relative," Antonia said. *"Brace yourself, this isn't going to be pleasant."*

Shizume scrunched up, but the call that reverberated through her brain felt like it was going to erupt through the top of her skull. *"AGATHA!"*

"My dear, there is no need to shout. I'm right here," another voice, this one cool and commanding, said.

"Here's your one chance, old woman, but we're coming with you to make sure this is done right, and you don't have a choice in the matter," Antonia said.

"Perish the thought. I'll need both of you there anyway," Agatha replied, then addressed Shizume. *"I'm Agatha Derlicht, the matriarch of my family many years ago."*

Shizume Mader, nee Noir, Shizume replied.

"Oh, you poor girl," Agatha said. *"I do hope this isn't too hard on you."*

"Enough with the chit-chat, let's go," Antonia said. *"Shizume, open your eyes."*

Shizume did so and now saw an iron-haired woman in an ancient long dress hovering over a featureless gray plane. Next to her was the woman she had helped, Antonia, a fierce expression simmering on her otherwise beautiful features.

Where are we? she asked.

"One could say we're in the landscape of the mind," Agatha replied. *"This is a realm that is normally outside time and space, which has now partly encroached on the physical world and caused all kinds of trouble."*

So that's what's caused the ripples in my city? Shizume asked.

"Yes, partly, the other part is that damnable deceiving Noir trying to come back to life," Antonia said. *"I can see their battleground over there. Let's get to them before they do even more damage."*

The three women linked hands and flew over to the area Antonia had pointed out, which was lit by flashes of light and strange sonic anomalies that made no noise yet shook the air around them.

"Mm, you have a good deal of untapped power," Agatha said to Shizume. *"Between the three of us, we should be able to subdue them. Then leave it to me. I've had three centuries to undo what they've done, and I know exactly how to handle this."*

"Remember, Agatha, we'll be watching you every step of the way, so make sure you do just that," Antonia replied.

"Naturally. Now if we do not hurry, we will miss our chance," Agatha said. *"After this, I will be done forever."*

The trio floated closer to the region, and now Shizume could catch a glimpse of what was over there. Thomas/Ryan and Jon/Mason had squared off, both still fighting, each only having eyes for the other. Around them eddied strange bits and fragments of other places, other times. As Shizume watched, things and people appeared, then disappeared just as quickly. A sobbing man sat in the ruins of a ravaged city, a tall pile of thick books at his side and a pair of thick, shattered glasses on his lap...a hospital room solidified into view, with a bandage-wrapped patient being attended by two of the ugliest physicians Shizume had ever seen, in fact, she couldn't even be sure they were human...a sweating, exhausted-looking man staggered around a strange square platform enclosed by three ropes, bulbous gloves of some kind on his hands, trying to avoid the relentless blows of what looked to her like an early *Sapien*-model human class robot...the gray plain around them changed to a bucolic suburban neighborhood Shizume had only seen in tri-documentaries, its quiet peacefulness shattered by a screaming, crazed mob pointing at one house, then another, and in every building they pointed to, the lights flashed on, then off, then on again...

What's happening here? Shizume asked.

"Surely you don't think your reality is the only dimension this place intersects, do you?" Agatha said. *"There are more things in heaven and earth, Shizume, than are dreamt of in your philosophy."*

Hamlet said it better, Shizume replied.

"But Shakespeare's point is well taken, and where we are is, in fact, one of those things," Agatha said. *"And right now, we're about to go to another."*

A few meters away, Jon broke Thomas's hold on him just as another scene appeared, this one of an old, wood-paneled room with a blazing stone fireplace in the wall and oil lamps casting a warm cheery glow. Inside, a tall, bearded man paced back and forth, occasionally casting concerned glances towards a room where strange sounds were emanating from, groans and labored cries, and a language unlike anything Shizume had ever heard. As soon he saw the scene appear, Jon ran for it, diving into the room with Thomas right behind.

"Now," Antonia said. *"Quickly!"*

The three women stepped into the picture, and Shizume was surprised at the smells and textures after the blankness of the gray plane. The wood fire popped and crackled, throwing off heat she could feel even from where she stood. She heard the wind roaring outside, and what sounded like hail rattling across the roof, even though a wooden block calendar on the wall read June 21st. The man continued pacing, walking right between Antonia and her ancestor without noticing either of them.

"Come on, we're going to lose them," Antonia said, grabbing Shizume's hand and dragging her towards the closed oaken door. When she saw the other woman wasn't going to stop, Shizume threw up her arms to protect her head—

—only to pass completely through the door as if it wasn't there. This room was smaller, darker, the only light provided by a guttering candle that twisted the shadows of the three people in the room into misshapen inky blotches. The place smelled of sweat, blood, and the heavy, cloying scent of some kind of burned herbs.

A young woman on her back in a small bed took up most of the available space, her swollen, flushed stomach heaving erratically. On one side was a middle-aged woman in a stained cotton skirt and sweat-soaked blouse, her sleeves rolled up and arms wet to the elbow. On the other side was the woman tending the burning herbs, a tiny, wizened thing, her face a mass of wrinkles. However old she looked, her eyes gleamed deep with intelligence, and the cadence of the singsong foreign language she was chanting never paused for a moment.

"Come on, Gretchen, you have to bear down, your children must come out. Now when I say, push!" the midwife said.

"I've...been pushing...for eight hours...now...these *verdammt* sons of his won't come," the prone woman gasped, squeezing the mid-wife's hand in a grip of iron. "Ah, *Gott*, they're like to tear me apart!"

Near her, wreathed in the shadows cast by the candle, the insubstantial figures of Jon and Thomas Noir watched the struggle of their own birth, both seemingly oblivious to the other.

"Now, now is the time to strike, when their attention is diverted— " Antonia said, moving forward.

Wait, wait a flash—I mean a second, Shizume said, trying to remember the garbled message her grandfather had tried to tell her. *Possession—switching bodies—Jon going back—*

No, she said. *We have to wait. Just a little bit longer.*

"If we wait much longer we'll miss this chance altogether," Agatha protested.

Trust me, it's almost here, Shizume said. *Jon talked about going back and changing the past so that he would be first, but he has to actually be in this time to do it. Well, I know what he's going to do.*

"Ready, Gretchen? Three, two, one. Push, girl, push;" the midwife said, positioning herself to assist the first child out. "Send them on their way."

"I'm *trying*," Gretchen spat, her huge abdomen shuddering as she strained. The other woman attempted to wipe the sweat from her brow, but Gretchen shrieked at her to get away. And still the shrunken crone never stopped her ominous chanting.

Gretchen heaved her bulk up, then bore down with all the might she had left. The crone looked on and increased the tempo of her chant. Apparently that was what the brothers had been waiting for, because they drifted up to Gretchen's gritted mouth and, transubstantiating into columns of slender white vapor, began insinuating themselves into her, riding her breath into her body.

Now—we go now, Shizume said. *One of you take us all inside,*

"Are you both sure you want to come along?" Agatha asked. *"What you are going to experience will not be easy."*

Shizume and Antonia exchanged glances, then both nodded.

"Very well, this is my *domain,"* Agatha said, gripping the two other women by the elbows. *"What do they say at the* doktor's—*ah yes, just try to relax."*

Shizume looked at her, but it was already too late. With a shock, she realized that her body was fading to that same ethereal mist into which the brothers had transformed themselves. *Oh, this part I didn't think through—*

But it was too late. As they went, Shizume thought

she saw the old black woman's eyes widen in surprise, but then she was inside another living person's body. Shizume, Agatha, and Antonia were drawn past the teeth, down the throat and esophagus, and into her stomach.

"This way," Agatha said, taking them all past the lining of the stomach and the uterine wall, into the distended womb itself. Both babies were there, and so were the spirits of Jon and Thomas, both still fighting each other. Below everything, Shizume could hear that endless chanting, reverberating through her bones, affecting her more on an instinctual than intellectual level. Suddenly she was filled with the desire to push toward the bottom, where the opening was, to escape this dark chamber—

"I thought this might happen," Agatha said, her thoughts snapping Shizume out of her temporary hypnosis. *"They are both trying to accomplish different goals. Thomas wants to possess Jon's body for the power he holds, while Jon just needs to destroy Thomas's infant form so he can be the true 13th son. So, while they squabble, we go—"*

"But, they are just infants—" Antonia began.

"Remember what these 'infants' are doing to your world," Agatha replied. *"We end it here, now, forever."*

Agatha floated to the other body and tried to flow into it but was repelled. *"Hmm, this child is stronger that I thought."* She tried again, with the same results.

"Agatha, what's the problem?" Antonia asked.

"I am having difficulty entering this child," she replied. *"Both of you, come here. We will all have to enter him at the same time. He will not be able to fend the three of us off simultaneously. Are you ready?"*

"*Y-Yes, I am ready,*" Antonia said, although her words quavered a bit.

Shizume looked down at the two infants jostling each other beneath her. *Do they know what their destiny is?* she thought. *How can two babies be responsible for so much destruction?* Then she remembered the fallen Zippers, the ruined buildings, the smoking New York skyline. *All of that was caused by them, millions of lives lost because of them—*

Let's do it, she said, her voice steel.

"*All right,*" Antonia replied. "*On my mark. Drei...zwei...ein...now.*"

Shizume flowed down towards the first infant, following the streams of Agatha and Antonia. The babe moved its head around, struggling against this new enemy, but the three women were everywhere, its nose, its mouth. She heard the chanting take on a faster pitch, the words echoing all around her. The child's tiny hands tried to ward them off, but it was too late. Agatha curled into him and displaced his infant consciouness, sending a wisp of soul drifting aimlessly away, leaving only dying flesh behind.

"*Now the other one,*" Agatha said.

The three women began to move towards the other child but now were stopped by another stream of white vapor. Its features solidified into a face Shizume recognized—

Jon...

"*Shizume, don't let them do this,*" Jon said. "*Thomas is gone now, thanks to you. I can remake the world into*

*a better place, just let me take this child and do what I
was meant to do—"*

And what is that—destroy my entire world? Shizume
said. *No way,* brother.

"*I can hold him off,*" Agatha said. "*You two take care
of the child.*"

"NO! I WILL BE BORN! I WILL HAVE WHAT IS
MINE!" Jon's insensate rage buffeted the three of them
like a tidal wave, tossing them around in the womb. His
face began to distort and grow, becoming a grotesque
parody of his normal features. From far off, they heard
a longer, gutteral scream that shook the very walls of
the womb.

"*Go! Now!*" Agatha said, interposing herself between
Jon and Antonia and Shizume. "I don't know how long
I can stop him!"

"*Good-bye,* großmutter," Antonia said, her voice
breaking.

"*Good-bye,* enkelin," was all Agatha had time to say
before a furious Jon Noir swarmed over her.

Shizume guided Antonia to the other infant, both of
them not looking back as a high, keening sound of agony
reverberated in their minds.

Go, go, don't stop, don't look back! Shizume said. The
child they sped towards seemed to be just as disoriented
as they were. It offered almost no resistance as they
entered into its mind.

"Noooooooooo!" Shizume heard both in the child's
mind and outside as they separated the child's consciousness from its body. At last, that infernal chanting fell
silent.

Trying to cling to each other, Shizume and Antonia floated back out of Gretchen, streaming from her mouth and nose as the woman gasped and bucked, a wordless scream coming out of her mouth along with them.

"Oh, *mein Gott*, the pain! What is happening!" Gretchen screamed. The midwife had disappeared between her legs, and as Shizume drifted away she could see the outline of a head press against the wall of Gretchen's abdomen, then receding back.

"One more time—push!" the midwife cried, but Gretchen was beyond hearing. The old woman was shaking her head, and her thin lips were set in silent disapproval. The midwife's head popped up, a look of utter terror on her face, then ducked back down again.

For her part, Shizume was just glad to resume her own body again. *I think we need to go, now,* she said to Antonia.

"Yes, we should leave," Antonia replied, looking exhausted by what they had just seen.

As they drifted towards the door, there was a commotion behind them. Unable to resist, Shizume looked back to see Gretchen convulsing on the bed, her limbs flailing helplessly. The midwife was trying to calm her down with no success, and her entreaties to the black woman for help went unheeded. The old woman got up, doused the smoking herbs in water and headed for the door, oblivious to the midwife's cries.

When she opened the door, Shizume guided Antonia through into the larger room. The old man rushed up, the look on his face one of mingled anticipation and dread. "Where is my son?" he rasped.

The old woman just shook her head and shuffled to a vacant rocking chair near the roaring fire.

The man's mouth opened and closed, but nothing came out. He ran into the birthing room, and Shizume heard the midwife attempt to explain, then she fell silent. Moments later a wordless keening began low, then rose to a banshee wail. The midwife scuttled out of the room on her hands and knees, then scrambled to her feet and ran out of the room, followed by the brief sound of a vicious wind elsewhere in the house, then the slamming of a heavy door.

The old woman stood by the fire, muttering something. The door to the chamber slammed open, and the man staggered out, looking like he had aged twenty years in the last two minutes. His hands went to his face, and he tore at his beard, the stones clacking madly as he did so. Not watching where he walked, he stumbled against the table, knocking over the oil lamp on it, which shattered and flared into bright flames.

"Over—it's all over—" he kept mumbling. "Never have thirteen again—my son—my vessel is gone—it's all over!"

The old woman stabbed forked fingers at him, then proclaimed something loudly in a language that had never been spoken in North America and never would be again. Pulling her shawl around her shoulders, she shuffled off to the kitchen, leaving the man to his despair.

The liquid flames had dripped off the table onto the rug, and now the entire room was aflame. The man stood in the middle of the conflagration, mumbling and laughing wildly to himself. When the walls went up, he screamed once, then ran from the room.

Shizume couldn't help herself; she followed him

through a hallway and into a foyer, where a thick oak door stood ajar, revealing a blinding blizzard, the wind whipping heavy sheets of snow and hail into a wall of white. The man didn't seem to see it but plunged outside, heedless of the terrible weather that engulfed him, obscuring him from view in a matter of a dozen steps.

Antonia, we have to go now, Shizume said. *Help me find the way back, please.*

"*It will happen automatically, although I don't know what kind of world we'll be returning to,*" she replied. Antonia drew her close, and the two women held fast to each other as the disaster faded around them into a now comforting grayness.

Shizume looked around, only to see the gray plane on all sides, stretching off into infinity. There was no room, there were no other dimensions, everything was gone. There was nothing but the two of them, alone. Antonia lolled next to her, apparently unconscious.

Antonia...Antonia, wake up, you have to help me. I can't find the way back by myself, Shizume said, panic stabbing through her. *Grandfather—Ryan—anyone!* she called out.

A faint voice answered her. "*Antonia...my love...where are you...?*"

Who's there? Shizume asked, whirling around in the grayness.

"*There...she is...my beloved...*" An indistinct form appeared from the shadows; one second he wasn't there, the next second he was. The immaculately dressed man shambled towards her. Ordinarily he would have been handsome, with thick black hair and classically strong features. His eyes, however, revealed a tragically different story.

Mason? Is—is that you? What happened? Shizume asked.

He looked up to stare at her. *"Reality happened...that's what. Fate, if you will, happened."* He reached out a translucent hand to brush an unconscious Antonia's hair away from her face. *"Even to the last...she was right...she knew what could happen...she tried to warn me...but I didn't listen...so sure I was right—and now it's too late—she's won, you see."*

He's—a spirit—trapped in here now, Shizume thought. *Who's won?* she asked.

"Agatha Derlicht," Mason replied, his features twisting into a parody of hatred as he spoke her name. He kept staring down at his wife, one manicured hand stroking her hair, just gazing at her, entranced.

There was a flash of white light in the distance, and faintly, as if carried on the wind, Shizume heard a woman's elderly, mocking laughter echo through the silence.

Apparently Mason heard it as well, for he cocked his ear, then looked up at her. The tenderness that had marked his face was gone now, replaced with a hard stare frightening in its intensity. *"She thinks she can beat me that easily, does she?"* he said. *"I can hurt her too. Just watch me."*

Mason reached for Antonia's throat with both hands and began to squeeze. His arms were still translucent, but now his hands had become very real indeed. Antonia's face turned a mottled pink, then redder.

Stop it! Shizume said, trying to wrench the unconscious woman away from her homicidal husband. Mason's face was set in that fearsome grimace as he came after her again, fingers curved into wicked claws.

A dull rumbling, the sound somehow echoing across the vast plane, reached her ears. *What was that?* Shizume cried, looking around as she tried to evade the psychotic man. With her burden, however, she couldn't outpace him. There was nowhere to hide, all around them was featureless gray, stretching to the horizon.

Wait, she thought. *Something's out there. Something's—ulp!*

Mason, uncaring, had caught up with her, his fingers wrapping around her own throat. *"I'll have my revenge,"* Mason howled like a man possessed. *"First you, then her! Agatha, watch what I'm doing now!"*

He's completely mad, Shizume thought. She wanted to fight him off, but something inside her told her to keep holding on to Antonia. Even though Mason was throttling her with all his might, it didn't seem to be affecting her at all. *Or maybe this is the final euphoric stage before I suffocate,* she thought.

The distant line she had spotted grew larger, speeding toward her. Shizume stared in horror as it got close enough for her to see what it was.

A boiling, churning barrage of black, lightning-pierced nothingness as high as the gray sky screamed towards her. The wind it pushed before it buffeted her, but she didn't move an inch. The furious, screaming wave loomed over her, lit from within by the crackling electricity. It seemed to pause for a second, a flat wall that had somehow come alive, and was savoring the moment before it engulfed them.

Mason had been so engrossed in killing her that he hadn't paid attention to the void until it was on top of them. He looked behind him, then looked again, his mouth opening in a silent scream as the wall inexorably advanced on them both.

When it touched him, Mason's body turned translucent, then misty, then dissipated. First his foot, then his leg, then his torso and arms, followed by his chest and head, from the back to the front. Shizume's last glimpse of him was a screaming face, locked in unimaginable torment.

The wall of energy curled over her like a monstrous black wave breaking on a gray shore. Shizume's last thought before the roiling wall swallowed them all was *What happens now?*

CHAPTER NINETEEN

"—what happens now?"

The words shocked Antonia out of her reverie. "I'm sorry." She turned from the window and looked back at the young woman sitting on the other side of her long, low desk. A steaming cup of tea sat beside the dark-haired reporter, her transpad cocked to capture Antonia's next words. "I'm afraid I didn't catch that."

"Well, after all the strides in technology, medicine, world agritech, conservation, communications, and space exploration, what's next on Derlicht Haus's agenda?"

Antonia looked around her office as if seeing it for the first time, impossible, of course, since she had spent the majority of her waking hours here for the past five decades. Everything about it, from the abstract Mekquon Te'lail antigravity sculpture hovering near the vaulted ceiling and lit by artificial sunlight to her one concession, an antique desk made out of a slab of polished granite, to the heated café au lait carpeting she often paced in bare feet while negotiating multi-billion dollar contracts with suppliers, contractors, and the government, everything spoke of subtle power combined with consummate elegance. Even her own clothes, a shimmering zero-gee wraparound silk suit from the designer Chrétian Luna, announced her success wherever she went, to whomever she met.

And yet, there was another time...a time of fear and fire...

Shaking off her temporary fugue, Antonia Derlicht steepled her fingers while she considered her answer. She reviewed her life as if seeing a tri-documentary of it, remembering trading her studies in folklore and ethnic history for a career where she could actually make a difference in the world. Her multiple degrees in business, bioscience, and law had served her well in her forty-year rise to the top. Of course, there had been the Derlicht fortune to help her along, but Antonia had been the one to bring it into full flower many years ago, and now she and the world were both reaping the benefits.

She glanced back at the shimmering ocean, the sunlight winking like thousands of diamonds scattered on the water. Looking down, she could see the busy streets of New York City, hydrogen and solar hover cars, buses, and personal craft flowing through the three levels of surface traffic, while personal aircraft whizzed by, all guided by the electronic heart of the seven kilometer long floating city, one of several built more than one hundred years ago over the submerged remains of the old New York City. The citizens that had returned had renamed much of the local areas, but the names of the boroughs and the city itself had stayed the same, as had one other place.

"I could quote you chapter and verse on the dozens of projects we have going, but you can get that through the research link we'll set you up with to complete your story," Antonia said. "But I'd rather answer your question with a true thought. A philosopher said long ago, 'Those who do not remember the past are condemned to repeat it.'

"George Santayana, I believe," the young woman said, tucking an errant coil of night-black hair behind one ear.

Although Antonia did not consider herself lacking in looks, she found herself admiring the young lady's smooth café au lait skin and expressive eyes. Her hairstyle was parceled into hundreds of tiny braids, a style that Antonia knew was the current fashion rage and which she had even considered getting herself. Her silk-suit was off-the-rack but well maintained, and she wore an accenting scarf that was fairly costly, Antonia knew, because she owned a controlling interest in the weaver's collective that made them. *A woman on her way up,* she thought.

"Very good," Antonia said, nodding. "I believe in that maxim, and after seeing it come true more often than not, have always examined the past before moving forward. There is a very rich history here, Ms. Mader. Although the city of Geistad has seen many changes over the last several hundred years, it still lives on, in the hearts of the people who live here, and in the streets we all call home. That, more than anything, I think, is what drives us forward."

A wood-walled room with an old man pacing the floor—some kind of disturbance in an adjoining room—a woman's scream?

Antonia shook her head and focused her attention on the other woman. "No matter what Derlicht Haus turns its attention to in the future, we will do so while keeping an eye on the past and remaining at the forefront of innovation." *Wow, did that sound canned,* she thought. *I've got to leverage a vacation sometime. I'm sure Mason, Alec, and Leah wouldn't mind.* "Is there anything else you'd like to ask?"

"I just have one more question," the woman said, rising to her feet and walking across the office to a framed painting floating in front of the wall. "I couldn't help noticing this—unique piece of art on the wall. I hope you won't mind my saying so, but it doesn't seem to blend with the rest of your décor. Is there a story behind it?"

Antonia came around the desk and walked over to stand beside the young woman. She gazed up at the painting, a study of a sprawling mansion going up in a large fire, its wings and roof consumed by the greedy flames. Even though the sun peeked out from behind a dark cloud, the rest of the sky was obscured by a powerful snowstorm lashing the conflagration, the strange juxtaposition of weather lending a surreal tone to the otherwise realistic picture.

"I'm not really sure," she replied. "It's called *The Fire at Noir Manor* and is based on a legendary disaster that happened more than three centuries ago when there was a snowstorm in Geistad, then called Geiststadt, in June of 1821.

"It's been in my family for generations. It's hundreds of years old, but we don't know who painted it, or exactly when it was finished. Despite its dark subject matter, it's come to symbolize good fortune for my family over the decades, and one of my relatives has always hung it on a wall in their business. A few years ago it was my turn, and it's been here ever since."

"Fascinating, and still keeping with your philosophy of looking back while looking forward?" the other woman asked.

"Yes, something like that," Antonia replied, staring harder at the painting. She squinted for a moment, trying to see through the wind-whipped snow. *Did the door of the mansion just open?* She wondered. *Did I just see a small man stagger out into the snow?* For a second she thought she could actually hear the howling wind, rising and blending with a cry of mortal agony. The painting seemed to shift again, the snow whipping around as the little man disappeared into the blizzard—

"Antonia?" the reporter asked.

As quickly as the moment came, it was gone. "Oh, I'm sorry," she said, her perfectly manicured fingers rubbing her temple. "Was there anything else you wanted to ask?"

"No, I think that should do it for, now. No doubt I've taken up too much of your time anyway," the woman said. "I may have a few follow up questions tomorrow, but we can handle those by viewphone."

"Please, don't worry about it," Antonia said. "Here," she touched a button on her desk. 'I'm beaming my personal office number to your celphone account. Feel free to give me a call whenever you need to."

"Thank you very much," the woman said. She extended

her hand, talking all the while. "I really cannot thank you enough for agreeing to see me. This will be the crowning touch for my internship at *New York City Business*."

"I'm happy I could help—something about your name, Shizume, triggers—I don't know—just this sense of déjà vu," Antonia said, reaching out to clasp her hand. When she did, it was like an electric jolt coursed through her for a moment.

A sterile white laboratory with a liquid-filled chamber—an old, old man decaying before her eyes, the chamber filled again, with another human form—a man dressed in outlandish costume and beard talking to her—the sensation that she was in the chamber, the liquid all around her, filling her mouth and nose—an old woman, her face so stern it looked as if it had been carved in stone—that same old, old room, with the paneling and a fire, a fire that burned down the walls—

"Ms. Derlicht, are you all right?"

"Please, call me Antonia, as I said before," she replied, recovering her poise. "I'm sorry, I just can't shake the feeling that I've seen you somewhere before."

The look on the young woman's face was comical for its surprise. "No—I can't believe you just said that..."

"What?" Antonia asked.

"Well—I thought this sounded brainflashed, but now maybe I'm not so sure," Shizume said. "Ever since I walked into this office, I've had the strangest feeling that I've somehow been here before, and you look incredibly familiar—I don't mean from the VR press releases either, although we certainly get enough of them from your

305

offices. No, *you* look familiar, like I've known you from somewhere else, but I just can't seem to access the memory. Strange, huh?"

Antonia chuckled. "I've heard stranger stories. I tell you what, when you're finished with your internship and earned your degree, come back and see me. I have no doubt I could use someone with your talents. As large as our PR department is, it's always hungry for more staff. Actually, insatiable is more like it."

"Thank you very much, Ms.—Antonia. I have to be honest with you, I'm still looking at VR journalism as my first choice, but it's so competitive. Those virtual anchors just don't do it for me."

"To be honest, me either, even though we pioneered that technology," Antonia said with a chuckle. "They're almost too perfect. All right, the offer will stand, but while you're at NYCB, consider me your inside source for business news and analysis. That should put a surprised look on the faces of Greenberg and Gorman when you start bringing them scoops. They are still the managing editors, aren't they?"

"Yes, and they're both in the office every day," Shizume said. "Best editors I've ever seen."

"Still as busy as ever, I suppose," Antonia said. "Learn as much as you can from both of them. Every byte of information will serve you well later on."

"My grandfather always said if you can't learn by experience, find the oldest person you know and watch them," Shizume said.

"Today that's not a bad lesson to take to heart," Antonia replied. The sound of a door opening made both women's heads turn.

"Mother, it's six forty-five," a blond haired, blue-eyed young girl said with all the imperiousness she could muster. "You said you'd be done by now."

Antonia smiled and said, "Yes, Leah, I know. Why don't you find your two brothers and bring them in here. And where's your father?"

The girl sighed, investing every movement with studied pre-teen angst. "He's on the phone *again*," she said, then flounced out of the room, leaving both women to stifle their giggles.

"She's adorable," Shizume said.

"Of course she is, you've just met her," Antonia replied. "Seven going on twenty-seven. Still—" she paused as the girl came flying back into the room as fast as her pumping legs could take her, followed by two boys, an older one trying to set an example for the other, and a younger boy with his head buried in a transpad, "—as enjoyable as my career is, I wouldn't give this up for a moment. Fortunately, in this day and age, I also didn't have to choose."

"I was going to comment that you seemed very young to have accomplished all this, but with the Derlicht clinics worldwide, it's within the reach of anyone," Shizume said.

Antonia nodded, introducing her sons Mason and Alec as her daughter entwined herself around her legs, staring up at her with pure love. She remembered the long nights of school and career, but all of that was many, many decades ago, and with the cloning advances made in the latter half of the 21st century, she and anyone else who wanted serial immortality could enjoy it with relative ease. This time around, she was the businesswoman and mother, and enjoying both immensely.

A tow-headed man's head atop a crisp Saville Row suit poked into the office. "Is this where they've gotten off to? Dear, I'm sorry, I told Leah she shouldn't interrupt you while you were working."

"It's all right, we were just finishing up," she called. "Be right there. My husband, Evan. By the way, I wanted to congratulate you on your own impending children."

"More like onrushing, if these two have their way," Shizume said. "I'm beginning my last trimester."

"You carry them well." Antonia tapped her temple. "Besides, the glow you're giving off could light my office at midnight."

Shizume blushed, making her look even prettier. "My husband, Ryan, was so nervous before the child license test, but we passed it with no trouble at all. I think he's almost looking forward to this more than I am. But he doesn't have to carry them around all day. I love them already, but they're so active."

"You think they're active now, wait until they get outside," Antonia said. "This has been a pleasure, Shizume, but I'm afraid we do have to be going. Can I have a company car drop you off anywhere?"

"Oh, I don't want to impose—"

"Nonsense, it's what we have them for. I'll have my secretary take care of it," she said, escorting Shizume to the door while the children followed. "And remember what I said, call me if you need any information, or just a juicy quote about something."

"Antonia, I cannot thank you enough for this," Shizume said. "I will be in touch."

"All right then, take care," Antonia said.

After the other woman left, her daughter looked up again. "Mommy, who was that?"

"Someone I thought I knew from somewhere else," Antonia said, a distant look on her face for a moment, then she looked down and ruffled her daughter's hair. "But she's going to be a reporter, if I don't steal her away from that rat race first, and reporters are always good to know. But that's not important right now. How was *your* day?"

Leah chattered gaily about what happened to her at private school, with Antonia listening and supplying the appropriate verbal cues and agreements. But another part of her mind was pondering where she had seen Shizume Mader before, and those images that kept popping into her mind during the interview. *It all seemed so real, like I wasn't just watching it, but* living *it*, she thought. *But nothing like that ever happened, did it?* For a moment, things seemed to crystallize, and it was coming together—something about a house long ago—and—two brothers—

"*Mo-om*," Leah tugged at her hand, scattering her thoughts to the four winds and beyond.

"What is it, honey?" she said, looking down.

"Everyone is *waiting*," she said, as if Antonia was causing a horrific scene simply by not keeping up.

She smiled and looked up to see the rest of the family in the sleek, autopiloted hovercar. "Of course, I'm coming." She and her daughter trotted out to join them, any thoughts of the oddity of that afternoon already fading back to where they had come from—nowhere.

EPILOGUE

S hizume's head was bursting as she got out of the hovercar. The interview had been spectacular, and she couldn't wait to begin writing her article. Only that bit of strangeness between Antonia and her still clamored for attention as she slipped through the busy sidewalk and into her apartment building. *Why did she look so familiar? And what were those flashes I kept getting, a fire, an old man, an old woman, what was that about?*

Shizume shook her head and pulled out her transpad, wanting to go over the filmed interview once more. She was soon so engrossed in the video that she didn't see the girl coming down the hallway until they collided.

"Oh! Oh, I'm sorry, I didn't see you coming. That was my fault," Shizume said, extending a hand to help her up. "Are you all right?"

The young girl was stared at her with, judging by the look on her face, the same expression of suspicious surprise. Her blonde hair was neatly combed and fell in a sculpted wave across the left side of her face, obscuring her eye behind a golden curtain of hair. She was dressed

in a tony private school uniform with a hover-pack carrying her own transpad and anything else vital to a
fourteen-year-old's daily survival floating behind her.
"You look familiar."

"Yes, but—your face is clean," Shizume said, wondering
at the same time why she had remarked on that. A vision
swam before her eyes of this same girl, her face smudged
and dirty in a ragged green jumpsuit, spitting on her.
Why would she do that? she thought. *I've never even
seen her before.* "Is your name Flaya?"

The girl started and stared even harder at Shizume.
"No, my name is Chelzea." She said, then paused, "but
Flaya is my middle name. Some ethnic thing my grand-
mother wanted. How did you know that?"

"I have no idea," Shizume said. "I—I know I've never
seen you before, but part of me says yes, I have."

"Yeah, me too, flash that, eh? What's all this about,
some kind of cosmic déjà vu?" the girl asked.

"I don't know," Shizume said. "Where do you go to
school?"

"Oh, I'm just home on for the weekend, but I go to
Derlicht University Inland. I want to be a bioagricultur-
ist."

Shizume smiled. "I think—I think you'll do well.
Uh—good luck."

"Yeah. I'm just going to go home and try to not think
too hard about this."

Shizume nodded in agreement. "Yes, I think that's a
very good idea. Good-bye." She walked backwards down
the hall, unable to take her eyes off the girl until she
reached the corner. *What was that all about? What a
day,* she thought as she palmed the lock to her apartment.

The warm, spicy smell of cooking permeated the air as she walked in and made her mouth water. "Is that you, hon?" a male voice called from farther inside.

"Yes, Ryan," Shizume replied. "You didn't have to go to all this trouble, you know, the autocook could handle it."

Ryan appeared in the doorway to the small foyer, an apron over his chest and a spoon containing a rich red sauce in his hand. "Yes, but my family would never forgive me. Here, have a taste," he said after kissing her on the cheek.

Shizume did, savoring the mixed flavors of merlot, peppers, and tomato. "Ooh, that's good."

"Well, get your beautiful pregnant body comfortable and tell me how it went," Ryan said over his shoulder as he headed back into the kitchen.

"What? Oh the interview. What a strange day," Shizume said. "It went great; she was a fantastic subject. I think I made my first professional contact too."

"That's great. Did you tell her I said hi?" Ryan said with a chuckle.

"No, Mr. Fifteenth Cousin, Twice Removed, I didn't want to come across as a brainfry."

"Oh, you wound me, my dear," Ryan said. "Besides, I'll bet half the city is related to her in one way or another. Speaking of relatives, your grandfather called."

"That old overprotecting coot," Shizume said with a grin. "What'd he have to say?"

"You know, the usual—making sure I'm taking care of you, saying you shouldn't be working now, he's really looking forward to seeing us at the end of the month, all that and more. He wants you to call him back."

"Oh boy, I'd better block out the rest of the evening then," Shizume groaned, massaging her bulging abdomen.

"How was the other appointment?" Ryan called out.

"Oog, just a minute," Shizume said, trying to settle herself on a massaging chair she had summoned from the wall. "The doctor says the boys are coming along fine, if a little active, but he said that's not out of the norm for them. Could have fooled me, though."

"So they're still bouncing around in there?" Ryan said as he walked over to her.

"Are your hands clean?" she asked.

"Of course they are," he said, kneeling down beside her and laying his head against her abdomen. "Hmm, I don't hear anything. Maybe they've quieted down for the night."

"Sure, I'll bet they wake up right after you leave for your shift. It isn't another ten-hour one, is it?" Shizume asked.

"No, dear, only eight," Ryan replied. "Summer is quieter for us. More folks staying outside. A mixed blessing, I suppose. Anyway, the shelter's only about three-quarters-full. I should be home by three-thirty at the latest."

"All right, I'll be working on this article anyway—Ow!" Shizume said, pressing a hand to her side.

"They've started again, have they?" Ryan said, then jerked his head away. "I think one just kicked at me."

"I'm sure it wasn't that, dear, they're just moving around," Shizume said, stifling another gasp of pain. "Although sometimes I think they're doing water aer-

obics. I really don't know what gets into them sometimes.
It's like they're trying to kill each other."

Inside Shizume's swollen uterus, swimming in amniotic
fluid, two babies lay curled up side-by-side, crowded
together in the warm soothing darkness. Their development had been relatively peaceful so far, but now one,
then the other, cocked his head, as if listening to something only they could hear.

Across space, across time, across dimensions, from
somewhere that by all rights shouldn't have existed yet
did, each child heard a low crooning voice speaking a
language that had died out centuries ago. The voice
whispered seductive promises of power and glory that
each baby understood on an instinctual level. All that
one or the other would have to do to receive this power
would be to make one tiny sacrifice—

Against all medical odds, the eyes of one male child
popped open. Seconds later the other child's eyes opened.
The tiny, perfect features of each baby frowned into a
look of utter hatred directed at the other.

Soon, each one thought. *Not yet, but soon...very soon...*

ALSO AVAILABLE

THE TWILIGHT ZONE
BOOK 1: SHADES OF NIGHT, FALLING
by John J. Miller
ISBN: 0-7434-5858-3

Geiststadt, New York, has always been considered a strange place, beginning with the mysterious disappearance of the original Dutch settlers in the 1650s. Centuries later, Thomas Noir—the thirteenth son of a thirteenth son—seeks power in all forms, whether it be physical, financial...or magical. And he will allow no one to stand in his way of obtaining it: not his father, not the members of the Derlicht clan—Geiststadt's premiere family—and certainly not his twin brother, Jon.

Unfortunately, that all-consuming desire will have profound effects on not just the Noirs and the Derlichts, but on every resident of Geiststadt—now, and for generations to come....

THE TWILIGHT ZONE
BOOK 2: A GATHERING OF SHADOWS
by Russell Davis
ISBN: 0-7434-7471-6

Set in present day New York, *A Gathering of Shadows* introduces a new generation in the saga of the Noir and Derlicht families. Here we meet Mason Noir—the great-grandson of Thomas Noir; once again, there is a Noir male who is the thirteenth son of a thirteenth son.

If all goes as planned, Mason will inherit the vast family fortune, along with the temporal and magical power he's dreamed of for most of his life—but gaining such power and wealth will come with a heavy price to pay....